A HOOD LEGEND

This is a work of fiction. The authors have invented the characters. Any resemblance to actual persons, living or dead, is purely coincidental.

If you have purchased this book with a 'dull' or missing cover——You have possibly purchased an unauthorized or stolen book. Please immediately contact the publisher advising where, when and how you purchased this book.

Compilation and Introduction copyright © 2004 by
Triple Crown Publications
2959 Stelzer Rd., Suite C
Columbus, Ohio 43219
www.TripleCrownPublications.com

Library of Congress Control Number: 2004106285
ISBN# 0-9747895-6-9
Cover Design/Graphics: www.MarionDesigns.com
Author: Victor L. Martin
Editor: Leah Whitney
Production: Kevin J. Calloway
Consulting: Vickie M. Stringer

First Trade Paperback Edition Printing July 2004
10 9 8 7 6 5 4 3 2

Printed in the United States of America

ACKNOWLEDGEMENTS

In the summer of 2004, yes, I'm still holding it down on H-Conday-by-day. But N-E way, thanks to Liberty City, B.K.A.-Pork-n-Bean's. From Holmes Elementary to Brownsville Jr. High, the streets of Miami were my home and yes, I'm due South once I hit that free world once more- 62nd, 4th Ave, Pack Jam, USA Flea Market, Dem Bulls at Northwestern and my peeps from 65th, you know who you are. Yes, Ramica A. Lloyd, dis your old flame, Vic, who bounced to N.C., -Babyface (Sunshine), yeah, I remember!

I can't give out many female names but thanks to those that believed in me when I first picked up this pen and started this thang. Oh well! But a few did Karen from New Bern was the first to plant the seed, and boy did it grow. Tiffani L MartinShe gave me the sunlight that I needed at a time in my live that needed when I wanted to wither away. Yes, our minds will meet again; I'm thanking and thinking of you daily. My typist, Kim A. Carroll, thank you deeply for everything and we were right, friendship is priceless.

This would not have been possible with out the help of all my test readers, thank you. You know I must hold it down for all my peeps from Johnston County, Selma and Smithfield, no doubt. Big Chubb (Keep your head up!) You said I would make it. P.K. (Holla!) and Shan Freeman (If you would have thrown this away ain't no telling where I'd be. We'll get up.) I would also like to thank, Fang, D.P., Jamaica, Big Pun, M. Peacock, and a moment .

of thought to all those resting in peace before their time.

To my grandfather, James McMillan, to my father, Gregory Martin, and my sister, Tremika Smith. Much love and thanks to the H.Q.I.C (Head Queen In Charge) Vickie Stringer, I'ma just let my actions speak louder than my words. And Tammy, thank you, for allowing me to get on your last nerve with my 1.5 million questions about my book. To my editors and to everyone I know and don't know who helped place A Hood Legend on the shelf. THANK YOU. T.C.P.

DEDICATIONS

To God, My Family and Friends. To my mom, Sandra Martin, Sister, Niece and Nephew, I love you all deeply. Many of you know how I could of lost my life on that cold December 13, 2002 night (Friday the 13th), but yet, here I stand. But build on this February 13, 2004 (Friday the 13th) I got my card from Vickie about my book, I'ma tell the world Vickie, this is for you. I'll stay humble and I'll stay true, and deep down inside. It's for the strength of you.

TrillVille (Neva Eva)

Triple Crown Publications presents

A Hood Legend

V.Martin

CHAPTER 1

Burberry Escalade ESV

Miami, Florida
Friday Afternoon
**It was two weeks before spring break and the sun and heat
were relentless.** The temperature there was in the upper nineties,
with Kool-Aid blue skies. Sitting on twenty-six-inch spinners, the
canary yellow Cadillac Escalade ESV pulled to a stop on Sixty-
Second and Seventeenth in Liberty City, near the Pork-n-Beans
projects.

"The world is mine. Yo, ya hear me, son?" Menage said into
his Nokia cell phone as he lowered the tinted window to check
out the two shorties walking past his SUV. He pressed a switch,
closing the window, and settled back into the coke-white and
yellow Burberry print leather seats with his phone to his right ear
and waited for the light to change. "You hear me, Dwight?" he
repeated. "Hot as a bitch out here!" he added as he activated the
AC by voice command.

"Yeah, man. What's up?" Dwight replied over the cell phone.

"You get my message about DJ?"

"Yeah, about five minutes ago," Dwight said. DJ had brought
a black DB-7 Vantage Volante into the chop shop the night
before. Both men knew that the going rate on a DB-7 was close
to $170,000, so Menage would make a lick once he tagged it.
"How the hell he pull that off?"

"Don't know yet. I wasn't in when it came. I'ma holla at him later on, but for now I'ma let it sit," Menage said.

"That's a good move—hope it's not out-of-state." Both men knew that transporting stolen goods across state lines would wake up the big dogs—the feds.

"Nah, nigga, I know the rules on that."

"Word…so where you at now?"

"In the beans, 'bout ta head on over to 103rd to check on shorty I met last night at the strip club. Yo, Dwight, shorty thick to def," Menage said as he adjusted the rear view mirror.

"Bruh, you trippin'. What's up with you and Chandra? You need to stop trying to live up to your name."

Menage frowned. "Nigga, please, since when you became the Pope? Yo, I'ma holla." Before Dwight could reply, Menage had snapped his phone shut and tossed it onto the passenger seat. He activated the sound system, cracked the tinted windows down a few inches and slid the sunroof open—all by voice command. The ESV slowly cruised down Sixty-Second with its four, fifteen-inch Alpine speakers thumping a hit by Outkast. Menage was in his element. He wore an all white, silk and mesh Sean John baggy jogging suit with a matching sun visor turned to the side. Around his neck hung a diamond-encrusted rope that swung below his chest. Attached to it was a matching medallion that spelled out his last name. Dangling from his left wrist was a custom-made, iced-out Millennia Bulova watch—a perfect match for the six platinum teeth in the front bottom row of his mouth.

As Menage made a right turn on Twenty-Seventh Avenue, his left wrist draped over the chrome and oak steering wheel, he thought of the girl he'd met the night before. The Bounce Back strip club was his second home, and the instant Benita hit the stage in high heels and thongs she had his complete attention. She had said that she was twenty-two as she gave him a lap dance up in VIP. She was built like a dream, and she had a face and body that any man—and from what he had seen last night—even a few women would lust for. Without heels Benita stood at 5'10" with thick juicy thighs and smooth, blemish-free mahogany skin to match. She had a rule about dating guys she met at work, but for some reason she made an exception for Menage. His lean, 5'11" 190-pound frame stood before her and he looked into her eyes, knowing she expected him to zero in on the two natural thirty-eight double-Ds that were smack dead in his face, spilling out of her mesh Fendi bra. He played it cool; he didn't want her to regret breaking her rule for Menage Unique Legend.

Benita was looking forward to the date to see what Miami was really all about. For two months she had been staying with her cousin, Lisa, who was a full-time nurse at Jackson Memorial. For five years, Miami, which was a whole lot different from Kinston, North Carolina, had been her home. Since Lisa worked more hours than she could stand, she really didn't have the time to show her cousin around. In the meantime, Benita was content with attending Dade Community College, making a few bills at the club and crashing out on the couch in Lisa's one-bedroom apartment. Lisa and Benita Alston acted like two sisters instead of cousins. Lisa was in her early thirties and kept her 5'8" petite body in the best of shape. She was easy to get along with, just as long as you didn't tell her she looked like Amerie—something she'd heard over a million times. "I'm taller and my tits are bigger than hers," she would always say with a smile, knowing that it was the truth.

"Girl, who is that out there with that loud ass music!" Lisa said sticking her head out the bathroom door holding a towel around her naked body.

"I think it's for me, girl," Benita said all bubbly as she peeked through the blinds. "Yesss, it's him," she said to herself. Outside Menage waited for the gulwing door to raise before stepping out of the stunning ESV. "Lisa, how do I look?" Benita held her arms out, turning around for Lisa to check her over.

Lisa smacked her lips. "Just don't stretch my top too much with your big tits."

Benita dropped her arms. "Girl, please."

"Hey, I wanna meet him."

"Not while you're nude you ain't."

"Girl, he done seen some breasts before," Lisa teased playfully.

"That might be true, cuz, but he won't be seeing yours." Lisa rolled her eyes and shut the bathroom door. Benita turned to open the front door just as Menage started to knock. "Dang he's so fine," she thought as he stood in the doorway flashing his twenty-thousand-dollar smile. She knew that Lisa would try to be nosy and she quickly moved things along. "Lemme get my tote bag and I'll be ready," she said hoping she didn't say anything stupid.

"I'm not in a rush," Menage said watching the glare from his jewelry blind her.

Walking toward the ESV, Benita tried to play it cool as the passenger door slowly lifted. "Nice," she said as it slowly closed on its own with a soft click. "I…didn't know they made 'em like this," she added running her fingers over a silver slab of wood on the dashboard that surrounded one of the five Panasonic plasma screens.

"They don't." Menage was trying to see where her head was. Last night she had turned him down for some one-on-one and since she presented a challenge, he pressed even harder until he got the digits. He figured she didn't know what he was worth, but he didn't play himself by saying what he had. But he wondered if maybe he went a little overboard by slipping five hundred in her g-string, which was really a small thing for him. Most nights he would leave with a stripper who gave up the ass as soon as they got into his whip. So far, Benita didn't act all childish over his material things, so he gave her a few points.

Menage had plenty of nicknames around the hood. The most common one was, "The Most Wanted Baby Father." His man,

Dwight, always said, "Why waste time when you have a main girl?" Menage cared deeply about Chandra Lovick but if he cared so much for her, why was Benita sitting next to him? Well, if you let him tell it, he'd say because she had a phat ass and juicy tits, but that was in his world—and he set the rules.

"So I'll give you your first official tour of the M.I.A.," Menage said as he lay back in the Burberry seat. "I guess we can just play it by ear...roll through the hood and whatnot. How you feel 'bout dat?" He managed to steal a glance between Benita's thighs. Now he knew what inspired Ginuwine to write that damn song, because he sure as hell wanted to get in those jeans.

"That's straight," she said putting on her seat belt.

"Hey, can I ask you a question?" Menage said sitting erect.

"Go ahead." She turned her hips in the seat to face him. Horns blew from the heavy traffic as the ESV cruised down Seventh Avenue, but Menage's attention was on Benita as he fought to control his raging hormones. She was definitely having an affect on him.

"Yo, do you feel odd knowing I done seen you half naked? No disrespect, ma, but when you came out on the thong song..."

"It's okay. I don't feel odd at all because it's a job to me," she said smiling, moving her bang from over her right eye.

"I know dat's right!" Menage knew they had all day to kick it, so he told her to sit back and enjoy the ride. Benita couldn't stop the goose bumps as they drew attention at the light; the Alpines mercilessly vibrated the pavement with Mobb Deep's hot beats.

***

In a lavish condo in North Miami Beach, Dwight McMillan flopped down on a leather couch as his woman, Tina Townes, nagged endlessly. The twenty-eight-year-olds were at odds again.

"Dwight, baby...it's been...it seems like since day one you've been letting Menage tell you how to handle your affairs!" Tina snapped, standing in front of him with her hands on her thick hips.

Dwight let out a deep breath and rubbed his face with both hands. "Tina", he said looking up at her, "for the last time, no one is in charge. You know he's fair and if it wasn't for him, do you think we'd have all this?" He made a sweeping gesture with his arm, adding emphasis to his statement as he glanced across the living room with its two-inch-thick plush carpet. "So why are you stressing twenty-four seven? You got the ride you always wanted, you wear designer clothes...what more can you ask for, Tina? If it wasn't for Menage, we'd still be trying to make ends meet." Dwight stood up and wrapped his arms around Tina's waist. She stepped closer to him, resting her head under his chin.

"Baby, I'm sorry. I guess I do need to look at the whole picture," she said softly.

"Menage has come a long way, Tina. That was a tough block he grew up on in Liberty City on Sixty-Fith. And I can say this: He hasn't forgotten where he came from. He was the one that gave money to the city and the NAACP to build that new park in Liberty City." He raised her chin with his right index finger and lightly kissed her on the lips. He then gazed over her shoulder through the tinted floor-to-ceiling window and watched a few cruise ships heading out to sea. The view always lifted his spirits.

"Baby, he's just so..." Tina searched for a word to describe Menage. "All those girls he fools around with, you know he's gonna break Chandra's heart if she finds out." And he's so damn conceited, she wanted to add.

"I'm trying to talk to him about that...and you're right." Dwight looked at her with a warm smile.

Tina gripped his shirt, pulling him closer. "I love you so much," she whispered, standing on her toes to stick her warm, wet tongue into his mouth. She shivered as his soft hands slid under the edge of her tight-fitting Miami Heat Jersey dress, cupping the bottom of her butt cheeks.

"No panties?" he said breathing heavily as Tina began to take off his shirt.

"Not when daddy's home." At the last shirt button and just as he managed to slide a finger into her sex, the phone chimed. "I'll get it," Tina said pushing him playfully down onto the couch. She swayed her voluptuous hips as she walked toward the bar, knowing that she had her man's full attention. Flinging her hair from her face and ear, she picked up the phone on its fourth ring. "Hello?" she said softly as she leaned against the bar and looked back at Dwight, now sliding his sex-coated fingers into his mouth.

"Yo, Tina, what up shorty?" Menage's voice seemed to taunt her, and her mood quickly changed. She rolled her hazel eyes and gripped the phone.

"Look, boy! I'm not your shorty, ok, so don't call me that!"

"Damn, Tina, calm down, you know I'm just trippin'." Anyway, let me holla at Dwight."

"Hold on, boy!" Tina trudged over to Dwight and dropped the cordless phone on his lap before going back to the bar for a drink.

"What's up, bruh?"

"Hey, Dwight, meet me at the Omni Mall 'bout six tonight."

"Why, what's up?"

"Oh, this the remix for "Twenty-One Questions?" Relax homie, and bring Tina, too." "Where you at now?"

"Damn, Dwight...I'm at Bayside wit' shorty I told you about. But we need to handle some money figures tonight. You feel me?"

"Yeah, bruh, I feel you."

"One," Menage said.

"Two," Dwight replied and pushed the disconnect button. He scratched his chin and laid the phone on the mirrored end table.

"Let me guess," Tina said sarcastically, handing Dwight a glass of Bacardi Vanilla Rum, "General Legend wants private McMillan to do his bidding today, huh?"

Dwight jumped up from the couch, nearly spilling his drink. "Tina!" He raised his voice, causing her to take a step back. "Will you please cut the bullshit? Matter of fact, he wants both privates—that's you and me. We're going to the Omni tonight." He hated that he had raised his voice at her. Tina was shocked and unable to speak. Dwight lowered his drink onto a coaster, then took Tina's and did the same. "Listen, baby." His tone was considerably lower now, and he reached for her hips in the cut out space on her jersey. "Many people overlook the good things he do. Sure, he's a player, or whatever. Remember when he came over with that girl last weekend?"

"The one that's only sixteen!" Tina snapped looking up into his eyes. Tina was tall but Dwight was taller at 6'4".

"He's not sleeping with her, if that's what you're thinking."

Oh, really!" she laughed. "Menage in a platonic relationship with a female? Please!"

Dwight let out a deep sigh and backed away from her. "He used to talk to her sister."

"You mean fuck her sister!" Tina said with her hands on her bare hips.

"Will you stop cutting me off? Anyway, that young girl was depending on her sister to help her go to college if she couldn't get a grant. Apparently she didn't get it and her sister got passed up for a promotion, so the funds weren't there. When Menage found out about it, he offered to help, and he paid for the girl's full education. And for your information, he was taking her to see her boyfriend in jail that day. Now tell me how many guys you know like that?" Tina changed the subject, voicing her other plans for the night, but Dwight made it plain and clear that she would have her black ass at the Omni. He left her standing in the living room, avoiding a stupid shouting match with her. After finishing her drink, she went into the bedroom expecting to find him and discovered that he was in the shower. Slipping off her jersey, she joined him.

"You still mad at me?" she said standing behind him, looking at the soapy trail sliding down his body.

"I'm never mad at you, Tina," he said washing his chest.

"Oh really," Tina said stepping in closer to join him under the hot spray of water. She pulled a rag from the gold bar against the wall behind her, soaked it and started to wash her man's back. She saw his muscles tense and flex under her touch. As she moved the rag down lower, she let it drop and started to rub his ass, causing him to groan. "You like it when I touch you like this, Dwight?" she said sliding a hand around his waist to find him already hard. Wrapping her other hand around him, she pressed her body tightly into his, causing her breasts to flatten against his back. Dwight braced himself up against the marble wall as Tina brought him to a healthy climax.

Bayside
Biscayne Blvd
After tasting her first spicy Jamaican meal, Benita pointed out an empty bench near the waterfront. "Finally some shade," she said. Menage still had his eyes on her—from her white tilted fedora to her stylish, shoulder-length, silky black hair with tinted red tips…and it was all hers. Her mahogany skin looked even smoother now, and the scent of her invigorating perfume made him not want to exhale. He has asked her what the name of it was as they ate. "Glow, by J-Lo," she said, feeling she was getting her money's worth since the fragrance was a little pricey. He

even asked about the Nude and Glitter lip-gloss on her lips. They were two separate products, but she liked to mix them so her glossy, sexy lips could show off a few specks of glitter. The yellow cotton tank top and white jeans were all by Lady Enyce. Even her bi-weekly pedicured feet got his attention in the pumps she wore. She was sexy without being revealing. In addition to her tall frame, Benita had a soft and curvaceous body with stats that many women would pay to possess. Her ample breasts, tiny waist and healthy hips were mesmerizing. Menage figured she'd be some naïve, money-hungry, no-goals-having, I'ma-strip-till-my-tits-say-quit chick, but she was none of that. She was smart, funny and didn't let her job run her life. And to her, that's all it was—a J-O-B.

As they continued to sit on the bench, Menage found himself still just wanting to inhale her sweet scent and stay near her. She was surprised at his behavior. At first, she regretted breaking her rule of dating guys she met at work. "But is this really a date?" she thought. She just knew he would try to bring up sex and she was ready to kindly say no. "This is beautiful," she said taking off her shades.

"They got places like this where you from?"

"No, boy," she said touching his knee. It's nothing like this...I can stay here forever." Menage thought about putting his hand on top of hers but she moved it onto her lap.

"Damn! I'm glad you don't sell drugs. I'm not trying to judge you, but one of my cousins met this guy and he came to pick her up for their second date with drugs in the car. It was just her luck that the car was stolen and he tried to put it on her when he got arrested."

"That's some lame shit. Did she beat the case?"

"Yeah—seven-thousand dollars for a lawyer and a two-year deal." Benita promised herself that she'd never go through any shit like that—no matter how good the guy looked. Now it was time to test him. "So what's on your mind," she said turning to face him. She quickly thought of how other men—or boys—usually replied to this question. If you wanna be on top or bottom. Wrong! Me and you and some whipped cream. Wrong! Me, you and your cousin. Definitely wrong! She just knew he'd be like the rest.

"Life," he said looking into her eyes. Benita thought he had to be joking, but after she looked into his eyes she knew he was for real.

"Well, I guess you have a lot on your mind." She was right, but he sure wasn't willing to share it with her.

"Hey, there's a million other things we can do than sit on this bench. How you feel about the zoo?"

"I'm game as long as I'm with you." Together they stood up, eyeing one another. They walked hand in hand back to the parking lot. Benita didn't know what to think. She was about to kiss him on the cheek, but he suddenly shoved her to the ground. She started to yell at him but the loud gunshots rang out, hitting the ground next to her.

***

Dwight softly massaged Tina's feet with scented lotion as she lay back on the king-sized bed. She wore a green, sheer Fendi teddy.

"You still mad at me?" he said sliding his thumb over her heel.

"Shhh." Tina slowly lifted her free foot to his mouth. He took her foot from off his lap and ran a hand up her bare thigh. She welcomed his touch, spreading her legs. "Don't tease me, baby," she said squeezing and rubbing her breasts. As he moved forward, she bent her knee to keep her toes in his mouth. "I love you so much," she moaned as he slid the teddy up around her waist. Tina watched through dazed eyes as he turned onto his stomach to feast between her legs, and her back arched the instant his tongue slid over her sex. She locked her heels around his lower back and started to hump his face as the sound of his wet smacking mixed with her moans. She practically ripped the thin teddy from excitement. "Oooooh, baby, yesss," she squealed as he slid a finger into her wet opening. He was sucking on her clit when the phone rang minutes later. Neither of them paid it any mind and it rang three times before the call was picked up by the answering machine. Tina held the back of Dwight's head, grinding her pussy into his face, when all of a sudden she stopped. The female voice on the machine was asking for her man.

Dwight moved Tina off of him and stared at the answering machine. "What the hell," he said as the woman begged him to pick up the phone. He picked up the receiver. "Who is this and how did you get this number?" he said sitting on the edge of the bed as Tina moved closer to his side.

"Th-this is Benita. I pushed redial on Menage's phone and—"

"Wait!" Dwight exclaimed. "Where is Menage?"

"He's been shot."

"Shot!" he shouted. "Where...oh shit!" As fast as she could, Benita told him about the drive-by and that she was at the hospital after following the ambulance in his ESV. By the time she was done, Dwight was dressed and heading for the door. Tina stayed on the phone with Benita to calm her down, but the call was cut off because of bad reception.

Dwight made it to Jackson Memorial Hospital in record time, locking the brakes on his blue Dodge Viper. After finding out what room Menage was in, he ran through the halls, ignoring the shouts from doctors and nurses asking him to slow down. He caught his breath as he reached Menage's room and noticed two uniformed cops in the hallway. He was close to losing his temper, as they wouldn't allow him into the room.

"What seems to be the problem, officers?" Dr. Wilson said as he walked up and stood next to Dwight. Dwight released a sigh of relief. Dr. Wilson smoothed things out in a matter of seconds and Dwight was given ten minutes to visit Menage. He entered the brightly lit room and said a silent prayer when he found his dawg lying on his stomach without any machines or IV.

Dwight stood at the side of the bed. "Bruh, you sleep?"

"Nah, just looking at my eyelids." Menage opened his eyes and smiled, but he winced when he tried to turn his head to look at his friend.

"Man, what happened?" Dwight asked before sliding a chair closer to the bed and sitting down.

"Got caught in a drive-by. Some cats rolled up in a Chevy and started dumpin'."

"Were they aiming for you?"

"Man, I ain't looked or asked no questions. I tried to grab my heat and bust back, but I had to cover shorty girl so I pushed her out of the way."

"Hold up, hold up. You risked your life for that girl you told me about!"

Menage sucked his teeth. "Yeah, man, let me finish. Anyway, I peeped what was going down, and then I realized I'd be better off to cover her. I caught a round in my back just as I dove on her. The police said the slug is stuck in my vest. I guess the impact knocked me out. But yeah, you can say I saved her life. Another guy got hit in the leg, so I really can't say they was gunnin' for me. Ain't like I started a war or somethin'."

"So why you out sporting a vest?" Dwight asked.

"Shit, it matched my outfit. Yo, who called you?"

"That girl you was with," Dwight said folding his huge arms. "She's down on the second floor. I cleared things with our friend, Dr. Wilson. Man, are you sure you weren't the target?"

Menage thought for a minute as he played the whole scene out in his mind again.

"Nope."

"That's what I figured."

"Well, ain't no need to sweat it. I'll be able to leave later tonight."

"What about the police?"

"Fuck 'em. I told 'em I had my back turned—ain't seen shit." Dwight was about to ask him about the DB-7 and why he wanted to see him and Tina at the Omni, but two taps at the door stopped him. Benita walked in with tears still in her eyes. She walked slowly up to the side of the bed.

"You ok?" she asked rubbing his arm. Sure, Menage had a sore back and had just escaped death, but the mere sight of her quickly aroused him.

"Yeah," he said, Ginuwine's song still on his mind. The visit was quickly coming to an end, and Benita gave Menage a kiss on the cheek and told him to call her as soon as he could. As she walked out with Dwight to catch a ride with him, all Menage could do was stare at her apple-shaped ass and press his erection into the bed. Damn! It shook like jelly.

Later that night, close to nine o'clock, Menage pulled into his three-part garage to his four-bedroom mini mansion on South Beach. It also served as an entrance to the stylish home. The sunken living room was decorated with a thirteen-foot Gucci leather sofa with matching loveseats and carpet that was two inches thick. Built into the wall opposite the sofa was an eighty-inch flat screen plasma HDTV. There was a two-person glass elevator on the left side of the screen, and on the right side was a wooden staircase. Both led upstairs to one of his bedrooms. To the far left, behind the elevator, was a state-of-the-art kitchen, fully decked out with blue marble counters and cabinets. A dim glow burst through his glass back door from the green tinted lights in his Olympic size pool. Each bathroom had heated floors and cobblestone shower stalls and hot tubs. Even though his home was fully voice activated, he still found himself giving direct commands to his two German Rottweilers, Vapor and Vigor. They sat side by side, staring at him as he flicked though the channels on the TV. "Vigor." The dog's ears perked up energetically. "Beer." Vigor, the larger of the two dogs, ran towards the kitchen and locked his mouth around the rubber handle near the bottom of the refrigerator. "Good boy, yeah, good boy," Menage said taking the bottle of Miller Genuine Draft from his mouth. "Vapor, hit the stash spot, boy!" He watched Vapor take off and head for one of the back rooms. In less than two minutes, the dog returned with a bag of weed and without being told, placed it in his owner's lap. Menage was about to light a blunt when his cell phone chimed. He knew who it was by the tone. "Hey, sexy," he said pushing Vapor out of his face.

"Boy, where your tail been at? I've been calling you all dang day," said Chandra. Chandra was a flawless black beauty with goals and she was in love with Menage—not for his money or the material things he could give her, but just for being him. She was 5'11" tall, slim and had a lovely figure. She was twenty-seven with no kids, majoring in medicine at Florida State and beside his mother, was the only woman Menage trusted.

"I switched cars and forgot to take my phone with me," he lied.

"Don't make it happen," she joked. "Mmm, spring break is coming up, so what do you wanna do?"

Menage pushed Vigor out of the way to stretch out on the sofa and since it was so long, Vigor moved to the middle. "Let's go deep sea diving again," he said turning onto his side. His back was still sore.

"You are so nasty, boy," she giggled. His version of deep sea diving was tying her hands and feet to the bed and going headlong after the grapes that he slid inside of her. "So you miss me, right?"

"You'll find out when I get you in my arms again," he said.

"I know that's right! How's your mom?"

"Same as yesterday. She asked about you."

"Well, I'll call her tomorrow. So what is my big baby doing all by his lonesome in that big ol' house?"

"Waitin' for you to turn it into a home."

Chandra was caught off guard. "So I bet we have a lot to put on the table, huh?" They talked more, but she had to cut the call short since she had to tutor a friend the following day. Menage pushed number 5 on his Nokia, and the phone at the other end rang four times.

"Ya'll shut the hell up and give dat boy his damn bottle!" Menage held the phone away from his ear. "Hello, who dis?" Katori said in her best ghetto sexy voice.

"What's really goin' on?"

"Ooooh, Menage baby, what up, nigga? Please say you 'bout to swing by. I swear I'm tryin' ta roll out dis piece—plus I'm horny as fuck…yeah, my baby daddy locked the fuck back up!" she said smacking her lips.

"Yeah, we can get up tonight," Menage said thinking about her tight little bubble ass. Katori was only eighteen and already had two kids. She was 4'11" and had a see-through gap between her legs.

"Yesss, now that I'm feelin', 'cause you know I be missin' the dick and how you stretch me open, baby."

"Yeah, whatever. What time you gonna be ready?" Menage heard a door slam in the background.

"Hold on a sec, boo-bitch. Don't worry 'bout who I'm talkin' to and no it ain't your brother…huh?" The phone disconnected. Menage was about to try Plan B—a Hindu chic in Opalocka, but his Nokia chimed.

"Hey, I'm sorry. Dat was my baby daddy crackhead sister.

Look, I had to give her a twenty to watch the kids, so you can come right on over." He was about to say no, but he thought of how she loved to suck his dick. He was on his way

***

Back at the apartment, Benita was telling her cousin Lisa what had happened at Bayside.

"Girl, you for real?" Lisa asked.

"Yes, it happened so fast," said Benita.

Lisa turned toward her bedroom mirror. "Well, I'ma take my behind to work. And yes, I'll see if I can find out how your...hero is doing. You sure you ain't give him no stuff?"

"Lisa!"

"Chill, cuz, just joking. Like, you get a dude to save your life on the first date and I gotta persuade dudes to go downtown." Lisa ducked the pillow Benita tossed at her. Minutes after Lisa left for work, Benita curled up on the couch to read the latest Honey magazine when the phone rang. The deep voice at the other end and the loud music in the background made her quickly regret picking up the phone. Big Chubb was the owner of the Bounce Back strip club.

"Hey Nita Poo, you off tonight, I already know, but Platinum and Silk can't find no babysitters, so can you come in?" he shouted.

"Chubby, my cousin is at work and you know I'm scared to catch a cab."

"I know, but check it: I got some NBA and NFL players in tonight, so I'ma have Dacle come pick you up...how 'bout dat?"

Benita rolled her eyes, but at the same time she knew she needed the extra cash. "Ok, Chubby, I'll be ready."

"Good lookin', I owe you one. She'll be there in half an

hour." Benita hung up the phone and went into her room to pack a bag. She gathered two sets of bikini tops with matching thongs and black leather form-fitting Prada shorts. An hour later she was in the dressing room at the strip club applying eyeliner. Her body was oiled from head to toe, with a double coat on her plump ass cheeks. Standing in front of the mirror, clad in black pumps and the low-riding shorts and bikini top, she was proud of her one hundred percent-natural body. As she was about to head up to VIP, two of her fellow dancers stepped into the dressing room.

"Hey, Nita Poo, girl," cooed the taller of the two.

"Hey, Sexion." Benita preferred not to be alone with the two lesbians. "Hey Plum."

"Ah, Nita Poo, do us a favor and watch out for us. There's fifty in it for you," said Sexion.

"Do what?" Benita said rolling her neck.

"Girl, relax. Just don't let nobody walk in on us. Just give us a couple of minutes," said Plum. Benita held out her hand for the money. Sexion smiled as she reached into her bra to pull out the bills, but in the process her bra popped open, spilling out her round 36Ds.

"Oh, sorry," Sexion said coyly, hoping Benita would join the fun. Plum sat on the stool by the door on her hands and knees as Sexion pumped her from behind with a strap-on dildo.

"Times up!" Benita said.

"Don't matter," Sexion panted, still stroking Plum. "I just wanted you to watch me fuck Plum." She burst out laughing when Benita raised her middle finger and left the room.

Bounce Back was on fire tonight. Up on stage were five strippers, ass up, face down, moaning and groaning as men sprayed whipped cream on them and then doubled their pleasure in a pussy-eating contest. Red tinted strobe lights flickered throughout the club and Benita could smell weed burning. Over at the bar, a stripper looked over her shoulder as she made her ass clap, while dollar bills fell all around her dark parted thighs. With all this sex and lust in the atmosphere, all Benita could do was think about Menage and hope that he would show up tonight or leave a message on her machine. She shook her head with disapproval as she went up the steps toward the VIP area. Near the pool table, a stripper stood against the wall holding her butt cheeks apart as a man knelt behind her, drinking the beer that another stripper poured down her crack. A loud cheer erupted when he stood up and pointed to the dry floor between the girl's legs. It was double the fun up in VIP. Benita spotted a stripper she knew by the name of Mink who was only eighteen. She sat between two men, giving them both a hand job. Benita knew it was a contest to see which of the men could hold out the longest, and judging from the way Mink's eyes were bulging and darting back and forth from dick to dick while biting her lips, it was obvious that she wanted to do more than just use her tiny hands. Even the music was on point; 50 Cent and Lil' Kim's Magic Stick was blasting full force.

It didn't take long for Benita to gain attention and be called over to someone's table. Her shorts fit her snugly, and she noticed her pursuer's eyes on her pussy as she stood before him at his table. Right away she knew he was in the NBA by his height and the three hundred-dollar bills he laid on the table next to a bottle of Moet. Catching the beat, she started to pull her shorts down while keeping her eyes on his. After stepping out of the shorts, she began humping over the print she saw growing in his jeans. Reaching behind her back, she pulled the string loose on her bikini top just as the remix to David Banner's Like a Pimp filled the joint. Cupping her breasts together, she jiggled them in his face as he tried to lick one of her nipples. Stepping back to show her ass, she looked over her shoulder while pulling up her thong to make it slide deeper into her crack. Backing her ass up, she let out a little squeal when he grabbed her soft hips and pulled her down onto his lap. "Be a good boy, now," she purred, trying to stay calm while reaching down to remove his hands. His grip was tight, and her struggling caused her ass to grind over his throbbing erection.

"Yeah, ho, that's it," he said reaching between her thighs to squeeze her sex through her thong. Benita closed her legs and tried to stand, but his grip was too strong. "Bitch, be fucking still. Just let me pull out so you can ride this dick!" Benita felt her thong being slid to the side.

"Um…let's not do it here," she said, hoping to make him believe that she was willing to take it elsewhere. "Look, what is wrong with you!" she said trying hard now to release herself from his grip.

"You the one that's wrong. So quit tripping, ho!" By now she felt his hard penis pressing against her thigh.

"Fuck this!" she said under her breath as she reached for the bottle of Moet. He was too busy trying to enter her to notice the bottle. "Stupid bitch!" he shouted and pushed her off of him out of sheer frustration. He quickly began wiping off his clothing. Benita tried to bounce, but he grabbed her wrist as she reached for her clothes.

"Ho, what's your problem?" he hissed.

"Let me go!" she said jerking her wrist, only causing him to grip her tighter. The first backhand stunned her.

"You know who I am?" He reared back to deliver another backhand, but he froze in mid swing as Big Chubb cocked the hammer on his silver and black .357.

"Nita Poo, get your paper and go to my office!" Big Chubb said with a toothpick hanging from the right corner of his mouth. Benita wasn't even halfway down the steps before Big Chubb hit the NBA player in the jaw, knocking him back and flipping him over the chair. Big Chubb straddled his chest and stuck the barrel into his mouth as blood ran down his cheek. "I don't give a fuck who you be or what set you claim—none of the shit! But nigga, you done lost your fuckin' mind to hit one of my girls!" He slid the barrel deeper, watching the man choke. "Breathe through your ass, bitch, 'cause that's what you is. Oh…you a pimp…huh…what…what nigga…you can't talk…huh bitch?

Don't cry now!" Keeping the heater in his mouth, Big Chubb reached into his pockets for his stash. Stripping him of his roll, he stood the man up and shoved him towards his two bouncers standing by. "Kick his ass out!" Big Chubb turned to see a few girls looking on in shock. "Get ya'll ass back to work and show that dookie hole," he said grinning and headed out of the VIP section.

Benita was fully dressed and waiting upstairs in Big Chubb's office, which overlooked the entire club through a one-way mirror. "Chubby, I…" Benita immediately started to speak when he stepped inside and closed the door, but he held up his big hands and pointed for her to sit.

"Nita Poo," he said, sitting on the edge of his desk, "I know you is new, but my girls come first. It was my fault because I pulled Lamont from VIP. I forgot he was up there by his damn self." He paused to count out eight hundred dollars. "Here, this is for your trouble… don't need no police up in here. Ya feel me, Nita Poo?" Benita nodded. "Well, you still have a job and ya did right, but I'ma let you call it a night. I'll get one of the girls to take you home."

"Thank you, Chubby." She stood up to hug him. "You still my big red teddy bear."

Later that night, Benita stripped off her clothes and stood in front of the bathroom mirror, thankful that she didn't have a bruise on her face. Even without the money Chubby gave her she would have kept her mouth shut because she didn't want her mom up in Kinston to find out that she was stripping. "Dang," she said seeing that she had no calls on Lisa's machine. After taking a shower, she went to bed with thoughts of no one other than Menage. She fell asleep five minutes after midnight.

***

Menage watched Katori's tits flop up and down as she rode him while making ugly sex faces.

"Uhhhh, it's hitting my stomach!" she moaned squeezing his chest. He didn't worry about her leaving any marks because she bit her nails. As she continued to ride him, he gripped her hips and forced his mind to think of something else other than her fist-tight sex.

Three years earlier, with a bad conduct discharge from the Marines, he moved back home to Miami with four thousand dollars to his name. A few days later, he came across a jit with a stolen Lexus. With his smooth game he drove off with the Lexus, having paid only five hundred for it. With the money he had left, he bought a matching body, identical to the Lexus from the junkyard, and within three weeks he switched the VIN from the junked model to the stolen one, making it a rebirth with a title in hand. He sold the Lexus to a dealership for twenty-four grand and never looked back since. However, his big profits didn't stop him from always keeping things under control; he had guidelines. Rule number one: No speedballing. His chop shop was currently moving six cars a month as a result of this rule but he made at least ten grand off of every ride. Money was coming in fast, so he got with Dwight who was struggling to make ends meet with his barber shop and the two quickly made a deal to become partners. A month later, MD Beauty Salon opened in Miami and it was the first of four shops. Their goal was to make a million each with their motto, "A two-man team with nothing in between."

Katori brought him back to the present by sticking her tongue in his ear as she continued to ride him. Pulling her tight, stretch-marked butt cheeks apart, he thrusted himself into her deeply. Then without pulling out, he rolled her over onto her back. Licking the sweat from her neck, he started stroking her as she lifted her legs and locked them hungrily around his waist. Moments later, he flooded the first of a box of five condoms that he had brought along with him as Katori reached down to fondle his balls.

CHAPTER 2

Big League

Saturday
"Hurry da hell up, girl!" Menage yelled walking towards his garage. Today he was Nautica from head to toe, white tank top and a pair of Carolina blue, cashmere buggy sweat pants. His eight-inch afro was picked out to its fullest. Vapor and Vigor sat still under the shade of the palm trees, the morning air cooling off their fur. Menage's Bulova read 7:47 a.m. and his man Dough-Low had left an early-morning message on his two-way about a cookout in Carol City for The Big League Car Club that he belonged to.

Keying the remote, only two doors slid open on his three-part garage. Beside his Escalade ESV sat a 1995 topless bowling ball green and black four-door Acura legend sitting on twenty-inch remote chrome and oak-trimmed free-spinning Dalvins. He yelled for Katori and put on his shades. He had brought her back to his house to continue their sex fest. She came out seconds later, and he couldn't help but smile at her tight little ass. Knowing that she wore no panties under her white tennis skirt pleased him even more.

"Man, my kitty is sore, so don't even be trying to rush me!" She stood on her toes to kiss his cheek, only to moan when he slid a hand under her skirt to palm her ass. "Hey, let's ride in the Escalade with the spinners," Katori said twirling a finger, giving the ESV a command. The front doors slowly rose in the air and the rear doors slid back. "That bitch is a fucking beast," Katori said running to plant her ass in the Burberry seat. "Your truck got me pregnant, boy," she said watching the door slowly come down with a soft click, "and man, my dookie hole sore."

"What? Ain't even get my head in...stankin' ass," Menage laughed, changing his CDs.

"Mmm, you ain't say that last night," she said reaching between his legs. Katori was far from shy, and Menage wasn't surprised when she told him to slide his seat back and tilt the steering wheel upward so she could suck his dick on GP—after she promised not to spill anything on the leather. She completed her task in four minutes and five seconds. After placing his .380 under his seat, he started up the SUV. Sliding the tinted sunroof back, he activated his sound system and Project Pat's Don't Save Her came booming through the sound system. Katori playfully punched him in his arm when she heard the song, knowing he was trying to be funny. It was another hot ass day—chicks beating the heat under whatever shade they could find as they waited for the bus, and ballers speeding down the avenue in old model cars with loud booming systems. Menage's ESV, as always, turned a few heads or broke a few necks as it cruised down the streets of Miami, and that suited him just fine. They stopped at Burger King and bought a breakfast meal at the drive-thru. Without Katori noticing, the chick in the drive-thru window slipped Menage her phone number.

Menage wasn't paying Katori for sex but he knew she was making ends meet as best she could. She was more than shocked when he gave her five hundred dollars and told her to use it for the baby before dropping her off at her place. It was almost eleven-thirty and he was on his way to the cookout, but he made a U-turn after remembering that he had scheduled a meeting with Felix Marchetti, the don of the underworld in Miami.

Menage walked into a dimly lit, small café on Collins Avenue and spotted Felix in the back smoking a thick Cuban Cigar. He had noticed two well-dressed huge men, Felix's body-guards, at the tiny entrance.

"What's up, old man?" he said pulling out a chair and spinning it around to sit in it backwards.

"Fifty-five isn't old, and how's your back?" Felix said squinting from the thick, rich smoke of his cigar.

"How you know about my back?"

"Dr. Wilson called me as soon as you were brought to the hospital. Remember, this is my city and I already have a few of my people looking into it." He paused to brush off his tailor-made Herme silk shirt. "So maybe you might wanna fill me in about this mess at Bayside." With a nod of his head, the waiter brought two glasses of red wine. After telling Felix more about Bayside, they finally got down to business.

"That DB-7 you say DJ brought in…you didn't inform me of the change of rules."

"What change are you talkin' about, Felix?

Felix flicked some lint off his seven-thousand-dollar overcoat. "The DB-7 was stolen from L.A., but I don't have the owner's name."

"L.A!" Menage yelled and quickly lowered his voice. "Felix, DJ know damn well that I don't deal with out-of-state shit…fuck!

"Have you spoken to him yet?" Felix asked tapping his cigar.

"Nah, but I sure as hell will today. Maybe someone will drive it from L.A. I'ma stop by the shop also. Felix then offered Menage the chance to come stay on his island if he felt worried about the hit at Bayside, but Menage declined. He briefly thought about skipping the cookout and going to see about the out-of-state stolen car sitting in his shop instead. He had a gut feeling that it was going to be a fucked up weekend.

***

Special Agent David Myers rubbed his temples as he sat behind his cluttered desk in sunny Los Angeles. Without opening his heavy eyelids, he called out to the receptionist sitting at a smaller desk outside his office. "Amy, can you please page Special Agent Lydia Nansteel for me, please?" He was past exhausted. He tried to straighten up his desk, knowing that it was pointless trying to flirt with Agent Nansteel. He was nearly twice her age and married, and he doubted that she dated white men. But hell, with all the blacks her age either in prison or dead, he thought that maybe he'd have a chance at the beauty.

She came in minutes later with a strictly business look about her. Myers knew her measurements from her last fitness reports, but the pants she wore hid her eye-pleasing, firm body. Nansteel was 5'8" and weighed 125 pounds. Her 34-25-35 measurements would make her a true rival for the workout guru Donna Richardson.

Yes, Agent Myers, you—"

"Call me David," he said cutting her off with a wave of his hand as she took a seat. "We're on the same team here." His intense, gray eyes quickly glanced at the outline of her perky tits showing through her simple, white blouse. Dismissing his wicked thoughts, he pulled a folder from his desk. "How are things on the Alistair case?" he asked.

Agent Nansteel softly cleared her throat. "Still no leads." She was shocked when she was put on the case last Tuesday. Robert Alistair, the eldest son of the Mayor of L.A., had been found in his condo with a single gunshot wound to the back of his head in front of a safe. After interviewing the Mayor, she found out that his son never kept more than seven grand in his safe. The only object missing was the black Aston Martin DB-7 Vantage Volante that he drove. After she gathered all the information, she withheld certain details about the case from the media; so when Myers told her he'd just received an anonymous call from someone in Miami mentioning the car and a name, Nansteel sat up in her seat with a surprised look on her face. The caller described the car down to its rims and apparently the tags were still on it. The name given was Menage Unique Legend. Agent

Nansteel quickly left to head for the records section to see what the FBI had on this man. This was her first big case, and being the only black female in her section with five years under her belt at the age of thirty-two, it would make her look damn good to solve it.

Before joining the FBI she tried to model, but the only modeling credit she had was gracing one of the pages of Jet for Beauty of the Week. And after walking in on her husband of four years to find him on top of their white, chubby next-door neighbor, she threw herself into her job. It wasn't fair. She was faithful to him, and the thanks she got was a woman, much less attractive than herself, sneaking around with her man. Then he tried to do a Kobe Bryant to buy her love and trust back—picture that. Her divorce became final eight months later. When word got out that her ex had slept with a white woman, a few white agents tried to push up on her. Thanks but no thanks was the position she always maintained. And her ex, still even two years after the divorce, never found out about the miscarriage she had due to stress. But through it all she forged ahead. However, sex or love was no longer a major issue in Agent Nansteel's life.

She returned to Myers office and informed him that the only charge Menage had on his record was possession of a stolen vehicle, and that was lessened to joyriding a year earlier. She also mentioned his bad conduct discharge from the Marines. Myers told her he made a few calls to Miami and found out that Menage was living rather large. He wanted to express his feelings of suspicion, but because Menage was black he didn't want to offend her. His sexual feelings aside, he had lots of respect for the young woman. Not only was she beautiful and highly competent as an agent, but she was even a black belt in some kind of Japanese fighting that he couldn't pronounce and fluent in six different languages.

Nansteel's second surprise of the day came when Myers told her she'd be going to Miami on her first undercover case. She flashed her ID at the gate, and a smile finally appeared on her face as she pulled her pearl white BMW 330ci into traffic. She knew she could handle the job and do what needed to be done—serve justice.

***

Menage knocked on Dwight and Tina's door for the second time. He was looking at his two-way when Tina opened the door. Sure, Dwight was his man, but shorty was looking good right about now. Tina already had a slammin' body, and standing in the doorway wearing a pair of denim boy-shorts and matching T-shirt with her perky nipples showing through made him swallow hard.

"Boy, come in," she said pulling him in by his elbow and motioning for him to sit down. "Oh man, I know Chandra threw a fit about what happened," she said sitting across from him with her legs open, allowing full view of her thick, juicy caramel hips and thighs.

"Damn, Tina, I need to get shot more often if you gonna treat me like this," said Menage as he sat down. And no, I didn't tell Chandra and I plan to keep it that way...hint, hint."

"Boy, you can't do that!"

"Look, go and get Dwight," he said looking at his Bulova. "I got a cookout to make." Tina sucked her teeth and left the sunken living room with the bottom of her smooth butt cheeks jiggling with each step. Menage shook his head, slumping back onto the soft couch. It was huge, with a full bar to his left and a two-hundred-gallon fish tank flushed into the wall in back of him. To his right were four black marble steps leading to the bedroom and a floor-to-ceiling tinted glass window was across from where he sat. The stylish condo was only a jog away from a sandy beach and rows of palm trees across the street.

"Well, if it ain't Superman," Dwight said walking into the living room. "You feeling okay, dawg?" They gave each other dap and ended with a secret handshake. Menage told Dwight about the DB-7 being stolen from L.A. "Say word?" Dwight said now sitting in plush chair, crossing his left ankle over his right knee.

"W-O-R-D—word!" DJ know the damn rules. He must got short-term memory or somethin'!" Menage said. He then told

Dwight that he would let the DB-7 sit for a minute until he holla'd at DJ. He knew he could get an easy fifty thousand for it off the street or sell it to a dealer and get eighty or ninety thousand. Menage only needed $150,000 to reach a mil. He had $850,000 in the bank that he didn't touch, but his balling paper was close to $75,000 the last time he checked. Dwight was $250,000 from his goal, so Menage suggested that he catch up by using the paper he was about to make off of a few brand new 6 series BMWs that he would soon have his team steal off the back of a car carrier. At first Dwight said no, wanting to keep the game fifty-fifty like always.

"Chill. We made a plan to reach this mil as one, and that's what we gonna do—plus it'll be spring break and I'ma be with Chandra, so get wit' Tony at the shop and do that for me."

Dwight gave in reluctantly. "So Chandra don't know about Bayside...yeah, Tina told me." Menage nodded his head, running his tongue over his platinum teeth. Dwight leaned forward with his hands clasped together, his elbows resting on his knees.

"Look, man. You being my ace and all, this on the real...when you gonna settle down with Chandra? You need to put that woman first."

"Oh, you Jaheim now!"

Dwight stood up abruptly. "Bruh, I'm for real. You need to grow up and quit this wanna-be-a-pimp life. What about H.I.V. and AIDS...STDs, come on, bruh!" Menage turned his head, stared at the fish tank and watched a baby shark glide through the clear water.

"Yo, Dwight, I ain't even gonna get into it wit' you about my personal life, so turn the page and close the book." Dwight let out a deep breath. He sat down and allowed Menage to change the subject. The young men shot the breeze back and forth until Menage's Nokia started chiming. Dwight passed on the cookout and told Menage he'd drop by later. He stood at the tinted glass window and watched the Escalade cruise down the street. He turned to find his woman bent over on the couch, sporting a belly chain and high heels. "I'm hot baby, you now what I want," she purred. Dwight was glad that he passed on the cookout.

Carol City

Dough-Low rubbed the dice over his belly and gathered them up into a tightly balled fist. He was 6'2", three hundred pounds and black as hell. With his bald head and mouth full of gold, he looked like a man that didn't give a fuck. He was Jack Master by trade and sold dope like g-strings to a strip club. His motto, "I'm thirty-two, and I'll stick a muthafucka up for his dreams if I catch 'em slippin'." He rolled the dice up against the wall. "Oh, it's true!" he yelled rolling an automatic winner. The group moaned and cursed as he scooped up close to nine hundred dollars. "Oh, it's true!" he said again as sweat rolled down his face. The game broke up and everyone headed back to the cookout.

Dough-Low stood in the door of his pearl black Yukon Denali XL with gold twenty-four-inch rims, counting his money. Standing nearby with their flashy rides were other members of The Big League Car Club. Leaving his two front doors up in the air and sliding the rear doors back, Menage made his entrance as two dark-skinned chicks began eyeing him intensely before he could even get out of his Escalade.

"My nigga, Dough, what up?" Menage said getting out of the ESV. Seeing that Dough-Low was counting money, he asked him who he had robbed.

"Nobody—yet. I beat Lil' Coonk, Jay-Po and dem in Cee-lo."

"Yo, man, look at Moet and her crew comin' in," Menage said leaning on Dough-Low's Denali XL. Both men watched the pussy pink Toyota Tundra double cab pull into the crowded parking lot. Five girls started to strip as Jacki-O's Nookie boomed from the system. Menage had his eyes locked on a brown-skinned chick wearing a g-string and a baby tee. Lil' Coonk jumped in the back of the pick-up truck and doused the girls with a bottle of Moet. "Get the one in the baby tee, Coonk," Menage yelled as the girls started to scream. All the members of the Big League were on the spot now. Pretty Lou was getting mad play, since he had released his second CD a week earlier. Menage was about to holla at him, but seeing a chick sitting in his lap and moving in an odd way in the cramped space of his silver Porsche 911, he let him get his smash on.

"Yo, nigga, let's eat," Dough-Low said tossing back a bottle of Old English 800 after seeing that the food was ready. His mouth watered as he eyed hot dogs, hamburgers, baked beans, steak and dessert. There was also a healthy supply of beer and weed and Menage caught a few getting skied up with powder. There was no need for a deejay. June-June's candy green Dodge Magnum, with its ten, fifteen-inch Kenwoods provided the music and Lil' John and the East Side Boys kept the party live. Chicks with big tits and no bras played a game of volleyball, and their running and jumping caused many dicks to swell at the sight of bouncy breasts under halter-tops and baby tees.

"Kamesa ain't comin'?" Menage asked pouring ketchup on his hotdog.

"Nah. She had to take her sister back to Florida A&M," Dough-Low said after swallowing a piece of steak. "I saw you 'bout to holla at Lou. That fool still trippin' 'cause you fucked one of his groupies?"

"Not really. And he ain't say shit a few weeks ago when he used my crib to shoot his video."

Dough-Low looked over at Lou, who was now being pulled into the girl's bathroom by a white girl with fake tits. "I don't too much care fo' the cat!" Dough Low said. "And oh yeah. Last week, Coonk and me was at the studio gettin' high and shit while Lou was laying a track. Anyway, there was these three blood-ass raw Ethnicity models gettin' smoked out too. Lou tried to feel one of 'em up and she treated that clown like an unplugged Sega." They began laughing hysterically.

"No play!" they simultaneously shouted.

"Lou ain't about shit, but I'd be a fool to waste my time beefin' with him. I got money to make. By the way, let me tell you what that nigga DJ did, Menage said." He gave Dough-Low the short version about DJ and the out-of-state DB-7. They were about to go to the grill for seconds when a young girl about sixteen or seventeen walked up and ran her blue nails through Menage's wild-looking afro.

"Let me do your head. I can hook it up with a fly X & O pattern." She sat on the table with him between her legs, doing just that in an hour flat and left a C-note richer. Revealing that she would be turning eighteen soon, she and Menage exchanged numbers and a few "what I'ma do to yous."

"I might need to give her a job at my salon," Menage said as the girl pranced off wearing a smile.

"Yo, I heard Lou's in a gang now," Dough-Low said with a smirk. "But I wouldn't give a damn if he was in the Cub Scouts! I told Lil' Coonk he was funny actin'. I'm waitin' fo him to cross me. CD or not, I'll blaze his ass and make him famous like 50!"

"More like Tupac, you mean," Menage said knowing that Dough-Low didn't usually aim to maim.

"Yo, Kamesa had some chickenhead she wanted you to holla at the other day." Kamesa was Dough-Low's shorty that stayed in Carol City. "Look, I gotta go hit the block, so holla at me later," Dough-Low said and hopped into his Denali. Menage stayed a bit longer and kicked it with Lil' Coonk. Everybody was asking him about Lou. Fuck Lou.

"Well, he 'bout to go to LA for a week. He leavin' tonight," was all Menage kept hearing.

Menage glanced over at the windshield of the Cadillac XLR parked next to his SUV. On the hood sat a tall and slender female, clad in a white skimpy tank top and a pair of red boy-shorts. He read the message on the top half of the windshield. It read DNNN. "What does DNNN mean?" he asked standing by the fender of her ride.

She cocked her head to one side and without cracking a

smile said, "Don't need no nigga." She said it good and slow, obviously wanting to make herself clear so she wouldn't have to repeat herself.

"So I guess I can get your number, huh?" he said letting his eyes travel up and down her long, dark, hairless legs. Little did he know that she was Lou's ex. She smacked her full lips and slid a strand of blonde weave behind her ear. She then stood up, her stiletto sandals increasing her height to 5'9".

"You don't get it, do you?" she said placing her hands on her hips.

Menage could see her nipples pushing against the thin top. "Nah, not yet," he said smiling. "You might not need a nigga but I know you want one, so what's your name?" She rolled her eyes. Most of the time a brother would call her a bitch and move on, which made no difference to her. Menage was right; she didn't need a man, but she sure as hell wanted one.

"My…name is Andrea," she said blushing. The game was spit and they discovered that they both wanted the same thing—sex. Menage got into his ESV and followed Andrea to the room she had rented at The New Radisson Hotel. Andrea had a body like Eve, and he wondered if that was the reason she wore her clothing line. Once in the lavish hotel room, Menage untied the strings of Andrea's tank top. He immediately began sucking on her breasts and helped her slide out of her boy-shorts. They fell onto the bed as they groped one another and Andrea began to nibble on Menage's neck with her blood-red coated lips, leaving prints all over his body. Menage slipped on his jimmy and Andrea reached for his dick without hesitation. With her back to him, she slowly slid down onto his erection. Menage gripped her tattooed butt cheeks, sliding deeper into her and enjoying every second.

***

Menage pulled into his driveway an hour later as the gate closed on its own. Vapor and Vigor came running from the backyard, begging for attention as soon as he stepped out of his truck. Entering his crib, he activated his answering machine by voice command as he made his way to his kitchen and poured himself a glass of orange juice. Throughout the entire mansion, the female computerized voice spoke in a soft tone: Good evening, Mr. Legend. Tthe time now is 5:29 p.m. You have a total of three calls…Saturday, 4:10 p.m.—message one: Menage…baby, pick up…helloo…well, I guess you're not in and you better know who this is…nah, just playing. The next call was played as Menage poured himself a glass of orange juice. Menage…baby pick up…helloo…well I guess you're not in and you better know who this is, nah, just playing. Anyway, I just called to say I love you. I'll call later, if I'm not in my dorm…just two-way me. Bye, love. It was Chandra, and he felt guilty because he was out sleeping with a girl he didn't even know while she was doing what she did best—loving him. The computerized voice spoke again: Saturday, 4:20 p.m.—message two: Boy, this is your mama! I told you about leaving all that loud rap stuff on this machine! Anyway, you need to call your nephew because he's acting up in school again and if you come up here, bring some church clothes. I love you. Call me later. Menage smiled. Vapor and Vigor shot out the door toward the backyard as a large flamingo landed on the picture-perfect lawn. They'd never catch it. Saturday, 5:10 p.m.—message three: Bitch-ass nigga…yeah, you can be touched up again, so don't get caught slippin'…you marked, nigga! End of messages.

The last message caused Menage to nearly choke on his drink. He could count the people on one hand that had the number to his crib. He played the message twice more to see if he could recognize the voice. Shit wasn't right. Whoever it was, was now touching too close to home. He wasn't used to feeling paranoid in his own crib, and he thought that maybe it was the weed. He went into his bedroom to a hidden stash spot in his walk-in closet. Vapor and Vigor were now back in the mansion. Facing the Rottweilers, he looked them both in the eye. With a closed fist he hit his chest twice, giving them the silent command to go on guard. Vapor and Vigor wouldn't let anyone on the estate and would attack with or without Menage around and would do so until an additional command was given. Vigor swiftly ran out of the bedroom and went outside, as Vapor took off to check the other three bedrooms and three bathrooms, which he inspected thoroughly, entering each room grinding his teeth. He then came back to his owner and watched his every step. Menage took off the safety of his H & K MP-5 tactical assault rifle and went back into the living room with a full thirty-round clip. A black bulletproof vest now covered the tank top he wore. By voice command, he called up the surveillance channel on his eighty-inch plasma screen TV that showed all surveillance shots simultaneously. Menage gripped the custom-fitted rubber grip and finally realized how close he came to being six feet deep. And now some fool had his home number. He was supposed to be safe in his own home—not walking around wearing a vest and carrying a loaded MP-5. Fuck it. He sure as hell wasn't going to call the police...picture that.

Menage studied the screen. Everything looked clear and when Vigor trotted in moments later, he knew that outside was clear. The two dogs rubbed noses, then sat down on either side of Menage. "It's gonna to be a long day, boys." Both dogs let out a low whine. Menage sat on the couch with his finger on the trigger...and waited.

***

Tina was now at the MD Beauty Salon headquarters on 175th Street in her office doing paperwork. Finally taking a short break, she looked at her watch. It was five-forty. Resting her elbows on the desk, she slowly rubbed her temples. Today had been busy since one of her manicurists had called in sick. Her desk, like her life, was in perfect order; she had a good man, a job, car...hell, what else could she possibly want? She picked up the picture of she and Dwight cutting the ribbon at the first Menage Dwight Beauty Salon, better known as MD Beauty Salon. "Why not DT or TD Beauty Salon?" she thought to herself. Her office was fully renovated with a plush, money-green, wall-to-wall carpet. Her name was written in faint gold letters in the center of the rug. In the corner was the sound system that filled the huge, two-story salon with the latest hits. There were over a thousand mirrors as well as a marble onyx floor in the luxurious space. A plasma screen was fitted and flushed into the wall in the waiting area, and upstairs kids under ten could play with the latest video game systems. Menage played a major role in designing this area of the salon.

Tina was about to call Dwight, but a soft knock on her door changed her plans. "Come in, it's open," she said folding her slender hands on the desk. Cookie, one of the stylists, stuck her head through the door.

"Hey, Tina, we gettin' a little behind. A new client just came in and I think all she needs is a relaxer. Can you do it?"

"Yeah, girl, just set her up for me. Let me tie things up in here and I'll be right out," Tina said slipping out of her silver, Gucci slingback pumps to switch to her sandals.

"Thanks, girl…and can you put on that new Kelly Price CD?"

"Yeah, I was about to take it home with me the other day," Tina joked.

"I'll have her ready for you, ok?" Cookie said. I just wanna tell you before you leave that I'ma need next weekend off." Tina made note of it on her desk calendar. She then turned on her answering machine and reached for her jacket. Before stepping out of her office, she checked herself in the mirror. She was flawless as always.

"Hi, my name is Tina. Welcome to MD Beauty Salon," Tina said as she put on some green latex gloves and tilted the new client's seat back to wash her hair. Benita, right?" Tina said making sure Cookie gave her the correct name.

"Yes," Benita said with her eyes closed.

"I hope you don't mind me asking, but are you new to this area? And let me know if this water gets too hot."

"Okay. Yes, I'm new…well, I've been here for a few months—ever heard of Kinston, North Carolina?"

"Uh, well, I can't say that I have," Tina said turning on the water.

"That's no surprise. Kinston is small and you'll ride right through it in no time," Benita said with her eyes closed as Tina washed her hair. Back and forth they had small talk, and Benita couldn't help but notice the stunning diamond encrusted bracelet on Tina's right wrist. She was still thinking about Menage, and she could have easily found him had she asked Tina what MD stood for. Lisa had already brought home the news that Menage had checked out of the hospital, but it was odd because there was no information left on him—no address or anything.

When Tina turned Benita around to face the mirror, she was stunned by her own work. Benita paid at the desk with her credit card, and as always, she drew instant attention when she stepped outside. Yeah, she liked it, but she ignored the horns and catcalls as she crossed the street to Lisa's cream Acura TSX. Pulling into traffic, her thoughts drifted back to Menage. It wasn't every day that a guy risked and saved a girl's life on a first date. They didn't even get the chance to kiss. She wanted to ask him so many things and there was something she wanted—something she wanted to give, but he had yet to call her. Maybe he'd call or show up at the club. Well, until then, she'd keep an eye open for that stunning, canary yellow, Cadillac Escalade ESV.

The digital clock on the dashboard read 7:15 p.m. Not wanting to get lost, she made sure to input Lisa's address in the navigational system—just to be on the safe side. Maybe her cousin was right; she needed to spread her wings and have some fun due to the simple fact that she was young and alive. Maybe she'd enjoy herself at the club that Lisa talked her into going with her to later on that night. But still in the back of her mind, she wondered what Menage Unique Legend was doing at that very moment.

***

Menage was coming out of the bathroom when the computerized voice announced a visitor at the front gate. He viewed the eighty-inch screen and saw Dwight sitting in his dove gray BMW 745Li with the twenty-inch chrome Dalvin spinners. Since Vigor had a shorter temper when it came to visitors, he had to stay outside, but it didn't stop him from barking at the glass back door. "Easy, boy," Menage said to Vigor, and he reached down to rub Vapor's head as Dwight came into the house.

"What's going on?" Dwight said looking down at the table full of cash.

"Everythang but the right thang," Menage said, then quickly told Dwight about the threat he received on his phone.

"Say word? I thought that line was private," Dwight said.

"It was, but fuck it, that's a bitch game. Well, I now know that dem niggas was gunnin' for me, and I'm not 'bout to sit and hide…let's hit the streets, man," Menage said. "You gonna call your girl and ask her if you can you go out?" he added smiling.

"Funny!" Dwight said wondering how Menage could put the incident at Bayside on the back burner.

***

They pulled up to a corner store on Sixty-Second Avenue. Menage came out with two ice-cold bottles of Old English 800 and a bag of Skittles. He was back in his element, gripping the steering wheel with the system knocking. Dwight finished his beer before Menage and the tight feeling he felt in his stomach made his mouth water for a second. Leaning back in the Burberry printed seat with his forearm across his eyes, he glanced at Menage, who was bobbing his neck to the booming system as he gripped the steering wheel with one hand and yelled at some girl on his Gucci Logo Nokia 3650 camera phone. Dwight quickly glanced at the screen on Menage's phone. There was a picture of a naked girl lying in bed. There was even an X-rated DVD playing on a TV screen that was mounted from the black chrome dashboard. Dwight was feeling good when he reached for his blunt. He only got high when he was with Menage. Tina wasn't going for it, so he made the best of it and didn't bug Menage about all of his women.

Menage didn't lead anybody on or sell any false dreams. Chicks saw the whip with its spinning rims and banging system—not to mention the platinum he wore—and they were hooked. He was also fine as hell, so they said. He couldn't recall the last time he waited over a week before sexing a new woman that he'd met. Hell, sometimes they made the first move toward the bed. "There's an art to this game," Menage once said.

Dwight watched him meet seven different girls as they cruised around Miami—same line, different chick. He did it all the time. And they flagged him down—flashing high beams, blowing horns...so how was he at fault? Dwight could only smile and shake his head.

"Where you going?" Dwight yelled leaning toward him as he turned down a side street.

"I'ma see some girl I met last week. Wait till you see her—badoonka-donk-type ass...oh, this my shit here!" he yelled turning up the system a notch louder as the latest hip-hop cut shook the Escalade. They pulled up to a housing project off of Twenty-Seventh Avenue past a football stadium. Dwight looked at his red gold Bulgari watch and saw that it was after nine. Menage backed into a parking space and before he took the key out of the ignition, a light-skinned female came outside in a tight pair of coochie cutters and a green bikini top. Her ass was huge! She walked up to the ESV, waved at Dwight and kissed Menage on the lips.

"You still going out tonight?" Dwight said.

"Yeah," Menage replied, then whispered something in the girl's ear. "Yo, man, it's too early to go to the club, but are you coming in?" he added looking at Dwight while reaching under the seat for his .380.

"Nah, bruh, I'ma chill out here," Dwight said placing a .357 on his lap. On nights like this, Menage didn't think about the chop shop or the money he laundered through his salons. It was all about how many girls he could get with. Dwight watched him follow the big-butt girl into the building and he could actually see them enter her bedroom on the third floor from where he sat. By looking at the digital clock on the dash, he noticed that it only took four minutes for the bedroom lights to go off. He eased back in the plush seat to get comfortable, switched on the plasma screen and watched Biker Boyz.

***

Armed with New York street smarts, DJ was slicker than baby oil between Lil' Kim's breasts. He brought his baby blue Lexus GS430 to a slow halt at a light on Biscayne Boulevard. DJ was twenty-seven, with the pretty-boy looks of Ginuwine. Menage put him back on his feet when word got around that he could steal a car with ease without breaking the steering column. Menage had saved him from a two-year bid and paid his bond of seventy-five thousand. DJ had walked out of the county six months earlier to find Menage sitting across the street in his roofless Acura Legend. He introduced himself, and DJ quickly found out who had paid his bond. Menage took DJ under his wing and showed him how to make real money. Two weeks later, he had DJ use his skills to snatch a brand new Ferrari off the docks as soon as it was unloaded off the cargo ship. That same night Menage drove him to a modest apartment in Hollywood with the Lexus GS430 parked in the driveway. DJ thought it was another job, but he was speechless when Menage gave him the keys to the apartment and Lexus along with twenty thousand in cash spread out on the bed inside the crib. Now DJ was his number-1 car thief, and he gained even more status when he brought in the DB-7, but he hoped Menage wouldn't flip once he told him when and how he got it. Money was money, right?

"Yo, be quiet while I'm on the phone, aight!" he said to the Jessica Simpson look-alike sitting next to him. Only the greenish glow from the Navi system filled the GS430. He quickly dialed a number by heart as he waited for the light to change. There was an answer after the second ring. "What up, sexy?" he said turning down the music with a knob on the steering wheel.

"Un-uh. I called you around six."

"I was tied up." His passenger did as she was told and kept her mouth shut, but since he didn't say anything about not touching him, she leaned over and zeroed her attention between his legs. DJ didn't turn her away. He gave into his need to feel her hands on him. "Can we get up later on tonight? You know I'm tryin' ta beat that." He held in his moan as his zipper slid down.

"Oh, really!" the woman on the other end laughed.

"Y-yeah…can we meet at our spot or what?" he said resting the phone on his shoulder and gripping his passenger's blonde hair. His eyes closed and he became silent as she took him deep into her mouth.

"DJ!"

"Y-Yeah."

"I called your name five times, boy! Anyway, I'll be there in an hour." She hung up before he could reply, but he didn't give a damn. Flinging the phone over his shoulder, he pressed the back of blondie's head down, calling out her name as she sucked him. Neither of the two realized that the light had changed until horns started to loudly blow behind them. Screeching off with the girl's face buried in his lap, DJ quickly took her back to the University of Miami in Coral Gables and made it to his second session in record time.

***

"So, how do I look, girl?" Lisa said turning sideways in her bed-room mirror to examine how her ass filled out the yellow Enyce bodysuit. Benita, standing alongside her, smacked her lips and tilted her head to one side. She wore the same body suit in black. Benita was also pleased with what she saw through her tinted frameless Miss Sixty shades. Both women knew they had the looks and body measurements that many women enied, and they were single. Lisa was ready for a man—not the thug on the corner who would end up in jail or prison; those collect calls and visits were over for her. She rubbed her full lips together after applying her lipgloss. Nails were done, toes painted, nose hairs pulled and make-up in flawless order.

"Benita, will you please bring your ass on here! I wanna stop at the store to buy some coolers," she said looking down at the print between her thighs. "I should have trimmed my kitty hairs some." Benita rolled her eyes and slid on the back of her earring. Grabbing their small Enyce tote bags, they headed out the door. Lisa opened the sunroof of her Acura and told Benita that Club Limelight held true to its reputation as she popped in her favorite CD and let it pump through the speakers. Benita was still thinking about Menage. Finally she met a man that didn't press her for sex out the gate—not that he got the chance. But she would have given him just that, which was something that no one had ever gotten with her. Everyone felt that because she was a stripper she'd spread her legs for that mighty dollar without hesitation—wrong!

"Maybe you'll bring a man home tonight and get some!" Lisa yelled over the music. She had yet to see Benita bring a man to the apartment.

"I'm not down with one-night stands like some freaks I know," Benita said laughing.

"Whateva, but I betcha I'ma get somebody to lick my kitty tonight," Lisa said snapping her fingers twice. Benita smiled at her silly cousin. Yeah, maybe Lisa was right; she should live a little.

***

"So what's the surprise, bruh?" Dwight sat on the hood of his BMW in Menage's driveway.

"Got a new whip," Menage said stepping into his dark

garage. He lightly ran his fingers over a platinum-colored Mercedes-Benz S600. It sat on triple chrome, twenty-one-inch custom- made Neeper concept rims. Everything was voice-activated, and the interior was done in Gucci leather. Three eight-inch plasma screens along with four twelve-inch Alpine speakers made his S600 a showstopper. Slowly it pulled out of the garage, a bluish glow beneath it. Dwight laughed to himself as he got into his BMW.

"Yo, I got sumthin' in store for you later on, but I'ma wait till we get to tha club," Menage said leaning his elbow out the window as he pulled alongside Dwight.

Dwight was thinking of Tina and stopped himself from using her favorite saying—Oh, really! "Let's roll, bruh," was all he said, brushing the collar of his Armani jacket. Menage pulled off first, nearly blowing a fuse as he pushed his speakers to the max. He sported his regular jewelry—watch and chain—but tonight he added a four-fingered diamond encrusted ring that read PIMP on his left hand. His gear matched the inside of his S600, from his leather fedora, green tinted shades and the twenty-seven-hundred-dollar flannel flight suit—all by Gucci. Dwight was still feeling a little buzz as he brought up the rear. He knew Tina would have a fit if she knew the condition he was in while driving. Smoking weed would really put him on the couch. He planned to be sober by the time he got home, so it would be all gravy. Thinking of her as he sped down I-95 made him smile. She had been in his life for three years and they stuck together through the worst of times. It was pure love he had for her and he placed her before everyone—even Menage. The thought of life without her made him speed up and pull ahead of Menage...now he was leading. Maybe Tina was right, he thought. She was afraid that Menage's cheating ways would rub off on him and Dwight thought her thinking was simply foolish; their love was too strong.

***

Club Limelight was a tri-level 7,750 square foot club that did hold true to its rep, but right now all the action was outside in the parking lot—parking lot pimping, you could call it, as everyone checked out the flashy rides. If you had the props and a costly ride, you were able to park in the VIP section, located under two huge lime green street lamps. Lisa and Benita sat on the hood of the Acura, waiting for the long line to shorten a bit. In the meantime, they enjoyed the action in the parking lot. There was loud music, mingling, souped-up bikes doing burnouts... and of course the police.

***

DJ pulled into the parking lot at Club Limelight. "Why are we stopping here?" asked his female passenger.

"I'm just riding through, that's all." DJ turned to look at her and saw that she wasn't pleased. "Just keep the window up, cant nobody see inside," he said grinning. She glared at him as he began to light a blunt.

"Will you put that mess out?" she snapped and pressed the button to lower the passenger window slightly. She snatched the blunt out of his mouth and tossed it out of the window. DJ didn't stress. He would just drop her off and return to the club later.

***

"Girl, check out that Lex. Now that is off the hook. Maybe I can buy me one next year," Lisa said. Benita turned to look just as the window inched down and a slender arm flung something out onto the street. The face couldn't be seen, but Benita could tell it was a female. It was the shiny bracelet on the woman's wrist that caught her attention. She wondered about the bracelet but with so much going on and being on her third cooler, her mind failed to stay focused. She watched the Lexus slowly pull out of the parking lot as the deep thundering bass vibrated from its speakers.

***

Dwight was in the Limelight parking lot waiting for Menage to reveal his surprise.

"Yo, Dwight," Menage said excitedly into his cell phone, "I'ma show you how to make a scene!" Right now nobody could tell him a thing. He was in his element, his world. He slowly cruised his S600AMG into the parking lot. "CD two, song seven, volume max, windows down." The four tinted windows and sunroof opened simultaneously. Seconds later music thumped loudly from the stunning Benz.

***

Menage hit the scene behind a gold Chevy G4 jacked in the air on three wheels, but his S600 stole the show.

"Daaamn!" Lisa said. "Look at this ride here." She pointed at Menage's Benz as it rolled into the parking lot. Benita turned to look and nearly dropped her drink. As the car pulled up, a crowd slowly formed around it. Sure, the system was so loud that she had to yell at Lisa who was right next to her...but why all the attention? She was unable to see the driver from the passenger side, but she soon found out why everyone was all keyed up. This time she dropped her drink. It had to be an illusion. She rubbed her eyes and figured that she'd had too much to drink, but when she looked again the view was the same. With the system at its max, the huge twenty-one-inch rims on the S600 started to slowly spin forward as the car remained motionless. The rims suddenly stopped and then started to spin backwards. Then they began spinning in different directions and speeds. The scene was hypnotic. Dwight was astonished by what he saw. Benita watched the S600 pull into the VIP parking space. She was about to find out who the driver was but Lisa pulled her away, telling her that the line had gotten much shorter. Benita missed Menage by just a few seconds and Dwight walked up as he got out of his car.

"Yo, nigga, you see what happened? Right now I can have any chick out here! You know it, I know it, they know it," he said pointing to the crowd. "I'ma fuck da world and make her mine, that's my word. They can't see me, they can't see me...I'm the nigga," he said pounding his chest with his fist. "Shorties dissin' their niggas—fuck 'em all! Dis how you s'pose to rep. It's all a game and I make the rules!" Menage was now trembling with pure adrenalin. A few members of The Big League Car Club showed up and Coonk and Dough-Low met up with Menage and Dwight. They all went into the club to get their party on.

***

The floor inside Club Limelight was packed. The huge, mirrored dance floor slowly rotated. Women in fishnet stockings and thongs walked around sippng Tanqueray. Menage stepped to the bar to order some drinks as a hit by Three 6 Mafia filled the club. He turned on his stool to face the dance floor. Everyone but he and Dough-Low was up in the VIP section.

"Yo," Menage yelled at Dough-Low, "where Lou at? I thought he was coming tonight."

Dough-Low shrugged his shoulder. "Said something came up. I don't know where the hell he at!" They sat at the bar checking out the women on the big dance floor.

"That's my song, yo, see ya!" Menage yelled before quickly finishing his drink. Minutes later on the dance floor, he was surrounded by two full-figured women jamming to a cut by the Ying Yang Twins. He let the loud music and flashing strobe lights hypnotize him. Life couldn't get any better—fast and fancy cars and women just as fast…and easy as switching lanes. And of course there was the money. It made his world go 'round.

Menage was quite aware of the problems that still existed in the world and he knew that no matter how much money he had, there were many people who would still judge him by the color of his skin. But his view on color was plain and simple: "We all the same when the lights go out." He'd been crossed and played by all colors, but he knew about the hate and envy amongst his own. He didn't look over his shoulder at the white man waiting to stick him up for his ride or his money. It was his own kind that he had to watch out for. All this created drama and stress—something he could do without.

Hands in the crowd flew up in the air when the DJ played an old school song. By now Menage had danced close to two hours and it was time for him to hit the bar again. Before leaving the dance floor, he tried to push up on the chick he was dancing with but she kindly held up her hand, revealing a ring. "Oh, well, that's life," he thought as he slowly made his way back to the bar. Not watching where he was going he bumped into someone, knocking the drink out of his or her hand. He yelled that he was sorry and quickly found the dark-skinned woman standing before him attractive. Together they headed for the bar. It didn't take Menage long to find out where her head was. Her name was Tanita, and she was down from Maryland visiting her sick aunt. She wasn't a beauty queen, but her looks were decent without a face full of make-up. They took a few pictures together in VIP and later talked about what things they had in common. He was sure he had her figured out, that is, until she pulled him on the dance floor and placed her head on his chest as a song by Musiq slowed things down a bit and changed the mood in the club. Holding Tanita in his arms, Menage closed his eyes. Her slender body was warm and soft. He gently kissed her neck and deeply inhaled, taking in her natural scent. Feelings of arousal swept through his body. Sex was easy for him to get and he never disrespected a woman or pressed her for it; there was no need. Tanita looked into his eyes, pleased with the respect he was showing her. No words needed to be spoken as she led him off the dance floor. He would've never guessed her age to be thirty-nine.

DJ sat across from Lisa, holding her hand. They carried a conversation over all the loud music, and it was clear that they were interested in one another. They finished their drinks and wondered what the night would bring. DJ already knew the mathematics: Hennessey and hormones was equal to panties around the ankle.

***

"Just take the car and I'll call you tonight...or in the morning," Lisa said to Benita later on in the ladies room.

"What!" Benita exclaimed. "Girl, you just met this guy and you going home with him?"

"Chile, please. I ain't married and it's been...what, two weeks for me, and I'm not looking for no relationship. What's wrong with a little safe and fun sex—on one of the very few occasions I don't have to work on a Saturday, huh? And I'm about to go on vacation, too...girl, please."

"Well, never mind, but if you're leaving now I'll just go on home," Benita said.

"You gots to be jokin'...all these fine-ass dudes up in here and you going home? It ain't nothing but..." she looked at her watch, "three something. God, girl, have some fun, will you!" Lisa said.

Benita rubbed her temples. "I can't...I'm still thinking about Menage. I just can't get him off my mind, Lisa. He saved my life. How would I look checking out some other guy that nine times out of ten only want some pussy and don't give a damn about me!" she said turning away.

"Look, just calm down. Take the car and go home. Maybe it wasn't such a good idea to come out here anyway." Lisa placed her hands on Benita's shoulders and turned her around so they could face each other. She continued. "I was just trying to cheer you up, that's all, but I'm sure he'll call," Lisa said softly looking into Benita's eyes.

"Okay, but you better call me so I'll know where you are and—"

"Yes, Mother," Lisa said laughing, cutting her off. They embraced and Lisa went back inside the club.

Benita was ready to get home to see if Menage had called. She was in such a rush as she started to back out of the parking lot that she almost hit a dove gray BMW that drove by. "Damn fool!" she screamed. Upon making it home, she was disappointed to see that Menage hadn't called. Tossing her body suit to the floor, she fell onto the couch and stared up at the ceiling. She thought of Menage with each breath she took. "Why do I have to be alone?" she thought as she turned off the lamp. Outside she heard a police siren. She looked at the digital clock, its red numbers piercing the darkness. It read 3:45 a.m. Letting out a deep breath, she rolled over and punched the pillow, ignoring her new eighty-dollar hairstyle. She was asleep in minutes.

***

Showing off was something that Menage mastered. He sat in his S600 in front of the club as everyone exited. The music pumped from his Benz as the rims slowly spun around and around. Directly in front of him, Tanita sat in her sporty Toyota Camry Solara coupe, no doubt checking him out from her rearview mirror. It had rained a little, and the slightly wet platinum Benz glimmered even more under the moonlight. Menage knew Tanita was down after excusing herself and going to the ladies room at the club, only to return with her silky thong balled up in her fist. "I have a birthmark I want you see," she had whispered in his ear. They stopped at the Waffle House and Menage then followed her to her hotel room. He wanted to do more than just see her birthmark. Just another day, he figured, as he stood at her hotel door, rubbing his fingers over the ribbed condom in his pocket. Safe sex it would be…no doubt.

Triple Crown Publications presents

CHAPTER 3

Fillin' Clips

Sunday
11:48AM
**"First, ask me do I give a fuck! Then look me in the face to see
if I care!" Menage said over his cell phone as he sat behind his
desk at the body shop.** "No…since you can't see me, listen really hard to see if I give a fuck. You done wrecked two cars, Rico—
two! Now this is the last time I'ma work wit' yo' ass and your sister won't change my mind. And by the way, where she at?" Rico
had called and said that he had crashed the forty-thousand-dol-
lar Chevy SSR that he had stolen. After lending his sister's serv-
ices to Menage, he promised that he'd have another SSR the following week. Menage already had a buyer willing to drop twenty thousand tax-free greenbacks for the SSR, and he told Rico to
make it happen. Since his cars commanded the biggest checks
once they were tagged, his name was gold to those that knew his
hustle. Why pay top dollar for a nice ride when you could cop
one from Menage for less than half price with less than eight
hundred miles? After dealing with Rico, he went back to the
garage where the DB-7 Vantage Volante sat covered, sitting next
to a fortieth anniversary Ford Mustang GT. His workers would be
in about two, so for now he was alone. He glanced at this
Bulova and figured it would be best to try to call DJ later. He was
heated and was itching to talk. DJ knew the rules and he knew
Felix was telling the truth about the DB-7 being from L.A.

The five-car garage was dark and smelled of oil and leather.

Menage walked towards a blood red Cadillac XLR with gold twenty-inch rims. It had been stolen from Tampa straight off the lot. A simple solo test drive and a trip to a parked van with a key copier had made a key. In less than thirty minutes the XLR was returned and it was stolen a week later. Rico just walked on the lot around midnight, got into the vehicle and drove off like it was nothing. The XLR would bring Menage a huge profit. He knew it was possible to move five cars a day and bring in crazy, stupid money, but he refused to be sucked in by greed and speedballing was out of the question. The game had rules—like not using your own product if you sold dope. Although Menage followed a set of rules, he looked at buying cars as some looked at buying a new pair of Air Ones; to him it was just an everyday thing.

The scratches Tanita had left on his back were becoming irritated by his bulletproof vest, so he took it off but planned to put it back on later. When his workers started to show up he changed his clothes and went to work on some cars that were in his shop for legitimate repairs. He got dirty just like everybody else.

He grew restless as the hours passed and he began working under the hood of a Dodge Ram SRT-10, amazed with its 500hp engine. "I gotta get me one of these," he said when he found out that the pick-up could reach 150mph and reach 60mph in 5 seconds. Once things were generally taken care of at the shop, he changed, washed up and headed to his mansion. Halfway home, he realized that he had left his vest at the shop but he didn't sweat it. Home was safe and today would be a good day, he told himself.

DJ sped through traffic with one hand on the wheel and his phone in the other. His meeting with Mr. Marchetti wasn't as bad as he thought it would be and he was glad that it was over. He had more important things to take care of.

***

Menage pulled into his garage at ten minutes to five. As soon as he stepped out of his car, Vapor and Vigor ran up to him, whining and fully agitated. He knew something was wrong.

"What is it boys, huh?" he whispered as he pulled out his .380. Before walking into the house, he quickly scanned both his front and back yards. Nothing appeared suspicious but he trusted his dogs. He rushed to his bedroom, picked up his MP-5, slung it over his shoulder and went into the living room. He switched his TV to the surveillance channel with Vapor and Vigor still at his side. He checked each camera as he slammed a fresh thirty-round clip into the MP-5. It all went down too fast. On the last camera shot of his front yard, he noticed four men trimming his bushes. It took two seconds for him to realize that they weren't due until Tuesday and that the van wasn't out front like it was supposed to be. He tried to figure out what the deal was but the camera suddenly revealed two of the men rushing toward his glass door carrying Uzis. They stopped inches from the glass and bringing the guns up to their chin, they opened fire. The glass shattered in tiny fragments as the deadly stream of lead ripped through the living room. Sheetrock began to fly, as the bullets tore ragged chunks from the wall. The eighty-inch TV exploded as it too came under fire. Menage had dove over the couch and into the kitchen before the first shot was fired. Finally the shooting stopped and he heard the sound of broken glass under boots. He knew they were reloading, but what about he other two? "Fuck!" Menage cursed as he pointed the MP-5 blindly over the counter, sending a barrage of bullets in the direction of where the men had entered. His military training now took over. The first man was hit in the neck, stumbling backward through the shattered glass door, spewing blood as he fell down dead. The second man caught a few rounds in the chest and the impact took him high off his feet like a rag doll. Gasping for breath, he slowly tried to get back on his feet and make it to his Uzi a just a few inches away. He knew he was still vulnerable to the man who had shot him and he was surprised that he didn't pick him off while he lay struggling to get to his feet. His plan of surprise didn't work, and he figured that Menage thought he was dead. Well, he'd sure as hell make him pay for that mistake, he vowed, as he got to his knees. The first man now lay in a steady streaming pool of blood. Clenching his teeth, the second man reached for his Uzi and set out to finish the job that he and his partner had started. He hesitated as a quick movement caught his eye. His mouth dropped in pure horror. Vigor lunged at him swiftly and silently, his fangs fully bared. The man screamed, and seconds later the dog broke though his weak shield of forearms, bit into his neck and gave him a deadly bite to the jugular. At the front door the other two now stood. Giving each other the go-ahead, they raised their Uzis and shot through the lock. Kicking in the door, they slowly eased down the hallway, Uzi's held under their chins. There was total silence; the thick carpet made their steps light and undetectable. Menage was still in the kitchen behind the counter and had heard the men kick in the front door. He loaded the MP-5 with its last clip. Vapor lay next to him, tense and alert. He growled softly, sensing the two men in the house. "Easy boy, easy," Menage said rubbing his head. Where was Vigor? Thinking the worst, he blocked his thoughts out of his mind. He then threw the huge plastic saltshaker over the counter, causing it to fall onto the glass from the shattered TV. His plan worked. One of the men ran into the living room, pointing his blazing Uzi from left to right. Glass shattered as he now fired into the kitchen and then back into the living room. Menage never gave him a chance to regain his composure. He tucked the MP-5 under his chin and sent three rounds right to the man's face. He dropped lifelessly onto the glass coffee table, shattering it on impact. Menage watched his headless body fall, but it would cost him. The last of the four men, now acting out of pure fright, darted into the living room, catching Menage off guard. He pulled the trigger, wildly spraying the already-destroyed wall and kitchen, but he found his target. The lead tore into Menage's left shoulder, spinning him around and onto his back. At first he was in excruciating pain, but he soon lost feeling in his left shoulder, now bleeding profusely. With his adrenaline working overtime, he clenched his teeth and got to his knees. The MP5 was nowhere in sight now. Vapor whined and drew closer to his owner, licking his face. Menage let out a deep guttural cry and stood up quickly. He fired his .380, emptying the clip of hollow tip slugs.

The last man stood against the wall as the slugs exploded just inches from his head. He held his Uzi to his chest with his eyes closed. When the firing stopped he slowly opened his eyes and looked to his left towards the living room to see a dog walking slowly through the shattered glass door, teeth grinding. The man panicked, nearly dropping his gun and let out a long, ten-round flurry of bullets in the dog's direction. Menage saw Vigor jump out of the way before the man could empty an entire clip on him. He tried to make it to his MP-5, but he didn't move fast enough. The man veered around the corner and yelled as he pulled the trigger, letting off another six rounds. They all found their mark. Menage was off his feet and lay crumpled on the kitchen floor. The man tossed his empty gun to the floor. Fear and shock made him forget about the extra clip he had in his pocket. He looked at all the blood and his faceless friend. Holding back vomit, he closed his eyes and picked up his dead partner's Uzi. He wouldn't need it. He had to finish the job as ordered—a bullet between the eyes. He slowly made his way towards the kitchen. Vigor charged through the front door behind the man, growling viciously as he locked onto his leg. The man yelled and tried to fight off the dog. Vigor slipped in some blood and lost his footing. Again he charged the man, this time not minding his weapon. The audible spit of the Uzi stopped Vigor in his tracks. The man then heard the familiar sound of an empty clip. Shaken and drained he slung the Uzi on the floor. It landed next to the MP-5. Before he could take one step, Vapor appeared from behind the counter, his hair standing up on his back as he bared his teeth and growled. The man froze. He saw the muscles tighten and flex in the dog's full chest. He was now prevented from grabbing the MP-5, and he winced when the dog barked. "Easy b-b-boy, it's okay now," he said and slowly took a step back. Vapor took a step forward, ignoring the soft mush of brain matter and blood under his paw. Standing over Vigor, he quickly dropped his head and let out a soft whine, never taking his eyes off the intruder. He nuzzled Vigor with his nose. Seeing his chance for escape, the man bolted for the front door. Vapor took off like a rocket after him, but he lost his traction in the blood. He quickly regained momentum but it was too late; the man slammed the door just in time for Vapor to crash into it, sealing it shut with his own weight. The man was about to head back to the van when all of a sudden, a Lexus GS430 smashed into the iron gate and came to a screeching sideways halt.

***

Dwight was a few blocks away from Menage's house. Even from a distance, he could see the front gates leaning at an odd angle; he knew something wasn't right. He nearly gave Tina whiplash as he floored the Viper. DJ ran toward Dwight's vehicle as it came to a sudden halt. Dwight jumped out with his .357 in tow.

"Tina, stay in the fucking car and call the police—now!" Dwight yelled. "DJ, what the hell is going on? Where's Menage?" he said looking at DJ, then down at the nine-millimeter in his hand.

"I…I just got here. I saw the place shot up, and I rammed into the gate. This guy came running out, so I smoked him!" DJ said gripping his nine-millimeter. Dwight looked down at the man in the driveway near the front end of DJ's Lexus. The back of his head was gone. Dwight turned away quickly. "D-Dwight, we need to check on Menage!" Dwight gripped his gun and rushed towards the house. Things didn't look good. If his friend were okay, he'd be out to greet them by now. With DJ beside him, he kicked open the door. Once inside he moved slowly along the wall, noticing all the bullet holes. He felt hard shell casings under the weight of his body with each step he took.

"Menage…answer me, man!" Dwight yelled. His heart was pounding in his chest. "DJ, you go to the back. I'ma check the living room and kitchen!" DJ went off without a word. Dwight stepped into the living room and nearly lost it. He had to step back around the wall to catch his breath. "Oh, my God," he said breathing heavily. The smell of human excrement made his knees weak, but he had to find his friend. He stepped back into the living room, ignoring the gushing pink substance beneath his feet. The once state-of-the-art living room was now a war zone. Tears filled his eyes as he saw Vigor lying on his side. His finger stayed poised on the hair trigger as he slowly scanned the scene before him. The gun felt heavy in his hand. He finally made it to the kitchen. He collapsed to his knees, dropping his gun. "Oh, please, God, n-o-o-o-o!" Dwight moaned. He looked at his friend, lying on the once-white floor; it was now red. Vapor stood next to Menage's body, growling viciously. Dwight's voice was weak. "Easy, boy…come on, Vapor, it's me, boy. Let me help Menage. Come on, boy." Vapor barked and whined and cocked his head to one side. He nudged Menage's head with his nose, whined again and sat down, staring at Dwight. Dwight, still on his knees, started to move forward, but Vapor's ears shot straight up and he started to growl.

"Freeze, don't move, put your hands on top on your head!" yelled the police. The house quickly filled up with cops and paramedics. Physical force had to be used to remove Dwight from the house until everything was under control. One of the officers used a stun gun on Vapor so the paramedics could get to get to Menage, but by the looks of what they saw, he was too far gone. Police cars and rescue squads packed the driveway of the house, and officers and paramedics ran from one spot to another. It started to rain, and DJ sat on the curb across the street wrapped in a raincoat…the weather forecast was wrong. Dwight and Tina sat in the back of an ambulance. She tried to get him to talk, but he was in shock. Squinting through the rain, he never took his eyes off the front door of Menage's mini mansion. The reverberating sound of the news and police helicopters hovering above the house drove Vapor crazy as he yanked his chain, attached to a palm tree in the front yard. The man lying in front of DJ's Lexus had already been covered with a body bag. DJ stood up when he saw a plainclothes officer yelling out to a uniformed officer standing in the front doorway.

"How many you say?" he yelled over the loud helicopters circling about.

"Two…bring two…no, three," replied the officer in uniform. DJ saw the plainclothes officer rush toward a paramedic, who then searched the back of an ambulance and gave him three body bags. DJ walked slowly up to the gate as far as he was allowed. Dwight was there too now. Helplessly they stood, eyes focused on the front door, waiting to see last of the living legend come out in a body bag. Vapor let out a long howl, causing everyone to shiver. Dwight clenched his fists. He desperately needed to vent his anger.

***

Chandra sat at her computer alone while her roommate was at basketball practice. Her mind drifted to Menage. She knew about the chop shop and occasionally tried to talk to him about getting out of the game. He made a promise to her that once he and Dwight each reached a million, he would get out and wash his hands clean. She glanced at the picture of him on top of her computer. He was standing in front of his Escalade with Vapor and Vigor. She was looking forward to spending time with him during spring break. She turned off her computer and ran her fingers through her soft, curly hair and recalled the day she met him.

It was a year and a half ago, and she was up in Raleigh, North Carolina, visiting a friend that attended Shaw University. They had gone to Crabtree Valley Mall to buy gifts for Christmas. She had to smile, remembering how Menage made his presence known. While she and her friend were leaving the mall, Chandra nearly stepped out in front of Menage's midnight black Acura RL. He was quick to get out to see if she was okay. With his smooth tongue, he persuaded her into letting him take her out to eat. They got along well, and what shocked her was that he waited around a few months to have sex with her. He grew to trust her with everything he had. She rubbed her stomach and wondered how he would take the shocking news that she was carrying his first child. She wondered if he was ready for what she had in mind—marriage. Putting on her Fubu tennis shoes, she started to head out the door to go wash her peach BMW X-5. Just as she was about to leave, the phone rang. She started to let the computer take the call but she went ahead and answered it.

"Hello?" she said.

"Chandra, this is Felix. How are you?"

"Oh, hi Felix. I'm doing fine. Menage tell you I'm comin' down for spring break?"

"Ah, yes, yes, he did."

"Felix, is something wrong?" She knew it was odd for Mr. Marchetti to be calling her. She slowly sat down.

"Chandra, Menage has been shot."

"Oh my God, Felix...no...h-how is he?" she said standing back up now.

"Listen, calm down and come to the airport. My private jet is on its way. How soon can you get there?"

"I...I'm on my way now...Felix, how is he?" she said, bursting into tears. She heard him take a deep breath.

"He's in critical condition and on life support. That's all I know as of right now. But it's important you get here, so drive carefully, Chandra, and don't worry. He'll pull through."

Chandra wanted to ask who was responsible, but she had to make it to the airport and get to Menage's side. His mother received the same call from Mr. Marchetti and an hour later, she, too, was aboard another one of his private jets from New York to Miami.

***

It had been almost thirty minutes since the helicopter had flown Menage off to the hospital. Detective Dominique Covington finally had the crime scene under control and he was thankful that it was no longer raining. Now he could stand outside and smoke his Newports. Earlier as he had finished taking statements from DJ, Dwight and Tina, the nosy-ass TV reporters rolled up in their vans. He had also confiscated DJ's nine-millimeter and Dwight's .357 until further investigation. DJ's Lexus, with its front end smashed, would be under investigation as well because of the blood on the fender. DJ didn't seem to mind; he was upset over what had happened to his friend. Detective Covington got down on one knee and pulled back the bag from the body in the driveway.

"Four dead bodies—three by gunshot wounds and one by a dog...fucking headache," Covington said to himself. At thirty-five, he was the head man on the street for homicide. Three things made him unique: He was the youngest person and the first black to ever hold the position. The other thing that made him unique he kept on the low. Crushing the butt under his shoe, he stood up and stretched. He pulled out another Newport but changed his mind. "Okay guys, let's not fuck up this scene. Collect all spent shells," said Covington.

"Oh, fuck, there must be over two hundred fucking shells in there!" a rookie cop replied.

"You keep talking and I'll have you do it all by your damn self! Now, as I was saying…collect all, that's A-L-L, spent shells, and please, please, make sure the CSI gets enough pictures of the bodies before they are moved. Peterson!"

"Yes sir," Peterson, a rookie cop replied.

"Order some pizza, I'm starving. Okay, girls, let's get to work!" Detective Covington said as he walked toward the house, looking up at the dark clouds overhead.

***

At Jackson Memorial Hospital, Dwight sat in the waiting room with his head against the wall, eyes closed. Tina sat next to him, stroking his hand. DJ sat in the corner alone, rubbing his throbbing, aching head. Mr. Marchetti stood looking out of the rain-streaked window with his hands behind his back. Next to him, facing the room, were his two bodyguards. Occasionally a doctor or nurse was paged over the intercom, breaking the silence. The only other thing that seemed to make any noise was the soft humming of the water fountain by the exit. No one knew what to say, and silence ruled. Outside the sky was getting darker and thunder could be heard in the distance. Time seemed to stand still.

"Mr. Marchetti, Mrs. Lovick has arrived," whispered one of his bodyguards, having received the information from a small mic that was in his left ear. Anyone who didn't know Marchetti would have mistook him for a government official and figured that his two guards were secret security agents. But in truth, he had as much power as the Mayor of Miami—maybe even more. Another pair of Marchetti's bodyguards escorted Chandra in, and he immediately got up and hugged her and then slowly walked her to a seat. He could see that she had been crying. As they sat down, she choked up on her words as she sought answers to what was going on. Dwight couldn't keep his eyes off Chandra, knowing what she had to be going through.

Menage's mother arrived about an hour later. At fifty-two she still looked young and in shape. She thanked everyone for coming, not really knowing what to say. Then she and Mr. Marchetti went to a corner to speak privately. Later on, sitting next to Chandra, she told her she was glad her son finally had some taste. She liked Chandra and the two seemed to get along well, considering the circumstances and them meeting in person for the first time.

"Baby," Menage's Mother said softly holding Chandra's hand in her lap, "my son would want you to be strong, so we got to be strong right now...come pray with me." She and Chandra got down on their knees and held hands. Mr. Marchetti got down on his knees as well and prayed with them. Then Dwight and Tina, followed by DJ, joined them. The two bodyguards, keeping their eyes fully open, lowered their heads. Chandra tried to be strong, but she had to lean on Mr. Marchetti for support and sobbed as Menage's mother began to pray: "Dear Lord...Oh Mighty Father...I ask you in Jesus' name, to save my son—your child. Oh heavenly Father, show your mighty power and grace and let the sun shine on his face again. Oh Lord, let him know that it's you who will bring him back. Oh Lord...oh Lord...let it be your will. My faith in you is strong, oh Lord, so I...so I now put it in your hands, Oh Lord, my Savior. Glory be thy name...oh Jesus...ohh Lord...in Jesus' name I pray and I thank you."

After the prayer, Chandra sat with Menage's mother as everyone continued to wait. When Chandra was able to talk, she told her that she was two weeks pregnant. Mrs. Legend, raising her head for the first time since her prayer, let a single tear run down her face. "This tear is for your baby—not my son," she said softly. DJ sat alone rubbing his eyes, trying to hide his tears.

After four hours of waiting, a doctor in a surgical mask and gown walked over to the group. Everyone stood with questioning looks on their faces. Mr. Marchetti directed the doctor toward Menage's mother. "I'm sorry, Mrs. Legend, but I must be fully honest with you..." He never got to finish. Chandra screamed at the top of her lungs. "N-o-o-o-o-o, God please, n-o-o-o-o!" She passed out and Dwight caught her before she hit the floor. Everyone began to yell and scream.

"This...this can't be...it can't be true!" Dwight muttered to himself as he held Chandra in his arms.

***

Detective Covington looked at his watch. It was almost eleven o'clock. He sat in his unmarked Ford Crown Victoria smoking a Newport as he watched a tow truck haul DJ's Lexus from the driveway. Things didn't add up from his viewpoint. He looked at his pad and glanced at the details of the case as the smoke burned his eyes. "Two bodies out back—one with one or two shots in the neck and the other...killed by one of the dogs." He let out a chuckle.

He then looked at DJ's statement regarding the shooting of the man in the driveway. DJ had said the guy ran toward him—unarmed—and he blew his head off at close range. Covington was now certain that something wasn't right. "It's going to be a long week," he sighed and looked down at his muddy suit. They had called the pound to pick up the dog. He seemed friendly, but as soon as some fool let it loose to go into the van, it took off toward the gate, dodging ten or more officers, including Covington, who slipped and fell face first.

He took off his muddy tie and tossed it onto the back seat.

The yellow crime-scene tape flapped in the wind, as he flicked his Newport out the window. Looking at the once beautiful mansion, he shook his head in disbelief, started the car and drove home.

***

Tina sat crying in her bedroom with the lights out, while Dwight sat in a bar getting drunk. He never experienced a pain so deep. Menage was like a brother to him, and Dwight knew that the only thing his friends cared about was the paper chase. Yet and still, Menage set rules, like no carjackin', or involvement with drugs or drug trafficking, so this all made no sense to Dwight.

"Why?" he whispered to himself. Jealous-ass niggas…it's all bullshit…just so…so…" He flung the bottle of wine he had been drinking against the wall. He knew he had to stay in control but he felt compelled to do something. However, there was nothing to do but wait.

***

Mr. Marchetti left two of his guards at the hospital as he flew back to his island. His gut told him that whoever did the hit on Menage had to have had a specific reason, being that Dwight or DJ weren't shot. He vowed to find out who it was and deal with them in his own way.

Tears slowly ran down Chandra's face as she looked at Menage. She carefully dabbed his lips with a wet towel to prevent them from drying. Chandra did her best to stay strong, since his mother wasn't able to stand the sight of her only son being kept alive by a machine. She refused to think of life without Menage, and she became hysterical and shouted at the doctor when he told her of the odds of him coming out of the coma. Menage's mother simply turned around and dropped to her knees and prayed. Over and over Chandra whispered in Menage's ear, begging him to fight and telling him how much she loved him. She once recalled seeing a special on TV about people waking up from deep comas, claiming to have heard music, so she relayed it to Felix, who quickly had someone get the CD she asked for, along with a portable CD player. After turning out the lights, she stopped and looked at all the machines that kept Menage alive, casting an orange glow on his face. Before Felix's bodyguard returned, she heard a song on the radio that caught her attention and the tears ran freely again. Closing her eyes, she buried her face in her hands and sobbed as the song Many Men, by 50 Cent, filled the room at a low volume.

Menage's medallion, which spelled out his last name, lay on the table behind where Chandra sat. The bullet that would have hit him in his heart had ricocheted off the letter D and created an imperfection. Even before this incident, Chandra knew her man had one foot in the grave because of the life he was living. She also knew that he had to pull through soon because his mother wouldn't let him remain this way for too long. She fell asleep inches from his bed as the music played softly in the background.

CHAPTER 4

Ante Up!

Four Days Later
Thursday
"You been to see Menage yet?" said Coonk.

"Nah...I don't get along wit' hospitals," Dough-Low replied. The two sat at a hand carwash on Seventy-First Avenue.

"Man, that's some fucked up shit. 'Nage cool as fuck, yo!" Coonk said frowning.

"Yeah, he don't be tryin' to shine on folks. I been thinkin' if he ever told me 'bout some cats he had beef wit' or somethin'. But you know as well as me, all he do is bang some shorties and make that paper," Dough-Low said. Coonk stood up and looked outside to see if his ride was ready. It wasn't.

"You know that new cat that took Menage's spot done raised the prices and everything, and the fool tried to get fly when I told him that me and Menage already had a deal. Word, Dough, I was 'bout to wet that bitch ass!" Dough-Low looked at Coonk to see if he was serious about what he had just said.

"What's his name?" Dough-Low asked rubbing his bald head.

"Shit...uh...DJ, yeah, yeah."

Dough-Low closed his eyes and tried to recall where he heard that name. "Damn, man, DJ... DJ," Dough-Low said slapping his forehead with the palm of his hand. Then he remembered. At the cookout, Menage had told him something about DJ bringing a fucked up ride to the chop shop. Keeping it to himself, he planned to find out what this DJ was all about.

Finally their rides were ready. Coonk pulled his BMW up next to Dough-Low's Yukon Denali XL. "Hey, yo, man, I'ma go see Menage later on, so I'll hit you on the two-way or something. Nine times outta ten, I'ma be on the block. What you 'bout to do?"

Dough-Low put on his shades and shrugged his shoulders. "Just hit me later on, partner. I'ma just chill."

"Bet dat!" Coonk said as he came off the clutch, smoking the back tires of his Z8.

Dough-Low fanned the smell of rubber out of his face and cruised out of the parking lot with his system booming. He adjusted his gold plated .380 in the small of his back at a stoplight. By his feet on the floorboard was his smooth action .40 cal.

Dough-Low pulled up to the front of Kamesa's apartment in Carol City. His truck was new and not as familiar as his Hummer H2, and he snuck up on two Cuban cats, Hector and Raul, who owed him several thousand dollars. They sat on the hood of a kitted-up Corvette. They'd been avoiding him for two whole months. One of them even had his girl tell Dough-Low that the law had sent him back to Cuba. The other one obviously didn't give a fuck.

Dough-Low pulled up behind them as they chatted with three other men.

"Yeah, amigo, its' true!" Dough-Low yelled with his .40 cal. pointed at the two Cubans. The other three started to back off. "Oh, no, move another step and it's on!" His gold .380 in his right arm froze them in their tracks. "Get on the ground!" he yelled at the three standing to his right. Two of them did as they were told but one of them, being a brave ass, cursed him in

Spanish. Dough-Low popped him in the kneecap with his .380. He fell to the ground holding his bleeding knee. "Oh, it's true, amigo!" Ignoring the man's cries, he turned to Hector and Raul. "So, you no gotta my money? You thinka you can play ol' Dough-Low for a fool, huh? Oh, what, you don't speak English no more!"

Hector spoke first. "H-hey man...we been looking f-for you, I swear," he pleaded.

"Yeah, after I set your ass ablaze, your thoughts come back! Nah, this how it's going down. You got two...no fuck it...tonight, I want my dough, understand? Now take your friend to the hospital—need ta get some fuckin' manners." Dough-Low took off before the police hit the set—if they were coming at all. He called Kamesa and told her what went down and that he'd meet her later on after he switched rides.

***

"Yes, I believe it was someone close to him but now I'm not sure," Mr. Marchetti said sitting across from Dwight in the living room of his mansion on his private island.

"That can very well mean me or DJ, and we know Chandra wouldn't do no shit like this. Really, Mr. Marchetti, I'm at a loss," said Dwight.

"Yes, I understand, but things just don't add up. Everyone in this city—this county—state—knows of my family and me. Yet someone had the balls to take a chance and put a hit—twice—on Menage who is like...like a son to me." Dwight pondered what he had said and remained silent.

"Look, Dwight. I brought you to my island because I don't like this one bit. If this was done by a rival family it would have been nice and quiet and I hate to say it, but we would be mourning Menage's death. But it was sloppy. Someone with money, but not enough—someone that knows my limit, your limit...and Menage's as well did this."

Dwight took a sip of his wine and leaned back against the Italian leather sofa. He closed his eyes and let his mind wander. Think, Dwight, think! Then he spoke aloud. "What about all of the women he slept with?" Maybe he messed with the wrong one!" Dwight's eyes were open now, and he waited for Mr. Marchetti's reply.

"But all this, including four men dead…over a piece of pussy? I don't think so."

Dwight glanced over at a long staircase with an ivory rail behind where Marchetti sat. "Maybe that girl he took the bullet for…Benita…I think that's her name," Dwight said leaning forward, his elbows on his knees rubbing his temples. "So what do we do now?" he said.

Mr. Marchetti lit a Cuban cigar with a gold lighter. "We continue, Dwight. I hate to sound harsh like this but we must go on," he said after filling his lungs with the rich smoke. "As you know, DJ will keep things running for the time being. At first he didn't want to take the position, but I talked him into it. Has he told you about how he stopped that guy?" he said looking off into the distance. "Maybe if that…piece of shit had lived I could have made him talk. I got my ways. I'm sure you're aware of that, Dwight.

"Yes, sir, but what about the DB-7? I'm sure you know it's from L.A.

Felix brushed ashes from his silk shirt. "I talked to DJ and he said it was an easy take, so he took it. But I advised him of the rules that Menage set and I asked him to follow them. For now it's best you let it sit. It's your call, Dwight…when will you be heading back to Miami? The helicopter will leave soon and I know how you get airsick," Felix said with a grin.

"Well, if it's not too much of a problem I'd like to stay here tonight—just to unwind. But I'll need to call Tina. I'm having a problem with my cell and two-way."

Felix smiled. "Not a problem." He was about to tell Dwight

about how he had a system that could block out all outgoing and incoming calls, but he figured he'd keep it to himself. Recording devices also monitored his phones 24 -7. "Dwight, I have rooms I haven't even seen myself," Felix chuckled. They both stood.

"I wonder how he's doing," Dwight said finishing his fourth glass of wine. He felt warm.

"No need to worry. I have a direct line with Dr. Wilson and his staff, so I'll be the first to know of any change in his condition," Felix said.

"I wonder…I mean, I can't believe that Chandra is having his child and he doesn't even know it," Dwight said softly. Felix told him not to worry again as he picked up the phone.

"Ah, senorita…yes…I'm fine. We'll be having a guest for dinner tonight, and fix up a room also. Yes, thank you…that will do." He hung up the phone and drew hard on his cigar. His eyes met Dwight's. "Dwight, we'll find out who did this and they will pay—that I can promise you. But for now, we wait. Time will tell and the streets will talk, so just go along as usual and let me handle things, okay?"

"Mr. Marchetti, do you think that if…I mean when he comes back, he'll stay in the game? I was just thinking…"

Felix put out his cigar and spoke slowly. "Truth be told, Dwight, at times I try hard to put myself in the next man's shoes to stay ahead in this game. But with…it's so different…he's in his own world…and he's playing the field." Dwight recalled the last night they had gone out and how Menage acted in the parking lot, as if he was on a stage. Menage thrived on attention.

"Well, I'm sorry, I have some business to take care of. But I'll be seeing you at dinner tonight."

"Yes, Mr. Marchetti."

"Good. Miss Welton will tend to your needs…and Dwight,

the last thing you need to do is feel guilty. I know how close the two of you are and I'm so sorry," he said taking Dwight's hand.

"Thank you."

Felix walked out of the room, followed by an Afghan hound that had been curled up by the door. Convinced that all he could do was wait, Dwight poured his fifth glass of wine. Standing in front of the huge, floor-to-ceiling window, he looked out at the Miami skyline. He then watched Felix's helicopter take off just a few yards from his luxurious yacht. He began to loosen his silk tie just as Miss Welton silently walked up behind him and tapped him on his shoulder. He was startled.

"Oh, I'm so sorry, Mr. Macmillan. I didn't mean to startle you," she said. Dwight looked down at the small woman. She was old enough to be his grandmother.

He smiled. It's okay. I'm fine. I'm just stressed, that's all. And you can call me Dwight."

"Oh...well, Mr. Dwight, if you'll follow me, I'll show you to your room," she said.

"Uh...Miss Welton...are you French? Your accent is strong."

"Yes I am, Mr. Dwight," she said leading him upstairs.

"Did Mr. Marchetti mention to you that I need to use the phone?" Dwight spoke in flawless French, surprising her. She stopped and slowly turned back to look at him with a smile on her face. She spoke back to him in French.

"Your French is excellent, Mr. Dwight, and yes, there is a phone in your room and a change of clothes to suit your taste is laid out for you."

"Thank you."

"You are welcome, Mr. Dwight, who speaks good French." They both laughed as she showed him to his room.

***

"Where can we meet?" Tina said standing in her bathroom taking off her make-up.

"Come to my place 'bout nine-thirty. Are you sure Dwight'll be staying at the island with Mr. Felix?" DJ asked.

"Yes, I'm sure. And where are you anyway?" she asked, not really caring where he was.

"Getting the system fixed in my truck," he lied.

"Oh…well, I'll be there."

"Hey, you gonna wear that see-through bra and thong set?"

"That's just a waste, DJ," Tina said laughing.

"So what are you doin' right this second?"

"Mmm…rubbing some scented cream on my thighs. I just stepped out of the shower, so I'm naked."

"You need to drop Dwight, girl," DJ said glancing at the new Jacob on his wrist.

"Oh, really! I don't think so, DJ. Your money ain't long enough, so don't go catchin' feelings for me!"

"So my money ain't long, huh? But how about my dick?"

"DJ, don't start. I told you day one how it would be, so do you want to see me or not?" DJ said that he did and hung up his phone.

"Stupid bitch!" Erasing her from his mind, he went back to counting the money stacked up on his kitchen table. He stopped at seventy-two thousand and he still had a few stacks left. He lit a blunt and headed back out to distribute his coke and make a few sales. DJ now had a good deal of control at the chop shop and did his best to fill Menage's shoes. He couldn't believe how

Tina had dissed him, but still she would be over his crib later on. As he pulled up to Lou's mansion, he smiled to himself, thinking about his new rank. He now had money and power. The money was good and the power, a glock .40, was sitting on his lap. As far as respect was concerned, he'd make sure he got it if he had to. He now hung out with rappers, fucked model chicks and lived the life he'd always wanted—in the limelight.

***

Dwight looked at his watch. It was now almost half past seven. He sat at Felix's large wet bar with its marble top and gold edges. He told the bartender he would pour his own drinks. He filled up his glass with Bacardi Limon. Resting his elbows on the bar, he let his mind wander. Tina…what would I do without her…my man is laid up in a coma…he thought to himself. He knew Felix was right; things had to move forward, but he knew it would be different without Menage around. He finished his drink in one swallow and refilled it. He lifted the glass to his lips and noticed that his hand was trembling. He closed his eyes and slowly placed the drink down. "Slow down, man, don't fucking over-do it." His mind was racing. Things would have to change. He now had the last word on how things would be run at the chop shop, but for now he would let DJ hold it down until he got everything in order. He sat alone in the dark. He desperately needed to hold Tina in his arms. Earlier on the phone she had told him to stay on the island to relax. He slowly stood, walked up the long staircase and made his way to bed. At first he thought sleep wouldn't come, but as soon as he fell onto the king-sized bed his exhaustion overcame him.

***

Tina stood in front of the mirror naked. On the bed were a mesh, Fendi g-string and matching lace bra. She cupped her breasts and thought of what DJ was going to do to her. She quickly got dressed and jumped into her two-door, deep shadow blue, pearl PT cruiser convertible. She didn't see anything wrong with sexing—no—fucking DJ, because it was only to help out

Dwight. DJ was fine and loved to please her, and he had no limitations on doing as she asked. She just hoped he wouldn't fall in love with her…maybe this would be his last night inside of her…well, maybe. Tina knew things would be different now that Menage was out of the picture. And to think that he turned her down one night…must be a fag!

***

Detective Covington took another picture of the flashy truck parked in front of DJ's apartment. He had taken several pictures of DJ going into hotels with two girls and then of him returning home. This was getting him nowhere. It was after ten now and he was about to call it a night when a PT cruiser with its top down appeared. It was too dark to make a correct call on the color. He quickly picked his camera back up again. "Nice…nice," he said getting some good shots of a woman getting out of the vehicle. He also got a close-up of DJ holding the woman in his arms in the doorway, kissing her with his hand on her nicely shaped ass. "Lucky man," he said as the door closed. All this action had him tired and horny…time to go home.

***

"You're late," DJ said locking the door.

"And!" Tina said as she led him to his bedroom. He couldn't take his eyes off the tight- fitting, Frankie B. jeans.

"Damn, you look good, Tina," he said as she stood by his bed. "Come here." She slowly walked towards him and into his arms, her breasts and nipples pressed tightly against the shirt she wore. Their lips met and their tongues danced back and forth. He brought her closer to his body, knowing she could feel his erection.

"Mmm…do me first, DJ," Tina purred as he licked her neck. He pulled her shirt over her head and tossed it onto the floor. He playfully squeezed her left breast.

"No teddy tonight?" DJ said as he undid her pants, rubbing her luscious set of hips.

"No, boy, just my birthday suit," she replied, breathing heavily as he slid her pants down to her ankles.

"You are so fucking sexy, Tina," DJ said running his fingers through her thick pubic hairs and finding his way easily inside of her.

"Wait!" she said pushing him away.

"What...what is it?" DJ said, hoping she wouldn't change her mind. He looked at her firm tits and eraser-sized brown nipples.

"Let's make it last tonight, DJ," she said smiling. "And leave the lights on!"

Don't I always?" he said slipping out of his pants. At 6'3", he stood in front of her in a pair of silk boxers. She chuckled as they rolled on his bed play fighting. "Lay on your back, boy—now, DJ." He did as he was told. Tina sat down next to him and smiled when she pulled his boxers down; his penis went past his navel. DJ moaned as she gripped it and slowly started to pump him with her hand.

"Oh, DJ, don't it feel good, baby?" she purred picking up the pace. DJ looked at her hanging breasts, the thickness of her hips and the hairy bush between her legs. "I'm talking to you," she said still pumping.

"Y-yeah...it feels so g-good," he said, his chest rising and falling with his quick breathing. Her hand was now a blur as DJ lost control and called out her name. He thought it couldn't get any better, but when she slowed down and started flicking her tongue back and forth across the tip of his head, he arched his back. Suddenly she stopped and DJ watched her roll onto her stomach. She looked back at him and wiggled her ass. DJ moaned with lust at the sight. His head was spinning as he started to rub her ass. Squeezing and softly smacking her cheeks, he glanced down at himself and saw that he was dripping pre-cum on the bed. "She's something else," he thought. She closed her eyes and bit her lip when she felt DJ pry her cheeks apart.

"Lick it, DJ...lick it, baby...then fuck me!" That's just what he did after he ate her ass and sex for close to twenty minutes. Putting on a condom, he got on top of her and deeply entered her wet opening. She closed her eyes and wrapped her arms around his neck as he drilled her just the way she wanted him to. They definitely weren't making love; they were fucking. Later that night, Tina brought DJ to the Promised Land. He didn't get the pleasure of cumming in her mouth, but he coated her breasts and chin and he was satisfied. She lay next to him as he rubbed the back of her neck.

"Do you think Menage will make it?" she asked.

"Hope not...but if he do, he won't be himself—a retard or something. Hell, God can't even help that nigga!" They both laughed.

"So how are things at the shop?" she said pinching his left nipple.

"Well, a few cats got mad 'cause of the changes, but they'll be okay. Money talks. I can pay them more by doing more cars. You gotta take chances in this game, you feel me?"

"I've been feeling you all night," she said moving her hand toward his crotch to fondle his now-flaccid penis. She worked him with her hands, bringing him back to life and he started to suck on her breast. "Do me, boy! Do me some more, DJ, please." He got on his back and had her squat down on top of his face. "Mmmm, boy, that's nice," she said running her fingers through his soft curly hair.

Maybe Tina really did love Dwight, but yet she lay naked with another man. She knew she would just about kill Dwight if he cheated on her. She knew this was her last night with DJ, but she didn't tell him yet. Why spoil the fun? She got a kick out of doing it behind Dwight's back. She felt in control, plus DJ would do anything for her when it came to getting between her legs. Tina understood the power of the pussy all too well.

After playing with DJ, she would focus on Dwight and marriage. Dwight was such a faithful, loving man and she would be his faithful, loving wife...well... "What he don't know won't hurt him," she thought as DJ made her cum with his talented tongue. He had turned her onto her back and she put her legs up on his shoulders. He pumped her with fast and powerful strokes. She knew it would be hard to stop seeing him and he made it difficult for her to even think about it when he hit her G-spot. The rhythmic sound of their bodies slapping up against each other filled the room. DJ gritted his teeth and added more power to his thrust. This shocked Tina; she never experienced him in this way before. It was pure bliss. Her mouth dropped open, but no sound came forth. She felt as if she couldn't breathe and it was getting darker.

"DJ!" she cried. Ignoring her, he pinned her legs behind her head, knowing she was double-jointed. Faster, harder, deeper, he drove himself inside of her. Tina's breasts bounced wildly about from all the pounding. "Mmmm...I'm...I'm....gonna cum....D....DJ, don't stop," she moaned rolling her hips as he continued to pound her. His face was drenched with sweat as he fucked her like he never had before. It was feeling so damn good...too damn good. Her sex gripped him like a suction cup and he began to stroke her deep and fast.

"Tina...Tina...Tina... Tina!"

"Yes, DJ, yes!" Their cries were simultaneous. DJ grunted when he felt Tina's wetness and heat all over his penis, still thrusting between her legs. Caught up in lust and pleasure, he buried his head in her neck. Tina reached down and stroked DJ's balls and he lost all control. He screamed out her name as his body rocked involuntarily and he came inside of her. Tina felt the hot juice running down her inner thigh as he jerked back and forth. Her mind went blank. Breathing hard, he rolled off of her. Tina slowly moved her hand down between her legs and felt what DJ had put inside of her, along with a piece of the torn rubber.

"N-o-o-o-o...please, God, n-o-o-o-o!" she wailed. DJ tried to comfort her, but she freaked out, yelling and crying at the same time, asking him to explain.

"Stupid bitch, it felt too damn good to stop!" he wanted to tell her, but he just sat on the edge of the bed with his head down. She could only hope that he didn't have any STDs, but more than that, she didn't want to get pregnant. She quickly got dressed, muttering something that DJ couldn't understand. She left without saying a word. DJ went into the kitchen and tried to calm himself. He didn't know what the fuck Tina was going to do. "Maybe she'll tell Dwight I raped her...nah...but that's one silly bitch," he thought. He could only wait now. He picked up a bottle of Martell and threw it against the wall. "This is bullshit!" he yelled. Looking at his clock he saw that it was almost four in the morning. He had to get himself together and he knew just how. He snuck across the street and tapped on the front door of a large, brick house. C'mon, girl, get up," he mumbled. The door opened a few seconds later. Standing in front of DJ was a short, white girl, a little on the chubby side with rollers in her hair. She wasn't something to walk in the park with, but she had what he needed—a nice hot mouth and a body that was always down for sex. And DJ had what she needed as well—a big penis to make her happy while her husband was at work. Quickly letting him in, she stepped out of her nightgown and dropped to her knees to unfasten his pants. He knew she could taste and smell the scent of Tina on his penis, but she paid it no mind and didn't spill a single drop when he blasted in her mouth. "Swallow it, bitch," he muttered through clenched teeth, gripping her head in the dark living room.

***

That night, Benita and Lisa returned from North Carolina after visiting family for a few days. Benita didn't want to go, but Lisa insisted that she come along to get things off her mind. Lisa unpacked her bags as Benita checked the answering machine. The two calls from DJ surprised Lisa. Dwight also called Benita, telling her to call him as soon as possible but the call was now two days old. She thought it was odd for him to be calling and thought that maybe he was calling about Menage. She was unable to stop thinking of him since their date. On her way to bed, she checked the DVR to make sure it had recorded her favorite program that aired every Sunday. Then she called it a night. She planned to ask Dwight what was going on with Menage and why he hadn't phoned when she returned his call. Lisa went right to bed; she had to work the next day and she wanted to make DJ sweat a little bit.

Friday Morning

"Tina, I'm home," Dwight yelled as he closed the door of their condo. He dropped his jacket onto the couch and walked to the bedroom to find Tina asleep wearing a purple Victoria's Secret teddy. He stood at the edge of the bed, gazing at the woman he loved. He gently moved the hair from her face. He didn't know what he would do without her. Just as he sat on the edge of the bed, she slowly opened her eyes.

"Hey, Boo," she said in a tired voice. She sat up and placed her head on his shoulder. "I missed you last night and I hope you don't plan on staying with Felix overnight anymore. I was so alone without you," she added sweetly.

"I'm sorry, but I've just had a lot on my mind, Tina. I guess I'm still in shock, and I'm sorry if I haven't been acting like myself," he said placing a hand on her thigh.

"Baby, don't be ridiculous. I fully understand, okay? So have you heard anything about Menage?"

"No," he said looking into her eyes. "But I'm going to see him today. Chandra is taking it really hard. Tina, I swear, if I find out who did this..." Dwight balled up his fist.

"Baby, calm down," she said kissing his cheek.

"Look, I'm not going in today. Can you handle it alone?" he said stroking her waist.

"Yes, but I'd rather go with you to see Menage—plus I need to talk to Chandra." Dwight was about to get up, but Tina grabbed his arm. "No, Dwight, I need you now...make love to me," she said as she slipped out of the teddy. Dwight bit his lip as her hand moved between his legs, caressing his bulge. Tina laid her on her back and Dwight sucked her breasts as he felt her hands fumble with his zipper. Moments later, he was burying his face in her cleavage as she rode him. "I love you so much, baby," she said with tears rolling down her face.

***

DJ sat behind Menage's desk at MD Body Works. He looked out the window as a sporty Toyota Celica GT pulled into the garage. He made a deal with the kid who brought it in for four thousand. At first he said no, so DJ offered him five thousand. The deal was made shortly afterward. DJ already had a body for the Celica to switch the numbers. He'd found a match at a junkyard in Carol City. Once the numbers were switched from the wrecked vehicle to the stolen one, all that was left to do was register it with the DMV as a restored vehicle, making it a rebirth, and then he could sell it for its base price and make a nice profit, having only paid five thousand for it. DJ knew how to make deals, but he was breaking a major rule—transporting drugs.

About an hour later, the kid left out the back in a black Honda Accord coupe and two thousand dollars cash. The Honda was a rebirth with full papers and tags that were filed with the DMV. Just minutes after the kid left, a Ford Excursion pulled in with a dented fender. It was all about the profit, which would be lovely; the Excursion would sell for over fifteen thousand.

Most of the rebirths were actually placed back on legit car lots and sold. MD Body Works was airtight and it did actual repair work. DJ was making a power move that would net him close to seventy-five thousand in one day. For the last two days, he had some of his runners test drive high-end vehicles with fake IDs. Their credit, as well as their appearance, was perfect. DJ even cleaned up a crackhead and sent him to a car lot to test drive the cars he had targeted. It seemed that DJ could do no wrong and his scheme was flawless. The deed was carried out without a hitch. The runners would convince the salesperson to allow them to make the test drive alone. Leaving a rebirth at the dealership, they'd immediately proceed to a parked van nearby where they'd hand the keys over to the car being test-driven and have them copied by a key-copying machine hidden inside the vehicle. When the copied key was tested, the driver would hand it back and return to the car lot. In broad daylight, DJ had things set to hit five car lots in one day. As payment, he would give his runners five thousand dollars worth of drugs and twenty-five hundred in cash making the total seventy-five hundred.

Everyone had to admit that DJ's operation was running smoothly. Tonight some of his workers would simply walk onto the lot and place a dealer tag on a car, then use the copy key to drive off. This was Menage's idea but he would never do so many cars in one night.

DJ looked at his Movado watch. He leaned back in the chair and looked around the office. A picture of Menage and Chandra sat on the desk. He picked up the picture and tossed it into the trashcan. His thoughts drifted back to the night before with Tina. It was a mess, but he smiled when he recalled the sensational feeling of being inside of her with nothing between them. He wondered what the outcome would be—if she would get pregnant…he hoped not. But he knew that Tina was able to overcome any problem, and she'd be able to overcome this one if the need to arose. Damn, he wanted her again—her flawless body. He tried to push her from his mind and he was about to leave when a customer appeared. DJ motioned him into the office.

"Welcome to MD Body Works. How can we help you today?" DJ said extending his hand across the desk.

"Uh…I'm looking for some air bags to put on my truck," the man said ignoring DJ's hand. DJ leaned back in his seat, enjoying the feeling of being on top. "What kind of truck do you have?" he asked.

"Yukon," the man said staring at the picture in the trashcan.

"I'm sure we can do that. Do you know what size you want?"

"Nah, not really," the man said looking around the office. "But I called a few weeks ago and talked to the owner. I forgot his name but he said it would take about a week to order everything."

"We're under new management now and I kinda run the place. But I'm sure we can still take care of your needs," DJ said.

The man smiled. "I see. Well is there a time that you can let me know when I can bring my truck in…and why were ya'll closed a few days ago?"

"We just had to take a few days off…you know, since I took over I had to change a few things." The man folded his hands on the table. "Will there be anything else." DJ asked. The man said there wasn't and he left after ordering the system he wanted. DJ made sure things were in place before stepping outside into the warm air. He walked to his flashy SUV and thought of how to spend the rest of the day. It was now after two in the afternoon.

Dough-Low thought about DJ as he turned at an intersection. He was heated after seeing the picture in the trashcan and wanted to smoke DJ on the spot. "So that's DJ," he said. "How grimy can a nigga get?"

***

"What the hell do you mean I can't see him!" Dwight yelled at the nurse behind the front desk at the hospital.

"Sir, I'm sorry, but your name is not on the family's list. I'm really sorry, but those are the rules," the nurse said.

"Baby, please calm down," Tina said rubbing his shoulder.

"Call Dr. Wilson. He'll clear all this shit up," Dwight said slamming his fist down on the desk.

"Dwight," Tina pleaded.

"Not now, Tina!" he said, cutting his eyes at her.

"Is there a problem?" someone said in a calm voice, coming from behind where Dwight and Tina stood. It was Dr. Wilson. Dwight turned around and let out a deep breath.

"Dr. Wilson, am I glad to see you. This… woman here," he

said waving his hand toward the nurse, "said I'm not...permitted to see Menage. Can you please clear this up right now?"

"I'm sorry to inform you, but she's correct. Beg my pardon, how are you, Tina?" he said acknowledging her then brought his attention back to Dwight. "These rules have been set by his mother and we have to fully comply with her request. Furthermore, Mr. McMillan, yelling and carrying on like this will change nothing. And with all due respect, try placing yourself in his mother's shoes. She has no clue who tried to kill her son, nor does she know you, so how can you expect her to trust anyone around him? Dwight, I ask that you please try to understand. I know this is a difficult time for you and Tina, but please lower your voice and calm down. I wish I could allow you to see him or at least tell you more but I can't. Please believe that. The best you can do is...well, to be honest, I don't know. Now if you'll excuse me, I have work to do...and Dwight, I really am very sorry." He nodded at Tina once more and then turned and walked down the hall.

"Dwight, let's go home...please," Tina said gently. They slowly walked out of the hospital hand in hand.

***

"Benita, I just talked to Dwight and he said Menage has been shot."

"Oh no! Not again! I need to go and see him!" Benita said hysterically.

"Calm down, girl. They said he couldn't have visitors or something. And who's Dwight?"

"Lisa, just give me the number, girl! Dwight, he the one who brought me from the hospital!" Benita said as Lisa handed her the number. Benita walked around in circles as she dialed Jackson Memorial. She couldn't believe Menage was back in the hospital. Maybe Dwight had made a mistake and meant to say that he never left the hospital. But something was wrong. Why didn't Menage call while she was away?

"Jackson Memorial…" said the female voice on the other end of the line.

"I need to find out Menage Unique Legend's room number," Benita said.

"Can you please repeat that name?"

"Menage…Unique…Legend!"

"One minute, please. Please hold."

Benita was now pacing back and forth in front of the TV as Lisa watched her, just wishing she would at least sit down so she could see the screen.

"Benita!"

"What!"

"Can you keep your ass still so I can see the TV!"

"Huh? This guy saved my life. He may still be up in the hospital and all you can think about is a show!"

"Hello…hello? May I ask who's calling?"

"I'm sorry," Benita said glaring at Lisa. "Yes, my name is Benita P. Alston and I would also like to see him. How is he?" She had to sit down as she waited for the reply.

"I…I'm sorry but I can't give out that information, and there are no visitors allowed at this time."

"What!" Benita said. She took the phone from her ear and stared at it for a second.

"Girl, what's wrong with you?" Lisa said, wishing she would leave the room to talk. Benita held up her hand to silence her. "What do you mean? I don't understand."

"I'm really sorry, Miss—"

"Yes, it's Miss!" Benita snapped.

"Miss Alston, that's all I can say and I'm sorry...really," the woman said in a professional tone. "But maybe you can leave a number and I'll be more than happy to pass it to a family member."

"Uh...yes, but hold on for a second please," Benita said pressing the mute button. Quickly she told Lisa what the problem was. Since she worked there, maybe she could cut through the red tape. Lisa took the phone.

"Girl, give me that. You don't know how to talk to my people," she said smiling. "Hi, this is Nurse Lisa Alston. I work in the Cardiovascular Unit and if you wish to check, I'll be glad to hold. I'd appreciate it if you could then pass me through to Dr. Wilson...thank you." Lisa looked at Benita and winked her eye.

"Yes...Nurse Alston, please hold while I direct your call to Dr. Wilson," the woman said after returning to the phone a few seconds later.

"Thank you," Lisa said turning down the TV.

"Dr. Wilson here, how may I help you?" He sat in a red leather chair with his feet up on his desk.

"Dr. Wilson, how are you? This is Nurse Alston from Cardio."

"Ah, yes, Nurse Alston...you still on vacation?"

"No, sir, but I need a favor."

"Hmmm, a favor...okay, and what might that be, Nurse Alston?"

"Well, my cousin has a friend that she wants to visit, but I'm getting the run-around trying to get his room number. Can you help me?"

"That's odd. What's the patients name?" he asked taking out his pen.

"Uh…Mak…Mer…Menage Unique Legend."

Dr. Wilson dropped his pen and swung his feet off the desk and onto the floor. He quickly and specifically recalled what Mr. Marchetti had instructed him to say. "Nurse Alston…that's not possible."

"Huh!"

"His family has set some firm rules—no visitors, and we can't reveal his condition. I'm sorry, Nurse Alston, but that's all I can say."

"What is he saying?" Benita asked impatiently with her hands on her hips.

Lisa waved at her to be quiet. "Okay, Dr. Wilson, I understand. Thank you." She smiled and hung up the phone. "Wait!" she said holding up her hands. "He wouldn't tell me anything, but I'll just wait till my shift starts tonight. Then I'll call back. It's no big deal. There's nothing more we can do…and don't stress me either!" She was listed in the books as being on vacation until the following evening. Benita knew Lisa was right, and all she could do was wait. She sat down on the couch and turned on the DVR to check out any possible programs that Lisa might have recorded while they were away. She pressed play as the phone rang again. It was DJ, and Lisa walked out of the living room and into her bedroom to talk to him. Benita was about to pop in a different tape when she saw that a special news bulletin had obviously interrupted one of Lisa's favorite shows. She decided to lie back on the couch and watch the bulletin.

"This is Elaine Woods, interrupting your regular programming to bring you footage from Sky Five," said the anchorwoman. The scene switched to a woman with short, blonde hair, reporting from a helicopter:

This is Stacey Marks, and we are here at a quiet section of South Miami Beach, but this rainy Sunday evening, it's been turned into a war zone. Our ground crew has not yet arrived on the scene, but what we have learned is that …" she looked down

at her pad, "several shots have been fired at the location below and there have been several injuries. Just a little while ago a Med-Vac helicopter left the scene with one black male. We'll now show you what's going on down below...

The camera zoomed in on Menage's house. The gate was torn off its hinges. Two cars sat in the driveway surrounded by the flashing lights of police cruisers and several rescue squads. The camera zoomed in on a damagedLexus and Benita paused the tape. She remembered seeing the Lexus at Club Limelight. She also remembered that the woman who did her hair was in that car...at least she thought so. And then Benita recognized Dwight's Dodge Viper. But what made her get up and step closer to the TV was what she saw sitting in the opened garage— Menage's Escalade ESV. Benita yelled for Lisa to come into the living room.

"What, girl?" Lisa said walking into the living room, no longer on the phone with DJ. Benita, not able to speak, pointed at the TV.

"What the hell..." Lisa said. "That's DJ's Lex...and the...whatever that is, it's the same car you rode home in from the hospital."

"Are you sure that's DJ's Lexus?" Benita asked Lisa.

"Yeah, but what happened to it?" Benita said noticing the obvious damage. So what is this anyway—police everywhere...rewind the tape."

"It's Menage's house. Are you sure that DJ's car?"

"Yeah, his rims are one of a kind. Damn, what the hell happened!"

"Did he tell you he was at Menage?s house on Sunday?" Benita said pressing play.

"Nope," Lisa said sitting down. "Heck, I might not go in tomorrow," she added.

"Remember at the club that night, seeing DJ's car coming through? Anyway, I think the girl that did my hair was with him."

"I don't recall all that. But so what, it ain't like he's my man or something. What are you trying to get at anyway? And what makes you think you know the girl he was with?"

"I saw her bracelet."

"Girl, please, you had a buzz from them coolers!" They watched the rest of the bulletin and Lisa wondered why DJ hadn't said anything about what happened. Maybe someone else was driving his car that day. She found it odd that DJ and Benita knew Menage but DJ didn't know Benita, since everyone seemed to be in such a close circle. After they watched the clip twice more, Lisa got up from the couch.

"Majestic ain't he?" she said.

"Who?"

"Your hero—Menage. Look, I'ma carry my black ass to sleep. And if DJ calls again, wake me up and don't ask him shit. If he wants me to know anything he'll tell me, and you need to stop stressing about everything. And yes, I'ma call back to the hospital tonight." Benita never felt more helpless in her life.

***

Chandra sat in the waiting room waiting for Menage's mother to return from his bedside. She left his room out of respect so she could be alone with her son. To cheer herself up, she thought about all the fun times she shared with Menage. She remembered how he always treated her with respect, never pressuring her for sex. One day when she was in class he paid her a surprise visit. He pulled up in the parking lot by a promiscuous female that no man on campus would turn down. When Chandra left class she found him sitting in the rec area watching TV. They had a big laugh after the horny girl stated that Menage must be gay. He took her to Walt Disney World for the weekend and the subject of sex was never brought up—not even once.

Menage called her every day throughout their relationship. She knew about his fast and flashy life down in Miami, but she was happy with him. She didn't care at all about his money, and she didn't find out how much he was worth until after they had sex. From a million to a penny she would stay with him, and she hoped he fully understood how deep her feelings were for him. She loved him more than anything but she knew he was afraid of love. He ran from it, yet he wanted it. She showed him that everything in life was a chance. She needed him and he needed her. Chandra didn't just lay with any man and since he came into her life, there was no other but him. "Maybe the child will change him," she thought.

Menage slowly opened his eyes. His vision was blurred, his mouth was dry and he felt dizzy. He was weak and didn't even have the strength to look around the room to see if he had a visitor. His mother had left only seconds before to go get Chandra. He closed his eyes as a chill swept though his body. He was scared. He knew he had been shot but he remembered so little. Was it Vapor or Vigor that ran out the door when he went for his MP-5? He couldn't recall what happened after that. He opened his eyes again and stared at the ceiling. He thought of the life he was leading—money, power and sex. To him it was the key to life...and a big body Benz on dubs. Suddenly, darkness overcame him. He tried to fight it, afraid of going back into the cold, desolate world that pulled at his soul. The door opened and Chandra walked into the room. She sat in the chair next to his bed.

"Baby, I love you. I don't know why this has happened but I know you can fight it." She looked at the ceiling to regain her strength. She hated to see him suffer and not be able to help him, but she knew she had to stay strong. She looked at him and gently grasped his hand. "Menage, I need you. Baby, you have to wake up...please don't leave me like this. I'm...I'm gonna have your child and I need you to be here with me. She began to sob. "Menage, maybe you don't really know how much I love you, but my love goes deep, you hear me? I'm not perfect—no one is, so don't leave because I don't wanna go on without you in my life." She broke down crying, and several minutes later she

regained her composure. After breaking down again she felt him squeeze her hand. "Baby?" she whispered. She didn't have to press the call button because his vital signs were being monitored by a computer down the hall. Seconds later the door swung open, slightly startling Chandra.

"Clear out," a doctor followed by two nurses said. Things moved fast as the doctor checked Menage's eyes to make sure that he was out of the coma and there wasn't just a glitch in the machines. Hours later Menage woke up on his own, with no respirator or tubes down his throat.

"Ma," he called out weakly. The inside of his mouth felt like sandpaper.

"I'm right here," his mother said standing by his bedside. He tried to reach for her but failed.

"Mama…I can't move my—"

"Shhh. You had to have surgery on your arm." She couldn't bear to speak on the other life-threatening operations. "It will be okay. You just need to rest. And thank God, you hear me, son? You need to look at your life, you hear me? God has a reason for saving you and you better take the time out to look at what's going on around you. You know right from wrong, so you just rest up and I'll send Chandra back in a minute. I love you, son." She kissed his forehead and left. Menage looked out the window located adjacent to his bed on the far left side of the room. He was shocked after the doctor told him he had been in a coma for five days. He remembered the bullet ripping through his left shoulder but he couldn't recall being hit in the chest. However, he felt how sore it was and the thick bandage that covered it felt tight. He realized how lucky he was. He closed his eyes and welcomed the darkness. Chandra walked back into the room.

"Baby, you up?" she whispered. He opened his eyes and managed to smile. She sat down next to him with tears running freely down her face. "I love you so much," she said. "Try not to talk and just listen," she added when he tried to speak. He nodded slowly. She rubbed his arm and saw a tear running down his cheek. She caught it with her fingertip and placed it to her lips. She sat down on the bed and told him the details of what had happened. She carefully broke the news about Vigor and how Vapor was still missing. Vigor saved his life and had spared his own. Now he was gone. Menage squeezed his eyes shut as he thought of his dogs. Dr. Wilson knocked on the door and entered after Chandra answered.

"Mr. Legend, you have a call on line two." Chandra thanked him, hit line two on the keypad on the phone next to the bed and held it to Menage's ear. It was Felix.

"Menage, if you think I'm going to feel sorry for you forget it! You're coming to my island and that's an order—okay? I also have a plan." Before hanging up, he told Menage how the police had gone back to the house to find Vapor asleep in his bedroom with a fifty-pound bag of dog food ripped open in the middle of the floor. Apparently, Vapor had dragged the bag from the shed and made himself at home. He was now with Felix.

"Who was that?"

"C-crazy Felix...he...got Vapor," Menage managed to say.

His mom was back in the room now. Mr. Marchetti had already spoken to her earlier and they agreed on not spreading the word that Menage had come out of his coma. The preparations were soon made for Menage to be secretly moved to Marchetti's island. "It's gonna be fine, baby," Chandra said.

***

"Damn!" Dwight said slamming down the phone. He rolled away from the desk.

"What's wrong?" Tina asked. She was sitting on a bearskin rug doing her toenails.

All she wore was a silk see-through blouse by Dolce and Gabana.

"I can't find out a damn thing about when or if I can see Menage. This don't make no damn sense and Dr. Wilson's not around."

"Have you called Mr. Marchetti yet?"

"No, I'll call him later I guess."

"Baby, come here." Tina said in a husky voice before lying back and parting her legs. "What will you do if he don't come out of the coma?" Dwight didn't want to think of his best friend leaving him.

"Don't talk like that." He got up from his chair, went to the bar in the living room and poured himself a glass of Hennessey. "Well, if he don't make it we have to keep going. It'll be hard but it's what we'll have to do," he said over his shoulder, loud enough for Tina to hear him in the den.

"I feel the same, and I feel sorry for Chandra." Dwight returned to the den and sat back down at his desk. Tina was now playing with herself.

"You love me, girl?" he said looking between her parted thighs.

"Yesss baby, you know I do," she said fingering herself. She closed her eyes as he knelt between her legs, waiting for his hand or mouth to take the place of her fingers. She felt him caress her inner thigh. Thankful that DJ didn't get her pregnant, she now gave her all to Dwight. Everything was perfect and all she needed to do now was become his wife. He was about to remove his shirt when his two-way chimed. He pulled it off his waist and looked at the message. It read:

KEVIN IN JAIL

BOND 20G—8:49PM

"What is it?" Tina said. She was propped up on her elbows, her breasts swinging freely.

"I guess one of the runners got caught with a hot car or something. Kevin works for Menage ...I mean DJ, but anyway I have to go bail him out," Dwight said reaching for his shirt.

"Now?" Tina said. "Why can't DJ do it?"

"Baby, ain't no telling where he is! Besides, I know Kevin, so it's no big deal. I'll hurry back, okay?" He kissed her and rushed toward the door. Tina didn't complain because Dwight was now handling both the beauty salon and the chop shop.

Dwight's BMW 745LI moved gracefully down Biscayne Blvd. as it headed toward the county jail. Maybe Tina had been right about him running the show. DJ was making more money but taking bigger risks. That was part of the game...wasn't it?

***

Detective Covington looked at his new rookie partner, Steve Hamilton. Covington wasn't irritated because Hamilton was white; he'd just rather work alone. Covington leaned back in his chair and looked around his office. On the wall were pictures of he and his wife and a few pictures from when he was a street cop in Broward County. His office was small and behind him was a view of mostly buildings and the busy street below. It wasn't much, but it was enough for Covington. On his desk sat a box of Dunkin Doughnuts and a new gray coffee cup with Detective Covington written in black letters on the handle. Detective Hamilton sat at the desk directly in front of Covington's, his 6'2" frame hunched over, a doughnut in one hand and a file in the other. He spoke with his mouth half full.

"So, now, lemme get this straight. We got four guys dead and two were shot by...uh...how do you say his name?" he said looking up from the file.

"Meh-nage," Covington replied rubbing his chin. He dropped his jaw on the second syllable of Menage's name.

"Okay, that's one out back and the headless one in the house. The third man was killed by the dog—fucking Cujo. The man in the driveway was shot by Roderick Hopkins, aka, DJ. So is that the story?" He looked up to see Covington leaning on his desk with his chin in the palm of his hands.

"Yeah, but check this out: The guy we found in the driveway wasn't armed, but his weapon was found in the living room in the house. We got his prints all over the Uzi and they all carried one, so it's odd, too, I mean for it not to be with him, and he had a full clip for the it in a cargo pocket. But how does this sound to you? He ditches his empty Uzi with a clip in his pocket and runs out front right into Roderick, or DJ, as he rams through the front gate. He gets shot at close range...maybe two feet," Covington said. Hamilton ran his fingers through his spiked blond hair. He read the report again.

"Maybe the car just came in too fast...or maybe he thought he could trick DJ since he had on the lawn service uniform. But there was no sign of struggle and he was shot in the back of the head. He was weaponless, defenseless and helpless." Hamilton took a deep breath and rubbed his tired eyes. "This may sound crazy, but I think the guy might have known DJ...rushed up to talk to him, then bang!" he said forming his left hand into the shape of a gun and putting it to his head.

Detective Covington stood up to stretch and turned toward the window. "You're right. Well, at least I think so."

Detective Hamilton shot up from his chair. "Then why don't we haul his ass in—at least for questioning? What are we waiting for?"

Detective Covington turned back around. "On what grounds? All we have are assumptions, and that silly ass DA won't do anything but laugh in our faces. Hell, right now Hopkins is a damn hero," he said and sat back down.

"How's that?" Detective Hamilton said.

"The slugs they pulled out of Menage came from the Uzi that was used by the guy Hopkins killed in the driveway."

"So what do we do now?"

"We wait and watch. I got some pictures of him last night—nothing but a late-night booty call. That means he had a woman over." He knew Detective Hamilton didn't know much slang.

"Funny!" Detective Hamilton said before returning to the subject at hand. "It's still going to be hard to prove why he killed an unarmed man…and now the hero is our number 1 suspect?" he added before sitting back down.

"Hard to say."

Detective Hamilton reached for the last doughnut. "Oh, never mind," he said grinning and sinking his teeth into the soft pastry. It took a second for him to realize he'd been played. He slapped the empty box off the desk and stormed out of the office. Detective Covington burst out laughing. He was about to call his wife but his phone rang.

"Yeah," he answered.

"Hey, Detective Covington. This is Walter down in the lab. The slugs from the dog match the ones taken out of Mr. Legend, so I guess our friend on the front pavement shot the dog also. Maybe you can—"

"Walter."

"Yes?"

"Thanks, but I can take it from here. Did anyone ever tell you that you talk too much? If I recall correctly, I think I told you that yesterday!" Walter winced when the phone crashed down in his ear. Detective Covington used the next hour to catch up on his work and ended up going over the hit at Bayside to see if there was a connection to the shooting at Menage's house. One was a sloppy hit in broad daylight, while the other was done with a professional touch. Still the hits weren't successful. He wouldn't call being in a coma beating the odds, but the four men wanted to finish Menage off completely that day in his home. Calling it a night, he lit up his last Newport and headed home with a lot on his mind.

***

Lisa finally awoke. She rolled over in bed and looked at the clock on the night table. It was after ten o'clock. "Damn," she said, upset that she had slept all day. She got up and went to the living room. Benita was still up watching TV. She was curled up on the couch watching Comic View on BET.

"Anybody call me?" Lisa said digging in her ear and making a scratching sound with her throat.

"Nah," Benita said.

"Benita, it ain't shit in here to eat!" she yelled from the kitchen. "Ain't it your turn to go shopping? I'm 'bout to starve up in here." Benita stood up and turned off the TV.

"Let's go to IHOP," she said. Since Benita was paying, Lisa quickly got dressed and afterward she called the hospital. She had the same problem as earlier. Lisa thought Benita was going to have a fit, but she took the bad news with ease. "Let's go before I change my mind."

***

An important phone call was being made from a hotel in Broward county. It was an hourly rate hotel with a run-down look, firm beds and thin walls. The man making the call contacted the FBI in Washington D.C. After a series of beeps and a short static tone, he knew the line was clear.

"Things are going as planned, sir," he said.

"Good, good...now, how soon can we bring Felix down?" the official on the other end said.

"One week or two, and I found out why our people in L.A. are so uptight."

"You mean the case on the Mayor's son…was that you who tipped them off?"

"Yes, sir. And I will need more men to take our Mr. Machetti down."

"No problem. I'll take it to the big wigs first thing in the morning, but consider it done. I'm thinking a small military operations unit or something," the official from D.C. said.

"Thank you, sir."

They ended their call. The man in the hotel room stood in the darkness and then walked to the window. Looking through the torn blinds and rusty bars, he adjusted his holster, which held a black Beretta. He worked to get this mission and he knew he would see it to the end with Felix Marchetti dead. He focused on a street lamp with a busted light and watched a bum stagger into a nearby phone booth. He answered his cell phone on the first ring. The bum spoke French in a clear and sober voice.

"Once the job is done, four million will be placed in two Swiss accounts—two million in each, and we must have undeniable proof." The man in the hotel said nothing. He reached into his pocket and pulled out a hi-tech penlight. He pointed it at the bum and flashed it twice. He then looked for the silent code. The bum hung up and went back into his flawless act, staggering along the sidewalk. He bumped into a black couple and asked for some change but was only pushed to the side. By that time, the man in the hotel had disappeared into the night, letting the darkness hide his face and movements.

***

Dwight dropped Kevin off at his apartment in Northern Miami. Kevin was only nineteen and he had worked with Menage off and on as the middleman, bringing in cars when he ran across kids in the hood that wanted to sell a hot ride. Dwight smiled as he headed back home, thinking of what Kevin had told him about the interrogation.

"Yo, check it, D," Kevin had said sitting next to Dwight as they sped down I-95 North in his BMW. "These dumb ass DTs come with that lame, old-ass game talkin' 'bout, 'Hey, son, you facing ten to twenty years and we got some of your friends who will turn on you' and all that bullshit, right? And they wanna know where I'm taking the car, so I like lower my head, right, and I make him think I'm about ta cop out and shit. They say, "Okay, so you wanna tell us and help yourself out? I say yeah, real sad and shit, right? And they say where...and I look up and say...your Momma!" They both cracked up during the entire ride to Kevin's apartment. Dwight gave him twenty-two hundred just on GP because he knew Kevin had two mouths to feed.

Dwight's mind drifted back to Tina and then Menage. It was a quarter to midnight when he pulled into his garage. If his best friend wasn't up in the hospital, he knew that nine times out of ten they'd be at some club or party. Tonight he was going to relax and spend time with his woman.

***

Kevin was about to go upstairs to his apartment when a white male dressed in an all black jumpsuit stepped in front of him and flashed a badge. Since it was dark, he couldn't tell what kind of badge it was. Kevin guessed he was here to ask him about the stolen car or some other bullshit. He didn't see a gun and thought that maybe the man was a narc or something.

"Yo, man, what the fuck you want?" Kevin said with his long arms spread, looking down at the shorter man. The man didn't move.

"Do you work for Felix Marchetti?" the man said with no emotion, looking Kevin square in the eye.

Kevin responded quickly. "Look, yo, if you ain't got no warrant, you need to get the fuck up outta here." Kevin knew not to make a physical approach, and he stood his ground.

The man spoke again slowly. "Do...you...work...for Felix

Marchetti?" Kevin didn't feel like playing his game. He also sensed that something was wrong with this guy.

"Man, fuck you. Ain't got time to be playin' games, yo. Go go get a warrant if you wanna ask some questions." He stepped past him to go upstairs. Kevin took just two steps when suddenly the man reached up and grabbed him. In less than a few seconds, Kevin had a gun pressed firmly against his temple.

"On your damn knees," the man hissed. Kevin knelt slowly to his knees. He was scared; police didn't use silencers. He had to keep this man from going upstairs to his family but he had no gun. He knew he was in a tough spot. "Now let's try this again. Do you work for Felix Marchetti?" Kevin was still on his knees with the gun to his head. His heart was beating in overdrive. He knew of Mr. Marchetti, but he didn't know him personally. He never actually even saw the man. But worst of all, he didn't know how to answer the question and he became nervous when the man repeated himself.

"N-no...I don't even know him...I mean not personally. I swear, man...do it look like I work for him? Come on, please." He opened his eyes when he felt the gun removed from his head. Kevin quickly jumped to his feet and rushed toward the stairs. From about twenty feet away, the man spun around and aimed the Beretta at Kevin's head. He pulled the trigger. The gun coughed. The slug was a black talon shell, made to go through the flesh and expand on impact. Kevin's head exploded like an eggshell as the slug hit his skull. He lay face down, halfway up the steps as blood flowed down the iron stairwell. The man reached into his pocket and tossed out a few grams of rock cocaine in plastic bags a few inches from Kevin's body. Now it would look like a drug deal gone bad. He then fired two shots through an apartment window, then turned and ran to his SUV. He smiled, knowing that he didn't have to kill the kid, but he didn't have a reason to let him live either. He tossed the Beretta out the window as he crossed a bridge. He decided to relieve some stress before taking a rest. He drove to Overtown and picked up a petite brunette after handing her a twenty-dollar bill. He sat on a hotel couch shortly afterward as the girl gave him a hand job in the darkness. Little did she know that this would be her last trick.

***

Federal agent Lydia Nansteel arrived in Miami quicker than she had planned. She was fully briefed on Menage's shooting and was trying to get answers. The case had her full attention and she was sent to work on it even though he was still in a coma. She sat in the government Lear jet going over the file and her contacts in Miami. Her new name would be Latosha Mandrick. If anyone did a background check, the record would say she was a saleswoman for Luster Hair Care and a single female graduate of North Carolina Central University with a degree in Sales and Marketing.

She was thinking of ways to get a lead on the DB-7 with Menage in a coma. No one knew the caller who gave the tip. At least that's what Myers had told her. If she could find that person it would make things a lot simpler. The FBI had given her a two-bedroom apartment near the University of Miami and the car of her choice. She picked a blue Lexus RX330, an SUV taken from an imprisoned drug dealer. She looked at the picture of Menage that was in her file. It showed him stepping out of a Yellow Escalade ESV. He wasn't wearing a shirt. "Attractive," she thought.

Nansteel was tired, but she made it from the airport in the RX330, which was parked where Myers said it would be. Now known as Latosha Mandrick, she opened the door to her assigned apartment. Turning on the lights, she glanced at the black and white flower print furniture she picked out and let out a sigh. "Perfect," she said. Her temporary dwelling was cozy and spacious. In the corner sat a large TV and DVD system. She walked into the master bedroom and looked at the queen-sized bed with a mirrored headboard. "Someone trying to be funny," she thought. She put her briefcase on the bed and placed her cell phone on the dresser. As she unpacked, she pulled out her black government-issued .45. She placed it on the bed and began to undress. She removed her blouse, revealing her perky breasts. She looked at herself in the mirror, thinking that she could still be a Jet Beauty. "Maybe I should have stuck with it," she thought.

After taking a shower, she put on a halter-top and boxers and went to bed. Saturday would be a busy day. The first stop would be the hospital and then…she didn't even know. It would be all work as usual. She had no problem sleeping solo; after her divorce from Paul she often went to bed alone. She briefly thought about him. She didn't think she'd ever be able to forgive him but she manged to move on, like any other strong black woman would, pouring all of her time into her job. Love was something she hated.

CHAPTER 5

Never Change

11:48P.M.
Felix Marchetti stood on his balcony with two of his body-guards. His private island was four miles long and one mile wide with a small airstrip. His mansion was worth twenty-five million. It had twenty rooms, an indoor, heated Olympic size pool, tennis courts and a horse stable that kept his eight prized Arabian horses. He looked at the full moon as it cast its glow on the ocean.

"They're coming now, sir," his guard said.

"Hit the lights in the landing area and wait till he gets out. Then wait for my signal," Felix instructed. The helicopter came into view, slowly moving sideways toward the landing pad.

***

From inside the helicopter, Menage could see the island come into view. As always, it was breathtaking. Chandra sat next to him, still holding his hand ever since they made their secret getaway from the hospital. The landing was smooth and the pilot waited for the rotors to stop before he opened the door.

I'ma try to walk," Menage said as the doors slid open slowly.

"Are you sure?" Chandra said as she rubbed his cheek. With the door now fully open, the smell of fuel and the sea blew into the passenger compartment. Menage took the first step and almost fell. Chandra was there to catch him. With her support, he slowly moved toward the mansion. They could both see Felix in the distance. "Dark out here, ain't it?" Chandra said softly.

"Uh huh...maybe I need to go work out in the gym or something."

"Yeah, right. Your butt need to be in that wheelchair and your mama told me to make sure you get your rest. As soon as we get inside you're going to bed!"

"Yeah," he said squeezing her butt.

"Boy, please!" she said as they slowly walked up the long path leading to Felix's home.

"Now!" Felix said. The guard to his left gave a quick order into his walkie-talkie. Suddenly Menage grabbed his chest and stumbled from Chandra's grasp.

Menage, what's wrong!" Chandra cried gripping his arm holding him steady. "I'm okay, just a chest pain. Help me up, baby." A cage swung open nearby. Vapor let out a low growl and poked his head out of the cage. He tilted his head and sniffed the air. He barked then took off running.

"Baby, look," Chandra said as she stopped and pointed down the beach. Menage followed her gaze.

"Vapor," he said softly. He was filled with joy and pain at the same time. He was happy to see Vapor, but he knew he was lonely without Vigor. Vapor was running down the beach at full speed, kicking up sand, his ears flapping in the wind. He knew Vapor wouldn't jump on him. With Chandra's help, he got down on his knees as Vapor ran up to him whining and licking his face. Menage hugged his beloved pet, unable to stop the tears that rolled down his face. Vapor's stump of a tail twitched back and forth as Menage held him tighlty.

"He hasn't eaten much since he's been here," said Felix

walking up on them. "He almost took off one of my guard's hands when they tried to feed him, but I'm sure you can take care of him now. I'm sorry about Vigor. Chandra, Rosita is here also." She was Felix's trusted woman of five years.

As soon as Chandra started to lightly snore, Menage snuck out of the room with Vapor. After feeding him, they sat on the third floor balcony and watched Felix's helicopter take off into the night. He looked towards the Miami skyline and thought about everything that was going on.

Felix wanted him to stay on the island, but it was killing him—well, maybe killing him wasn't the right thought—but he already missed being in the limelight—but why? Vapor stood up, stretched his front legs and shook his head from side to side. As he was about to sit back down, he slowly turned around and started to growl. "Easy, boy," Menage said rubbing Vapor's tense shoulder. Seconds later Rosita walked onto the balcony.

"May I join the two of you or is this a private party?" she said softly. Rosita had large, full breasts and a long, slender body. Her long brunette hair was soft as silk and it stopped at her mid back. She was simply breathtaking. Menage could only nod his head in her presence. "I see you can't sleep either. I often come out here myself just to look at the stars. So how is Chandra?" she asked sitting down in a lounge chair across from him.

"In bed knocked out— same as Felix." The slip she wore was nearly see-through and it did nothing to cover her breasts. Menage swore she was naked underneath the slip.

"Menage, I need to tell you something. Felix really cares about you."

"Yeah, I know," he said taking his eyes off of her. She smiled.

"He said you always keep him laughing with your smart mouth. He really wants the best for you and I often hear him speak on wishing you would get out of the game." He looked into her eyes. Could Felix really want that for him? Why?

"Rosita, I don't even know what's the best for me."

"Life is a chance, and you have to choose between two things."

"And what are those two things?"

"Heaven or hell. Look, I know I'm young, but I know a lot of things, Menage." He sat back and closed his eyes. He didn't feel like speaking on religion at first but he changed his mind.

"I sin every day and I have evil thoughts all the time, so how can I think about God...or whatever?" He opened his eyes and Rosita walked over and knelt down in front of him. He couldn't help but to look between her legs. She wore a pair of black panties. She held his hand and spoke.

"For all have sinned and come short of the Glory of God: Romans chapter three, verse twenty-three." Menage knew right from wrong and didn't wish to argue with her, and he could sense that she knew what she was talking about. "You can't keep playing the field, Menage."

"I—"

"Shhh...I can see it in your eyes. Don't try to sneak off the Island. Chandra needs you more than ever and you know I'm right," she said before kissing his cheek. "Don't stay up too long," she said before standing up and tracing his chin with her finger.

After Rosita left, Menage walked back to his room with Vapor on his heels. Chandra was sound asleep on her stomach. Vapor yawned, walked around in a circle twice and curled up on the floor. Menage took off his clothes and got into bed. Still half asleep, Chandra kissed him, rolled on her back and allowed him to snuggle up close to her breasts. He closed his eyes. So much had changed and he knew it was the start of the ending. Chandra's steady heartbeat quickly sent him to dreamland.

***

The night had come to an end and DJ wound up at a sorority house in Coral Gables. He forgot all about Lisa and Tina, which was a surprise. As for Dwight and Tina, she talked him into making a sex tape. Dwight was more than willing to do it, and he never once stopped to think of Tina's increased sex drive.

Saturday Morning
Menage walked into the huge dining room with Vapor by his side. He was feeling much better after getting some much-needed rest. Now he was about to eat his first real meal since coming out of the coma. He wore a pair Gucci, print slacks and matching silk pullover shirt. Chandra joined him in the dining room just seconds later. She looked beautiful in a chocolate brown sheer top with a matching sleeveless cardigan by Prada and a pair of diamond earrings. She also wore a pair of lizard sling backs by Ernesto Esposito. The entire outfit cost over five thousand dollars. She filled out the tan skirt she wore with her full hips, her smooth hairless legs covered in a pair of light brown stockings. She walked over to Menage and gave him a quick peck on the lips.

"Mmm…you look good enough to eat," he said licking her ear.

"Maybe later, mister, if you're up to it," she giggled.

"Yeah, right," he said pulling out a chair for her. "Why you dressed up like that? All we havin' is breakfast—like it's the BET awards or somethin'!"

"It was all Rosita's idea. If it was up to me, I'd be in jeans and T-shirt…but I do like the earrings though," she said lightly plucking them with her index fingers.

"I bet you do," Menage said. He sat down and wondered why she hadn't told him about the baby yet. He had heard every word she said when she thought he was still in a coma. Maybe she had her reasons. He wanted to call Dwight last night but Felix was against it, and he knew about the phone system so Chandra's cell phone was useless. He looked at Chandra. He'd been a fool taking her love for granted and he made up his mind last night as they lay in bed that he was going to change and be faithful to her.

Vapor lifted up his head and whined as Felix and Rosita appeared. Rosita wore a lightweight leather jacket that was unzipped, showing her ample cleavage through a silk chiffon blouse, and her skirt matched the waist-cut jacket. She wore a pair of Manolo Blahnik pumps. Felix stood with his chest out in a Giorgio Armani two-piece suit.

"Why everybody dressed like this? This the BET awards or somethin'?" Menage said looking around the table.

Boy, be quiet!" Chandra said pinching his leg underneath the table as they began their breakfast. They both had a plate of grits, eggs, bacon and pancakes. Felix and Rosita ate something they couldn't even pronounce.

"Hey, Felix," Menage said as he slipped Vapor a piece of bacon. "Who's the painting on the wall by?"

Felix wiped his mouth. "Julian Schnabel. I got it for one point five mil at an auction in Italy."

"What! One point five mil for one picture! Man, shit!" Felix smiled and pointed at Menage's platinum Rolex. "That's different," Menage said wishing he had worn the Bulova instead. The group laughed and joked, filling the dining room with cheer. Menage was soon eager to go back upstairs to be alone with Chandra.

"Baby, do you know how much that outfit cost I had on at breakfast?" Chandra said as she rubbed some medicated cream on Menage's chest. He was still waiting for her to break the news about the baby. He also thought of Felix's so-called plan, which Felix said he would fill him in on some time during the afternoon. He closed his eyes as her soft touch relaxed him. She now wore a Baby Phat halter-top with a matching tennis skirt and a pair of Nikes.

Menage had a child on the way and he had no clue on who tried to kill him—not once, but twice. And the possibility of Chandra being harmed was something he didn't want to think about…it was already enough that they killed Vigor. He couldn't imagine his life without Chandra—not in this lifetime. He recalled what Dwight had told him about being true to her. Maybe he was right.

"Finished," Chandra said. "My big baby, Menage…"

"Talk to me," he said with his head resting on her lap.

"I love you so much and I thought I was going to lose you," she said looking into his eyes. "You love me?" she said playing with his ear. "Don't play me, Menage."

"How much you love me?"

"More than you may ever know," she said caressing the side of his face now. "And you know I don't want you for your money or all the material things that you claim life is all about. You think you're invincible when it comes to pain and love…and loving me. Baby, I know you're intelligent and it's obvious you have good taste," she said pointing to herself. "But I thought I lost you and I was really scared. Now that you're with me," she said leaning forward to kiss him, "I don't plan on letting you go." Placing her hand on his firm, flat stomach, she began to move her smooth palm around in a slow circle. He took a deep breath and looked into her eyes. She knew the vulnerable areas of his body as well as every scar, old and new. And each time Menage was with her, it felt like their first time. But why did he still sleep with other women? It wasn't as if he didn't care if he hurt her.

"Baby…I know you're carrying my seed," he said. Her hand became stiff.

"H-how? I mean, who told you!"

"I was conscious when you said it at the hospital. I was just too weak to respond. I know I'm not perfect," he said reaching for her hand, "but I'll do my best to be a father to our child and more important, Chandra...a husband to you." She gasped as he continued. "I'm not good at this but I just want you to know that I'm sick of running from you and..." He took a deep breath.

"Baby...what are you trying to say?"

"I wish it wasn't like this but I feel the time is right, so..." He rolled off the bed and got on one knee. "Move, boy," he said pushing Vapor out of his face. He took both her small, soft hands in his and watched the tears flow down her face. "Chandra, will you marry me?" he asked meaning every single word. She tucked in her bottom lip and muttered something he couldn't comprehend.

"Y-yes, yes, I'll marry you," she managed to say this time. Her smile was brighter than platinum. He felt as if all the pressure in the world was lifted from him and he felt something he never thought he could feel again—love. He raised himself up and sat beside Chandra. He hugged her, rocking back and forth as she cried. Vapor whined and crawled on his stomach and when he was close enough, he put his head on Chandra's lap.

"Shhh. No more tears, baby." Menage gently pulled Chandra's hands away from her tear-stained face and kissed her.

"I...I'm sorry," she said.

"Sorry for what?" He raised her chin with his finger.

"Baby, just make love to me...now!" After putting Vapor in the next room, Menage looked at Chandra as she lay on her back rubbing her tear-filled eyes with the palms of her hands. He stood at the edge of the bed and motioned for her to lift up her feet so he could take off her shoes. He rubbed the bottom of her bare feet as she watched his every move. He could see the hairy print between her legs through her yellow thong. Removing her feet from his grasp, she scooted up on the bed, still on her back. He licked his dry lips as she lifted up her hips and tugged down the tennis skirt. Then she sat up, pulled off her top and tossed it in the corner. She got up on her knees and slowly reached behind her back to unsnap her bra. It, too, got tossed into the corner. She reached out for Menage, pulled him down onto the bed and laid him on his back. His boxers came off with ease. She kissed him deeply as she ran her hand down his stomach and then grasped his hard penis. He began to moan as she slid a nipple into his mouth. She stroked his penis while he softly bit her nipple and played with her other breast. Menage sent volts of pleasure through Chandra's body with his tongue. He hadn't noticed, but she had come out of her thong by pulling the Velcro strap on the thin waistband. He stopped her from jacking him off and rolled her onto her back. Now he was on his knees on top of her. There was a look of lust in her eyes. He quickly glanced between her parted legs and fought the will to plow into her softness. Kissing her stomach, he slowly touched the lips between her thighs, hidden under neatly trimmed, V-shaped pubic hair. Chandra was already on fire, and Menage felt as if he was caressing soft, wet, silky velvet. She began grinding her hips along with the motion of his fingers and he slowly moved his head toward her sex. He could now smell her natural, sweet musky scent and her pubic hairs tickled his chin. He kissed her chocolate inner thighs and lying down on his stomach, wrapped an arm around each of them, holding them apart. She bit her lip and grabbed the headboard when she felt him open her wet lips. He softly licked her from top to bottom. She moaned and arched her back. Soon he was licking her intensely and brought her to a stunning climax by doing things to her clit that he'd never done before. And he eagerly lapped up her creamy nectar. Menage rubbed his sore jaws. Had he worn a watch, he would have been shocked to see that he had been going at it for more than thirty minutes. Chandra was in a sexual daze of pure pleasure. He was about to enter her when she suddenly made him lay on his back and told him to close his eyes.

"Come on, Chandra, I'm 'bout to die," he pleaded.

"No, close your eyes," she said with a seductive tone. There was something in her eyes that he had never seen before. He closed his eyes as she straddled him. He felt her swinging nipples against his chest. "I love you so much," she said into his ear. Taking his throbbing penis, she rubbed it against her wet lips, only letting the head enter her. It was driving him crazy. When he tried to ease himself deeper inside her, she raised up higher. "Be still and keep your eyes closed," she said kissing him, tasting her juices on his lips and becoming excited. Then he felt her lips and tongue on his chest and wounds. He thought she was going to please him with her hands as she had done once before, but what she did next made him open his eyes with shock and disbelief. He felt her hot breath and tongue on his penis. He wanted her to stop but she said no with her eyes. It was her first time doing it. He had never asked her to, nor did he plan on asking her. She looked in his eyes as her lips locked around his throbbing penis. He tried to speak, but no words would come and he curled his toes. She slowly lowered her head, taking him deeper into her mouth. She didn't know what to expect; it really was her first time. Her roommate gave her some pointers and even pulled out a porno tape she kept under her bed. She held the base of his hard penis with her right hand and played with his balls with her left. Each time she came up she was careful not to bite him, keeping her teeth away from his skin. She enjoyed the feeling of putting him off guard, and she seemed to lose herself in the new erotic sensation she felt in her mouth. His pre-cum seemed to make her ache for more. She moaned and looked into his eyes as he placed his hand on her head. She was happy to be able to please her man with her new...she couldn't think of the right word but she was enjoying herself. She remembered the tape; she saw one girl take it all the way down her throat—something she wasn't going to try. She sucked him fast, bobbing her head up and down and licking him from top to bottom. Then she lost control, rubbing his penis all over her face. She was totally fascinated by this new act. She moaned as she put his penis back into her mouth. Menage breathed deeply through his mouth as Chandra continued to suck him. He knew she had no experience but he had no complaints about the feeling she was giving him. "B...baby...wait...stop...I'm...I'm about to cum," he said through his clenched teeth. She ignored him as her saliva trickled down toward the base of his penis. He reached down to stop her, but she pushed his hand away as she felt him twitch inside her mouth. She knew what was going to happen next. Her roommate told her this act was only to be done to a loved one and she decided she'd go for it. She slowed down as he arched his hips into the air and called out her name. The first shot surprised her, but she swallowed and took what he had to offer. She licked him clean and purred like a kitten.

"Baby...I need a doctor," he said trying to catch his breath. Moments later she got on her hands and knees as he entered her. His two hands almost met as he held her around her small waist. They couldn't seem to get enough of each other. The sound of their bodies slapping, flesh on flesh, filled the room.

"I love you, girl," Menage said as they sat in a black marble hot tub.

"I know," Chandra said rubbing his shoulders. "What will we name our little girl?"

"Huh? You mean boy. And I haven't really thought about it yet," he said with his eyes closed.

Saturday Afternoon
Lisa stood in front of the mirror putting on lipgloss when Benita walked in and leaned against the edge of the dresser with her arms crossed.

"Why are you getting ready so early? It's only three something."

"Mind your business, I'm just seeing which gloss looks right...so you think the lady that was with him Saturday night at the club was the same one that did your hair?"

"I think so," Benita said as she sat on the bed. "But like I said, all I saw was the bracelet."

"Oh, come on, girl, get real...and the shit was probably fake. And besides, what's the big deal anyway?" Lisa said wiping the gloss off her lips and reaching for another one.

"Well, nothing, I guess—just another girl, I don't know," Benita said nonchalantly, but she had a feeling that something was up. She just couldn't piece it together.

"Well if she was all that, she'd be the one going out with DJ instead of me. Anyway, that was then and this is now."

"Please!" Benita said. "Hey, I bet DJ don't even know that I know Dwight and Menage."

"Benita, will you stop? Anyone could've been driving his car that day and for all I know, it might not have even been his, you feel me? And so what if you are right and know some of his friends and one that's half dead and..." She caught herself and looked at Benita. "Girl, you know I didn't mean that. I'm sorry."

"Don't worry about it," Benita said sounding slightly hurt.

Lisa sat down next to her. "If DJ don't bring it up, I won't speak on it. I really don't see no reason to—do you?"

"Yeah, I feel ya. I'ma chill out today. Can I use your car?"

"Yeah, but please just fill it up this time."

Benita got up and went back into the living room. She still wanted to see Menage. She had so much to talk to him about.

***

Dressed in a cream blazer and matching slacks by Armani, Dwight stepped outside his condo and put on his shades. It was another hot and dry day. Today he had to make his rounds from shop to shop. Tina was already at the main salon doing hair. He locked the door and picked up his briefcase that contained eight thousand dollars in cash and a black calico. There was no word from Felix or Dr. Wilson, but he trusted both of them to inform him of any change in Menage's condition. As he got into his BMW, he wondered if no news really was good news. He pulled out of his driveway and turned up his system as Pete Rock and CL Smooth's They Reminisce Over You, brought back the good times he shared with Menage.

***

Six men sat in a hotel room. Five of them came together to meet Scorpion, their head man who needed a big favor, and so far the meeting wasn't going well.

"I want to do more than just kill Felix; I want him to suffer and I want that shipment he has on his Island that's going to Berlin," said Scorpion. The five men were hired mercenaries— all with some kind of military training.

One of them spoke up. "How will we go about it, sir? Do you have a plan?" asked Myrmidon, a tall and stocky mercenary.

"Yes," said Scorpion. "We'll sneak on the island and take that bitch of his. He'll break down, seeing that he can be touched…we'll snatch her right out of his hands!" he hissed.

"I like the idea but I don't think it'll be easy."

"I know this. But I want it to happen soon—even before my contact in D.C. makes a move."

"How much will we be paid?" Myrmidon asked, unofficially becoming the speaker for his comrades.

"One million each." No one said anything, and he took it as an okay sign. "Here is the intel on his island," Scorpion said handing over a brown folder. "The island, gentlemen, as you see, is by no means small and the estate is on the southernmost point. Intelligence has confirmed that radar is in operation there with a radius of approximately between thirty and fifty miles. We've got one or two options to get our target: First a high altitude, low opening jump and a helicopter to fly in an hour before the jump to drop off a small PVC raft for our exit once we get the girl. Or, we can go by air and hit the island. I'll let you go over all the information to come up with another possible plan." They all nodded and one by one, stood up to leave.

Myrmidon stopped and turned to Scorpion. "I say, if we see Felix we should kill him on sight."

"No, that's not the plan. I want the drugs. We'll get him later."

"You better hope you're right, Scorpion."

"Just have your men ready. I'll have everything that will be needed, "Scorpion said. Myrmidon did a flawless about face and walked out of the room followed by his men, leaving Scorpion alone. Making sure they were gone, Scorpion locked the door and went into the bedroom. The petite brunette he had picked up the night before was naked and tied to the bed. Panic overcame her when he entered the room, and she began to yell through the gag in her mouth. It was useless. Scorpion ran his fingers up her leg, stopping at her tangled pubic hairs.

"Shhh," he said as he started to take off his clothes. "I'll let you go when I get my money's worth. How about a little role play?" he said. She closed her eyes as he got on top of her, shoving his erect penis inside of her. She had guys that were crazy before, she thought, as he started to pump, but no one ever left her tied up all night or screwed her without protection. She threw her hips forward to meet his thrust and she moaned when she felt his hand on her breast. Pleasure took over fear. "Mmmm," she moaned. At least he was paying her well—two hundred bucks. Crazy or not, she was getting her money's worth. She wished he would take the gag out of her mouth so she could breathe better and tell him that she was about to cum. She couldn't remember the last time a john got her off; it was usually a quick blow job and out the door, or some old wind bag grunting on top of her for three to five minutes. And she'd always fake an orgasm to make them happy. Her stomach felt fluttery, as if she was going down a rollercoaster. She shut her eyes and wrapped her legs around his thrusting hips. "Please don't stop," she thought as her head banged against the headboard. She knew he would pull out before he came, but she hoped that she would cum first. She locked her legs around him and started to tremble. She was relieved when she came, and Scorpion reached his climax seconds later. Still pumping her steadily, he slid his hand under the pillow behind her head. The orgasm had her weak and filled with pleasure, and the first impact of the five-inch blade going into her side went unnoticed. Scorpion stabbed her with quick, strong jabs while still inside of her. He got up and fell to the floor with the knife in his hand as blood poured from the deep cuts under her right breast.

***

Agent Lydia Nansteel, aka Latosha Mandrick, had one thought on her mind when she woke up earlier that morning. How in the hell could she get a lead on the DB-7 or anything with Menage being in a coma? She knew she didn't have much time in Miami, so the first thing she planned to do was stop by the MD Salon. She though that maybe she could pick up something there. She thought of ways to break the ice and get something started. "Miami's all right," she thought as she took in the sights on her way to the salon. And she was grateful that she at least had an appointment that was being paid for by the FBI.

Everything seemed to be moving at a slow pace. A candy gold Benz pulled up next to her at a stoplight with its top down, playing music so loud it made her rearview mirror tremble. The dark-skinned, bald headed man driving was hunched forward with the steering wheel under his chin. He smiled at her with a mouth full of gold. His passenger was an olive-skinned girl in a bikini top. It really was too hot to wear anything else. When the light changed, the Benz hit a right turn on three wheels. Lydia could only shake her head, figuring the the guy probably had two or three baby's mothers, stayed in the projects and drove a…from the looks of it, the Benz cost more than the ride she had back home.

She parked at MD Beauty Salon next to a BMW 745Li that sat in front of a sign that read H-N-I-C, which stood for Head Nigga In Charge. She was shocked by the lavish set-up of the salon when she walked through the green tinted doors. Had she gone down to the barber shop section, she would have seen the wall covered with hundreds of Jet Beauties, and she would have noticed the picture of herself…likes to read, cook, swim and finished second in her class at the FBI academy was listed along with her photo. She took a seat and picked up the latest Essence Magazine. A young girl with micro braids came up and asked Lydia to confirm her appointment. A few minutes later, she was seated in a chair getting her hair washed. She had her head laid back and her eyes closed when Dwight walked in and stood with his back to her. She didn't know who he was and she started to doze off.

"So, how many days you need off, Tylisha?" Dwight asked one of the salon workers as he tapped a pen on the edge of the clipboard he was holding.

"Uh…'bout three days, that's all. My cousin finally gettin' married," Tylisha said combing the woman's hair in her chair.

"Are you sure that's all you'll need?"

"Yeah. If I stay any longer they gonna be buggin' me about when I'ma find a man. Shit, I'm only twenty-two."

Dwight smiled. "Maybe they have a point, Ty."

She looked up at him and rolled her eyes. "Don't even start. How's Menage doing?"

"I really don't know, Ty. The hospital won't release any information," he said. He reached out to touch her bare shoulder but quickly pulled back his hand.

"Well, I hope he pulls through. I know how tight you two are." Dwight couldn't find anything to say so he left and went back to his office.

Lydia's mind began to race at full speed when she heard Menage's name and learned that this Dwight guy, who was right in front of her, was close to him. She made up her mind to use her cover of selling hair care products, which would actually be shipped. She kept her eyes closed and listened as the women started to gossip. The woman doing her hair spoke first.

"I know you'll find a man one day, Ty…if you stop actin' so dang silly all the time!"

"Child, please. I'm not even thinking about settling down. Mmm…I wish I could have Dwight on top of me," Ty said smiling.

"You'd love to have any man on top of your hot ass," said the woman doing Lydia's hair.

"I think I can break him down and get him in my bed. I can see it now..." Tylisha rolled her hips in a sexual manner, making some of the women laugh.

"Ty, you better slow down before your hot ass is out of a job...now cut that."

Tylisha waved her hand at the woman doing Lydia's hair. "Ya'll see that BMW he got? It's hot like fire!" Tylisha said.

"Ty, you and Felicia both need to watch your mouth with all these kids up in here!" said the older woman doing nails.

"Well, ex-c-u-u-u-se me!" Tylisha exclaimed. They all laughed. "I even hear that Tina is fucking around on Dwight," Tylisha said in a lower voice this time.

"What!" said a woman putting in a weave.

"I'm just telling you what I heard," Tylisha said.

The older woman doing nails put down her file. "See, Ty, there you go runnin' that Jerry Springer-Ricki Lake mouth of yours, gettin' shit started. How do you know what she doin'? Ain't none of your concern...matter of fact I don't wanna hear no more about it!"

"Yeah, whuteva!" Tylisha said.

Lydia thought things would get out of hand, but all the women who worked at the salon all lived in the same area and some even grew up together. They attended the same church and their kids went to the same schools. Menage had canvassed the housing projects to find girls who did hair in their kitchens or living rooms. With money out of his own pocket he paid for their schooling, down to the last penny. Now they all had a job, a new place to stay and were no longer on welfare.

"I do hope Menage is okay," Tylisha said. "Not to tell my biz, but girl, he is all of that…ooh…that fine chiseled body, handsome chestnut complexion and much…you hear me girl, much sexual charisma," she added recalling their trip back to her homeland Brazil.

"Did you sleep wit' him, girl?" said the woman doing Lydia's hair.

Tylisha looked at her and grinned. "Did I sleep with him? Hell, we didn't get no sleep at all, girl. He had me cummin' all night long."

"For real?"

"Yes, girl, and I gots to see him again," Tylisha said slapping her thigh.

The older woman spoke up. "See, that's what's wrong wit' ya whorish ass now."

"What happened to watch your mouth with all these kids up in here? Quit hatin' from the sideline. You need to give it up and try to get your groove back. Forty-five ain't too old to be sexin'." Everyone laughed and even Lydia couldn't hold back. She was under a dryer now and getting her nails done at the same time. She now had a way to find out a few things about Menage and the DB-7. And the thought of Dwight's cheating woman…maybe he had his weaknesses, but none of the girls said he messed around…or maybe he did it on the DL. Maybe he was in love. She was curious about his personal life because of her own lack of love. Most of the men she worked with were white and she didn't have any harsh feelings toward them at all, but she wasn't going to let what Paul had put her through destroy her feelings for a black man.

***

Scorpion stepped out of the shower and walked back into the bedroom. He ignored the dead girl as he waited for a call from

D.C. The phone chimed right on time just as he finished dressing. He waited for the beeps and tones to stop before he could speak freely. Scorpion was passing as an undercover FBI agent. He really worked for the CIA—unbeknownst to the FBI. Scorpion spoke first.

"Any new info?"

"Yes," said JoeTroublefield, the Director of Central Intelligence. "We now know for sure that Felix has a godson or something. His name is...just a sec...okay...here we go...Menage Unique Legend—black male, twenty-four, which tells us nothing. But I heard the FBI has thier eyes on him...you gave them the tip. It's a coincidence, don't you think, him now being tied to Felix? But I'll leave that up to you. Now back to Felix. The last time I checked there were only twenty armed guards on his island, but it's real lax. He's been there for ten years or so and nothing's ever happened. As of now, I don't know if the Secretary of State will approve of us snatching him up like we did our friend in Cuba. But for the time being, your mission is still max classified and the FBI Hostage Rescue Team will be able to help. And you are not to make a move unless the word comes from me."

"Yes sir, I fully understand," Scorpion said. He hung up the phone and smiled. He had other plans that neither the FBI nor the CIA knew about. In the end he'd cross both organizations. The FBI wanted Felix for several offenses, including drug trafficking and racketeering. Troublefield had told Scorpion that Felix was suspected of dealing with an enemy of the United States. Scorpion had his own ideas. First he'd take Felix's girl and force him to give up his shipment as ransom for her return. Then he'd kill them both and collect four million as payment from a rival crime family. "Life is so good," Scorpion said to himself. He knew he had to make his move before the FBI sent in the HRT. He wasn't worried about the money that he was supposed to pay the mercenaries. He pulled out a black Glock G30 and put the barrel in his mouth. This was how he planned to pay his help in the end. He loved the feeling of the barrel in his mouth.

Scorpion left the room in a disguise—a life-like, latex mask, known to no one—including the CIA and FBI and they could only reach him by phone. He didn't worry about fingerprints in the room because they didn't exist on any file, and when he paid for the room the night before, he had worn the mask over his face. Before leaving, he closed the dead girl's eyes and kissed her lips. "Thank you," he said and walked out the door laughing.

***

Detective Covington entered his office to see Hamilton reading Stuff Magazine. He walked to his desk and sat down, first checking his memo box.

"So what's up?" Covington asked.

Hamilton put the magazine down. "Well, you're the boss. I should be asking you. And you picked a fine time to come in…"

"Chill out. It's only a little after four."

"Well, I've been down in the lab all day—still nothing new though," Hamilton said.

"I think we should go back and check out Menage's place tonight. Maybe we missed something," said Covington.

Hamilton sighed. "Like what? We videotaped the search and ripped the place apart. All the prints were lifted…but if you got a feeling, I'm with you."

Covington searched his desk for his Newports. "Last night I went over the statements again and our friend DJ said the guy he shot was reaching for a weapon."

Hamilton rubbed his forehead. "I know. They say he was acting in self defense."

"Yeah, right on the money," Covington said tapping his new pack of Newports against the back of his hand.

"Maybe if Menage wasn't in a coma he could shed some light on the dark areas in this case."

"That would be nice," Covington said now searching for his lighter.

Hamilton reached into his coat and pulled out a red notepad. He flipped through it quickly. "I did a follow-up with the gardening service and they believe the break-in was early Saturday morning."

Covington lit his Newport. "That still don't tell us much. But whoever wants Menage dead ain't playing no games."

Hamilton closed his notepad. "We're missing something. I really don't need an unsolved case on my record—not now."

The men sat in silence. Covington felt relaxed as he pulled deeply on the Newport. Hamilton fanned the smoke from his face. Before either could speak further, there was a soft tap at the door. Hamilton turned in the metal chair as Sonya, the dispatcher, stepped into the office. Sonya turned every single head in the station with her shapely body that once graced the pages of Penthouse. She carried a lot in her pants. The breast job from her rich ex-boyfriend added to her sexy frame, and Covington had to admit that she was hot for a white girl. She stepped in with a box of glazed doughnuts that Hamilton gladly took from her.

"Thanks, Sonya," he said, not able to takes his eyes off her breasts.

"You're welcome…and how are you, Dominique?" she said sitting on the edge of his desk. She had a thing for Covington and he knew it.

"It's the same old shit—nothing new, nothing old."

"Why didn't you come to my pool party last month? I was hoping you would show up, Dominque," she said coyly. Hamilton rolled his eyes up toward the ceiling as he listened to the exchange between the two and grabbed a doughnut from off his desk.

"You know I'm married, Sonya, and we've been through this how many times... too damn many."

"Not hardly," she said. "I'll leave the two of you alone. But you, Mr. Covington, I'll speak to later." She made sure to sway her hips as she walked out the door.

"She never gives up. Hey, let me get one," Covington said eyeing the doughnut in Hamilton's hand.

"The answer is no. Remember yesterday," Hamilton said smiling.

"Man, please, you can't be for real. You got a whole damn box. Stop playing."

"Be convinced that I am not playing, Covington. Be very convinced!"

"Fuck it then...hope your white ass chokes."

"If I do, it will be on the last one and you still won't get any," Hamilton said.

"Be that way. Yo, what did you do last night? I tried to call you."

Hamilton slowly bit into another doughnut. "Mmm...ain't you a detective? Figure it out."

"Funny," Covington said.

"I had a date. Is that allowed?"

"You!" yelled Covington, nearly choking on the smoke as he inhaled his Newport.

"Yeah, and why is that such a surprise, huh?"

"Come on, Hamilton—look at you...you got no class. But anyway, did you get any pussy?"

Hamilton closed the box of doughnuts and slid them to the corner of his desk, but seeing Covington's eyes, he changed his mind and placed them on the floor by his feet. "Ha, ha, very funny, but I keep my personal life on the low down," Hamilton said.

Covington burst with laughter. "It's down low, not low down…you crazy as hell, Hammie."

"Who cares about…about slang talk? It only means you're uneducated anyway,"

Hamilton said with a serious tone. "And it's Hamilton—not Hammie!"

Covington put down his burning Newport and leaned forward on his desk. "Is that so? Is it your high level of intelligence that prevents you from becoming acquainted with street language, Mr. Harvard, or is it your lack of concentration that makes it difficult for you to grasp the true meaning or aspect of slang—the simple alteration of the meaning of mere words? All that confusion makes you feel less invincible, huh?" Covington said. He smiled, picked up his Newport and inhaled and exhaled, blowing a cloud of smoke into Hamilton's face. Hamilton was speechless.

***

Dwight had just escorted Lydia out of his office. They had just completed an order for a supply of various Clairol tones for hair color. To show his gratitude for the decent deal she gave him, he didn't charge her for the manicure. They planned to have a business lunch, and at first he was unsure about it because he sensed she was flirting. But the pictures of he and Tina were plainly visible in his office. He was busy on the computer when one of his barbers knocked on his door. It was Jamal—his head barber from Haiti.

"Yo Dwight, do you have a second?"

"Yeah, come on in," Dwight said sliding his keyboard to the side.

Jamal closed the door and took a seat. "Who was that lady? Man, I swear I seen her face somewhere before."

"Latosha Mandrick…you might have seen her at a hair show or something; she sells hair products," Dwight said.

"Latosha…that name don't ring a bell, but man she was fly."

"Yeah, I know what you mean. But anyway, she's going to be doing some business with us, so you might be seeing her around."

"Now that sounds good. Hey, maybe you can like, put a bid in for me. I didn't peep no ring on her finger."

"I'll see what I can do. As a matter of fact, when I call her, maybe I'll tell her about this conversation and see if it's okay to pass her number on to you."

"Yeah, I can deal with that," Jamal said trying to remember where he had seen her face before.

Dwight stood up and walked to his filing cabinet. "You just keep your head up, Jamal. There's plenty of women in Miami, so don't rush it—okay?"

"Yeah, easy for you to say; you got a woman at home, and ain't it 'bout time the two of ya'll tie the knot?"

Dwight turned back to his desk and sat down. Yes it was time he made Tina his wife. He was ready and so was she. All he could picture was good times as long as she was in his life.

"In due time, Jamal."

"Well, I'ma get back to work, but hit me back when you hear something. And, oh yeah, check out my new whip."

"What is it?" Dwight asked not looking up from the paper in front of him.

"It's a black-on-black Pontiac G-6."

"Big wheel," Dwight said.

"Yeah, right. When I can buy my shorty a whip, own a BMW and have a Viper on the side, then I'll be big wheel. But I'ma check you later, Dwight." They gave each other dap before Jamal left. Dwight called Tina, who was at the other salon across town. The phone rang twice before it was answered.

"Hello, MD Salon…Akissi speaking, how may I help you?"

"Hey, this is Dwight. Is Tina in?"

"Oh, hi Dwight. Yes, she's in. Just hold one second." The line switched to a song by Brandy. Seconds later Tina was on the line.

"Hey baby."

"What's going on with you?" he said leaning back in his leather chair.

"Baby, it's busy as hell but that's good, right?" she said cheerfully, making him smile.

"You know it is. Do you have any idea what time you'll make it out of there tonight? "Hmmm…'bout eight or nine I guess."

"Okay. We might have a good deal on some hair color," Dwight said then went on to tell her about Latosha.

"That's great. Anything on Menage?"

"Nah, boo, it's the same story." He let out a deep sigh.

"I hope he makes it, Dwight…I really do. I know we didn't always get along, but it was all in fun."

"I know, baby, and he knows it too—trust me. I'd still feel better if I knew something… anything."

"I know, honey," she said softly.

"Oh yeah, I forgot to tell you…I called DJ over for dinner tonight to get things right so that we'll be on the same level. Just because Menage was in charge don't mean he'll automatically take over his job." He waited for her to say something. "Tina…Tina, you still there?"

"Oh yeah, I'm here. I...I was just thinking about what to cook on such short notice, that's all," she said. She couldn't believe that DJ would be under the same roof with she and Dwight. And right now she didn't want to see DJ at all. She closed her eyes and thought about that last night they shared together. She wasn't shocked to find herself wanting him inside her again. Fuck you, DJ. It's over, she thought.

"Don't stress it," Dwight said breaking her train of thought. "It's not a classy affair, but after I get off the phone with you I'ma call him. Just try to get off as soon as you can, okay?"

"Yeah, I'll see what I can do. Maybe I'll have Akissi close up," she said.

After saying their I love yous, they ended the call. Dwight sat back in his chair and picked up a picture of Tina. He loved her more than anything. She was perfect and made him happy—not to mention the sex. In his heart he knew it was time to make her his wife, for what they shared was real love.

***

Rosita and Chandra were tanning on the sundeck of Felix's 108-foot yacht. The Leight Notika was triple-decked, built at a Turkish shipyard. Equipped with a sky lounge and full accommodations, the yacht was able to comfortably carry eight guests and six crewmembers. Chandra was having a light discussion with Rosita, telling her how Vapor had come into the room while she and Menage were sleeping and snatched the blanket off the bed, running all around with it.

Menage walked out onto the pier of Felix's mansion and covered his eyes from the sun as he looked toward the yacht sailing in the calm waters. He pulled out his cell phone and called Chandra to tell her that he was going somewhere on the island with Felix. He knew that whatever system Felix had jamming the phones inside his home didn't stop calls from being made outside. He turned and walked back toward the mansion. Vapor was running down the beach trying to catch some seagulls.

Menage whistled and Vapor came at once. He let Vapor into the back of one of Felix's Hummers and then got in himself. Felix started up the Hummer and headed down the beach. Menage sat next to him eating a bacon, egg and cheese sandwich that Miss Welton had packed for their trip. The Hummer plowed through the thick sand with ease and Felix handled it with skill as it drove up a slope.

"Didn't you eat enough this morning?" Felix said as Menage reached for another sandwich.

"Man, don't you know I gotta get my strength back? And I have to keep up with Chandra..."

"I understand," Felix said smiling.

"Where we going anyway?" Menage asked, only seeing jungle and palm trees.

"It's a surprise," Felix said pulling out a Cuban cigar.

"When your damn lungs get as black as Vapor's, you gonna wish you never smoked. Those things stink anyway, but nope, you don't wanna listen to me," Menage said holding onto the door grip.

"Since when did you become the spokesperson for cancer?" Felix said making jabbing motions with the cigar toward Menage, while keeping his eye on the narrow path. He didn't light it up because he knew it would cause Menage discomfort. They rode on for another five minutes.

"Okay, here we are," Felix said as the Hummer shot out of the foliage and back onto the beach. They were now on the opposite side of the island at the northern end. Menage could make out what looked to be a small building just about where all the greenery ended. Vapor jumped out and walked around, sniffing the ground. "Come on, this way," Felix said walking toward the building. As they got closer, Menage noticed another Hummer parked behind the building. The door opened before Felix could knock. A young kid with long hair, dressed in shorts and a tank top motioned them inside and with a quick glance, Menage noticed that he was carrying a gun. His eyes quickly adjusted as they entered a dark room. The left wall was filled with TV screens, computers and what looked to be a radar screen. Sitting on a rolling stool was another kid wearing headphones. He was busy watching the screens.

"What the hell is this, Felix?" Menage asked.

"You don't know? Well, that's odd coming from an ex-Marine."

"Former Marine," Menage corrected him.

The kid with the long hair spoke. "It's state of the art…well, really, it's a small Russian radar outpost—nothing big, though. But we can see anything coming towards this island within a thirty-mile radius or more, depending on the weather, and it stays on twenty-four hours a day." He then pointed to the screen at Felix's yacht, and with a few commands on the computer it showed a digital outline of the entire island. Felix then led Menage back outside and walked down a path behind the building.

Menage was shocked when they reached an underground shelter. The four-inch steel door swung open and Felix led him down five steps and then to another door. They went down another ten steps. When Felix turned on a light, Menage's jaw dropped. The shelter was packed with wall-to-wall weapons. "My little collection," Felix said smiling. Menage walked to a crate marked Property of U.S.S.R. Next to it was a case filled with pistols that he'd never seen the likes of before. But what caught his eye was an H & K MP-10 sitting on a box wrapped in plastic.

Later on the drive back, Menage asked Felix why he had shown him the radar post and shelter. "So you and Chandra can feel safe," he said.

"Felix, only a fool would try to come out here. But yeah, I feel safe. I—"

"Can't stay on the Island...I know," Felix said interrupting him. Menage looked at him as he loaded one of the new Glock nine millimeters that he took from the shelter. "I got people thinking you're still in a coma. I figure that whoever did this will make some kind of slip-up...and...well, I really think that if you show your face back in Miami not knowing the enemy, you could end up dead. I know you can't stay here forever but just give me two days or so. I got a plan. Trust me on this one, Menage. Besides, you owe it to Chandra." He knew that his last statement would hit home...it did.

***

Back at the mansion, Menage stood on the pier looking toward Miami with Vapor panting alongside him. Felix's yacht now sat motionless in the blue-green waters. Chandra and Rosita were back in the mansion talking about baby clothes, wedding dresses and everything else in between. Menage was a father now...well, he'd be one soon...and no more being the center of attention. But nothing else had the same importance now—not even being so close to his dream of making a million. It all seemed so frivolous with a baby on the way. Still, he really wanted to get back to Miami and he was becoming restless. Moments later Felix walked down the pier.

"You miss it, right?" he said. Menage didn't reply. "You don't feel right unless you're in a flashy car, do you? I know you want to get back in the game, but now you have Chandra and the baby to think about. Look at all that I have, and yet you risk your life for a million. You're like a son to me, but you never asked for anything free; you've worked for what's yours and I fully respect that."

Menage put a towel over his head to ease the beaming sun. "Felix, I came a long way, from shit to sugar. When I was growing up in Liberty City I had nothing, but I don't fault my mama because she did what she could for me and made sure I never went to bed hungry. Now that she's happy, I'm happy. I didn't have to take this path but I did, so now I gotta live with it, you know? All this shit is bullshit man, really."

"Let's not get into all of that right now," Felix said pulling out his cell phone. "Hot out here, ain't it?"

"Yeah," Menage said scratching Vapor's ears. Felix's call was short. Moments later two small boats appeared in the water.

"What's going on?" Menage said. "Send Vapor back to the mansion." Felix was silent. Menage thought the boats were headed toward the yacht but they were slowly coming their way. "Hey, where those boats goin'?"

"Mine is going back to Miami."

"And what about the other one?" Felix slyly looked at Menage. "What? How...who shit is that? "No...Felix, I don't have a boat..."

It's yours, son—a gift for new fatherhood."

The look of shock was on Menage's face. "Say word?" he said as the boats slowed down. The Skater 46 was forty-five feet and seven inches long with a twelve-foot beam. The speedboat seated five high-backed yellow bucket seats. It could accelerate up to 170 miles per hour depending on water conditions, fuel and load. The only two custom modifications were the small cabin located on the lower deck and a solid gold throttle. The interior of the boat was painted money green and Menage's Way was prominently written on the stern.

"How fast can it go," Menage said after they stepped off Felix's boat and onto Menage's new one. Felix's boat was now heading back toward Miami.

"Only one way to find out," Felix said as he strapped himself into the passenger seat. Menage looked at the helm controls. Everything was digital. Taking a seat at the helm, he ran his right hand over the solid gold throttle. It was unbelievable, and it was his. Grinning like a five-year-old on December twenty-fifth, he began to strap himself into his seat.

"Just push the red button on the right. It's the quick-start," Felix said.

"Do we need to wear the helmets?"

"No, but I don't want you to open her up fully—not with me on it anyway."

"Chicken," Menage said taunting him.

"Yeah, you say that now. Push the damn button. Let's test her out," Felix said. Menage pushed the quick-start and the two thirteen hundred horsepower engines came alive. The whine from the engines sent Menage back to the time when he was a Marine, because the sound he now heard was similar to that of an AV-8B Harrier taking off.

"Felix, what the hell's pushin' this thing?" Menage said as he waited a few seconds for the engine to warm up. He sat back and relaxed as he grabbed the wheel with his left hand and gripped the throttle with his right. He looked forward and waited patiently as Felix pulled the straps tighter across his chest. He didn't quite yet trust Menage's boating skills. Menage slammed the throttle forward. For a second nothing happened. Then all of a sudden, the boat shot forward and quickly ripped through the waters like a knife. Menage eased off the throttle and glanced at the speed, as the boat felt as if it was floating on a cloud. The speed was 67.1 knots. He slowly pushed the throttle forward again, increasing the speed to 75.1 knots, then to 95.3knots...and 107.4 knots as he kept the boat on a straight course. Felix was now wearing a helmet and told Menage to do the same. Menage quickly did as he was told, as the boat seemed to be gliding on air.

"Can it go any faster?" he yelled, his voice filled with pure excitement.

"Yeah, but—" Felix's words were cut off when Menage made a sharp turn, now moving at a speed of close to 156.5 knots. Menage noticed that the throttle still wasn't wide open and he didn't know the boat's top speed, but the current velocity was incredible.

"I can't believe this!" he yelled. They tore through the

waters, racing to the unknown. Menage felt so free and the boat was under his full command. He decreased the speed and maneuvered the boat into a figure eight shape before coming to a full stop.

"This is the life ain't it, kid?" Felix said wanting to light up a Cuban cigar. The boat rocked softly with the moving sea as they dropped the small anchor.

"Yeah, this bitch is a fuckin' beast," Menage said slumped back in his seat with a towel over his head.

"So how you feel about getting married?"

"Change the subject," Menage said. He loved Chandra and meant what he'd said about making her his wife, but he looked down into the water to see if he could spot any fish—anything to get his mind off marriage. "Hot as fuck out here," he said wiping his face.

"Yeah, so what do you plan to do with your…uh…stable of women? And what happened to that older lady who had that stretch BMW."

Menage sat up and took the towel off his head and smiled. "Oh yeah, man, that chick was crazy. I mean, she was so stuck up just because she was rich—paid out the ass, trips to France, all that bullshit, you know. Anyway, like I told you before, I met her at Palm Beach and she had some guy come up and give me a card with her number on it. Come to find out, she never been with a black man. Get this, said she want a thug." They both laughed. "Anyway, I called and she was like playin' games. Call me back, or I'm busy, all that bullshit."

"How is that? I thought you were the player," Felix said.

"Fuck you Felix, but anyway, check it: One day I finally go see her and all she do is jack me off—no sex or nothing…and for forty-five she had a body—tits and a round, plump ass, gap and everything. But then, a few weeks later, she came to my crib and get this, yo, in a fuckin' helicopter. That's my word—landed in my backyard. Anyway, we got high and she wanted me to try that nose candy—no haps though, so shorty gets fucked up, Felix, gone. Man, that night was wild as hell. She even put dope on my dick and sucked it off, but when I got a hold of that ass, I put it to her good...all...night...long." Felix looked at him and shook his head. "Wait, I ain't finished. After I sexed her, she started flippin', talkin' 'bout she'll take care of me and move with her to Sweden.

"So what did you say?"

"I played like I was wit' it—I lied."

"What!"

"Damn right I did. I gave her a taste of how she ran me on the first go 'round, but I did have to hit that ass a few more times before I sent her on. She stopped calling about four months ago. I last seen her doing some event on TV in Denver...it's messed up, though."

"What's that?" Felix said smoking a cigar. He couldn't keep himself from smoking around Menage any longer but he was careful not to blow smoke in his direction.

"See man, I just wanna do my own thang, do it my way, you know? I don't fuck wit' nobody in a major way, but now look...a motherfucker tried to burn me."

Felix put on a straw hat and tossed his cigar in the ocean before pulling out another one. "Human beings are like animals; we must go against each other. You know the old saying: Only the strong survive...the weak are cast to the side. That's life, and it's not only the strong but also those who are smart. What good is a strong fool, huh? Think about that."

Menage stood up and put on his shades. "Things have to change, man. I can't stay on your island forever and I know I can't spray every chick that I see with a fat ass when I leave. But I feel like a pussy hiding out here. I gots to do something and you know I'm right. Are you feeling me on that?"

Felix put down his cigar. He knew that what Menage had said was right…well in a way. He knew enough about life to know that a man always had something to prove. He knew that Menage wouldn't stay on his island much longer and he also knew there was no way to talk him out of it.

"You know Chandra won't go for you going back to Miami. I know you wanna get in the mix of things, but son, you'll be a father soon and you need to put that in that thick skull of yours. You gotta see what's important in life. It's not sex and money and a Benz on twinkies."

Menage let the words sink in and sighed. Chandra would trip if he left the island. He thought that maybe he could sneak off, but he knew that would be too much on her and he had a weak spot for tears. Besides, he didn't wish to put her though any more pain.

"Any idea who's behind this?" Menage said as he sat back down.

Felix took off his hat and wiped his forehead. "If I knew I'd have him at the bottom of this ocean, but I don't have a single clue."

"I wonder what the police got."

Felix smiled. "If they had anything I'd know." He then told him that his nephew would reach him with the information concerning who was behind the hit. Other than that, all they could do was wait, he had advised. Menage began to smoke his first blunt since he'd been shot. He got so high that he was unable to drive the boat back. Felix called ahead and told Chandra that they were on their way back to the mansion. As he tied Menage's Way to the pier, Chandra was there waiting with a stern look on her face and Vapor was at her side, barking at the boat. Chandra wasn't too pleased when she learned that Menage had been smoking weed.

***

Menage ran down a dark street, unable to lose the thing or whatever it was that was after him. He didn't look back to see what it was, like the white people in horror flicks, and for some reason they would always fall and stay there. Bullshit! He ran faster, but now he felt hot breath on the back of his neck. He screamed and caught himself, abruptly awakening. He'd been dreaming, and Vapor was sitting at the edge of the bed, huffing and puffing in his face.

"Move, boy," he said rolling over and feeling slightly dizzy.

"Doctor's orders, huh?" Chandra snapped. "I'm shocked at you. You know you don't need to be smoking, and don't try to play me by saying it's for your pain." She got up, went to the bathroom and came out with a cool, wet rag. She put it on his forehead and sat next to him on the bed. "You okay, boo?" she whispered. He closed his eyes and rested his head on her lap.

"My head's killin' me and I feel like I can eat a cow. Call the help or somethin'."

Chandra called Miss Welton and ordered a meal for Menage. He put his arms around her waist and buried his face between her legs, like a whining baby.

"Oh, please. Don't try to get on my good side acting like a baby...all right, big baby, it's okay." After Menage ate, they made love again.

***

DJ smiled to himself as he headed down Northeast 151st Street. Things were looking good. His power move had come through the night before and he was on his way to pick up Lisa. He wore black Timbs, denim Esco pants and a lightweight pullover shirt zipped halfway down, revealing his new red gold piece. It was crafted in the shape of a man and a woman in a 69 position with the woman on top. It was almost nine-thirty, and he called ahead of time and told Lisa he'd be late. His truck drew attention as it slowed at a stoplight with the system knocking. He didn't know why Dwight wanted to see him, but Tina had called afterward and put him at ease. There was still no word on Menage, but he knew he was still in a coma. Yeah, just like the title of the Wu Tang song blasting, Bring Da Ruckus, is how he felt.

Now that he was a major player in the game, Tina might get back on his dick, he thought. The sex was good and so was the head. He laughed at how she was playing Dwight. "He put all his trust in that bitch and she ain't shit," he thought. It wasn't his fault Dwight was blind as fuck, but pussy always did that to a weak man. DJ knew it was his calling to be on top and he didn't care about anything else. A nigga gotta live, he felt. When he pulled up in front of Lisa's apartment, she was outside before he put the SUV in park.

"What happened to your Lex?" she asked as he backed out slowly. She wanted to see if he would tell the truth or lie.

"It's a long story…what Biggie used to say? Wreck it, buy a new one…"

"Well, at least he didn't lie," she thought. "Yeah, if you got it like that. Did you miss me, DJ?" She wondered if he could tell she wore a thong under her tight, Apple Bottom jeans.

"What do you think?"

"I don't know…you tell me," she said lightly rubbing his arm.

"Yes, I missed you. Hey, how was your trip?" DJ listened to her tell him about her trip and then she listened to him tell her about the little meeting they were headed to. She laid her head back and closed her eyes as they cruised down Seventh Avenue. They listened to music without speaking for a few minutes, and DJ turned down the radio and dialed a number on the phone that was mounted on the armrest between them. He used the speakerphone. After the fifth ring, the phone was picked up at the other end. Lisa was now gazing out the window.

"Hello?" Dwight said through the speakerphone.

"Yo, Dwight, this is DJ. What's the deal?"

"Nothing much, still waiting for Tina to get off work. What's going on?"

"I'll be there in a few. I'm on my way now and I'ma stop and get some wine or something. How about Chardonnay?"

"Yeah, that's fine."

"Look, I got a special lady friend with me. Is that ok?" He glanced at Lisa and smiled.

"No problem, she can chat with Tina while we talk. I'm sorry I didn't suggest it myself. So much is going on."

"I bet that's right," DJ thought. "Any word on Menage?" he asked. Lisa was all ears now, but she didn't look his way.

"Nah, I'll call Felix later on today, I guess."

"Okay," DJ said smiling. "I'll see ya when I get there."

"All right, peace out."

DJ pressed the end button. Lisa sat in silence. She wanted to tell DJ all about Benita and Menage, but she couldn't find a good reason to do so. So what he knew Menage—big deal.

"What about my place later tonight?" DJ said reaching over to rub her thigh.

"Huh?"

"I said...what about my place tonight?" DJ repeated, reaching to hold her hand this time.

"Oh...I don't know...I have to go in early tomorrow," she smiled and caressed his hand. She had already called in and said she wasn't coming in tonight, lengthening her vacation, and she didn't' want to push it. As they drove under a streetlight, she noticed him looking at her. "Damn, he's fine. I'm sure we wouldn't get any sleep," she thought.

"Come on, we can just chill and talk. It ain't all about sex," DJ lied. Once he got her under his roof, he'd run every trick in the book to get between her legs again.

"Yeah, right!" she said. "But I'll think about it."

DJ knew how to get any woman. Well at least he thought he did, and he had an idea and a song to help him. It was dark in his truck and the only light came from his radio's knobs and Navi screen. "Lisa," he said in a deep sexy voice, "I want you to show me something tonight."

She turned in her seat and looked at him. "Show you what?" she said. He didn't answer.

"DJ..."

"Shhh," he said.

Seconds later a song by Xscape, Softest Place on Earth, started playing. Lisa got the picture. The softest place on earth tonight would be between her legs—if she was willing. Lisa closed her eyes as the song eased her mind...and body. "Damn, he got game," she thought.

***

"Baby, are you ready yet?" Dwight said as he walked into the den.

"Yeah!" Tina yelled back from the bedroom. She felt a little nervous about DJ coming over, but after she heard he was bringing a date, she felt better. She was glad he was moving on...well a little. Now if she could just get Dwight to do the things that DJ did to her in bed, then he'd be the total package. Her low cut jeans fit her like a glove—might as well show DJ what he was missing. When DJ arrived with his date, Tina answered the door and he calmly introduced the two women. Lisa walked into the livingroom and was shocked by the lavish sight. Thick carpet, leather chairs and a huge fish tank flushed into the wall.

"Dwight'll be out in a sec, DJ," Tina said. Before she could turn around, Dwight appeared at her side and the introductions were quick. Tina took the bottle of wine from DJ and carried it to the kitchen. Dwight asked Lisa if she could excuse he and DJ for a moment.

"Tina'll keep you company. I promise we won't be long, and it's nice to meet you," Dwight said. He and DJ left the living room and vanished down the hall.

"Uh…Lisa, right?" Tina said handing Lisa a glass of Henny.

"Yes, thank you," Lisa said taking the glass.

"So, how are you tonight? And if you don't mind me asking, how long have you known DJ?"

"What! Nah, she didn't just ask me that. Who the hell she think she is?" Lisa thought. But all she said was, "I'm fine, thank you. DJ and I just met."

"Well, the two of ya'll look nice together," Tina said touching Lisa's knee.

"Ho, please," Lisa thought. She wished DJ would hurry the hell up so they could go. Hell, she might as well stay with DJ tonight. Lisa could tell that Tina thought it was all about her. But why shouldn't she? She had a good-looking man, nice crib and a huge diamond bracelet on her wrist—one she kept flinging around to make sure Lisa saw it.

"I been on my feet all day," Tina said."

"You work?" Lisa asked thinking that all she did was sit around drinking wine.

"Do I!" Tina said sipping her wine. "Girl, I pull eight to ten hours a day…six days a week most of the time."

Lisa was shocked. The woman put in more hours than she did. "Well, I can see it's paying off," Lisa said looking around the condo.

Tina laughed. "Yeah, but it's been a long, long road, girl. It would've been even harder if I didn't have Dwight, but maybe soon we can both slow down and enjoy the fruits of our labor."

"I can drink to that," Lisa said, thinking that maybe Tina wasn't so bad after all.

"So where are you from?" Tina asked. She could tell by the way Lisa talked that she wasn't born and raised in Miami.

"Kinston, North Carolina."

"Kinston…Kinston…" Tina said sticking her tongue in her cheek. "I think I did a girl's head last weekend and she said she was from Kinston."

"Really? Kinston's so small; I'm bound to know her," Lisa said playing dumb.

Tina thought for a second. "Yeah, and come to think of it, she was one of Big Chubb's new girls…oh, he owns the strip club. But anyway, she's a dancer and told me she was from Kinston."

"So that's what you do—hair?" Lisa said, her mind racing.

"Yeah, and I own the place—Dwight and I, that is. But most of the time I'm out on the floor helping out if I can get away from the desk. Maybe you should stop by one day. I'm sure you'll love the service and it'll be on me."

Lisa thanked her and sipped her wine. "If Tina was in the car with DJ at the club, what did it really matter?" she thought.

"Girl, I can't help but notice that bracelet; it's beautiful. Where did you buy it?"

Tina smiled and extended her arm out towards Lisa. "It's a custom piece. Dwight bought if for me on Valentine's Day last year."

"Hmmm…I hate to see the wedding ring."

"You and me both, girl," Tina said winking her eye.

Lisa thought of Benita…so her crazy ass was right…oh well. The two women talked about men, sex, clothes and everything they could think of. Lisa was also starting to like Tina. Like Martin had always said, she was stompin' wit' da big dawgs."

***

"Yeah, I put fourteen thousand in my account," Dwight said sitting behind his desk in his small office. DJ sat slumped in the chair across from him, rubbing his goatee. "And you move pretty fast, I've noticed," added Dwight leaning forward and folding his hands.

"Well, to you it may seem that way but to me it's normal. I fully understand that you, or should I say Menage, only did a small amount a month. All I'm doing is moving cars at a faster rate," DJ said smoothly, his eyes never leaving Dwight's.

"I can say that you have…let's say, more experience in the street aspect than I do, but I'm not saying I don't know the ins and outs. And due to recent events you now sit in a new seat, but I want you to hear me out, DJ. You will never take Menage's status—meaning every dime you make comes to me and then we'll split the pie; every move you make goes through me first. Now, do you have any problems with that?"

DJ shrugged his shoulders. "Nah, yo, I'm not trying to change nothing. But if you let me open the shop fully, I can give you…well, I estimate over a hundred grand a month. It's your move, though, like you said." DJ knew Dwight would find it hard to turn down that much dough, so he waited for his reply.

"DJ, look, just slow down—no speedballin'. And by the way, I want that DB-7 to vanish. I want our hands washed clean of it."

"Huh? You don't want me to flip it?"

"No! Dwight snapped. "No out-of-state cars."

"I feel ya."

"Well that's about it, DJ." Dwight smiled and stood up quickly. "Let's join the ladies, shall we?" As DJ walked out of the office, he thought Dwight had to be crazy as fuck if he thought he'd just ditch the DB-7. He knew he could get fifty Gs easy...fuck Dwight. He fucked his girl behind his back, so selling the car wouldn't be shit. DJ still had no clue that it was the Mayor's son he'd killed.

When the two men walked back into the living room, the two women looked up and smiled. DJ stood behind Dwight and eyed Lisa and Tina. He'd love to freak them both at the same time.

***

"Man, this is pure bullshit! All I see is this guy with different women and they're all fine as hell; that's all I got—a full roll of nothing on film. Hey, Hamilton, wake up!" Detective Covington yelled. He and Hamilton sat across the street about fifty yards from Dwight's condo in an unmarked squad car.

"Wha-what?" Detective Hamilton said. He yawned and rubbed his eyes. "They still in there? Christ, what time is it?"

"Yeah, they're still in there...it's ten past ten," Covington said looking at his watch.

"Gimme the binoculars," Hamilton said.

"For what?"

"Man, come on...so I can see in the damn dark, that's why!" Covington grimaced and reached for the night vision binoculars in the back seat. He picked them up and gave them to Hamilton. Hamilton slowly scanned the condo. "Did you ever get the address on that PT cruiser you saw at DJ's place?" he asked with the binoculars still to his eyes.

"No, why?"

"Did the tag on front say MD...uh...Salon?"

"Why?"

"Because it's parked in the garage. Are you blind or something?"

"What!" Covington yelled lunging for the binoculars. "Let me see this shit." He focused the binoculars. "Well, ain't this a bitch." He saw the PT cruiser beside a BMW. He only met...no, saw Dwight once, but he knew he had a woman. He really didn't know who she was and he couldn't figure out what the hell was going on. He thought that maybe someone else was driving the PT cruiser that night. He smiled. All he had to do was find Dwight's woman and compare her to the pictures he had. If Dwight's girl was sleeping with DJ, then maybe he could find out something other than what was obviously going on—late night booty calls. Covington knew it wasn't something to bug his uncle about just yet, and he would first try and put two and two together.

"So what do we do now?" Hamilton said rubbing his jaw.

"We ain't doin't shit!" Covington said as he started the car. "I'm going to the crib and lay up wit' the wife. You can take the car and do whatever. Maybe you'll find a chick, and that's on the down low," Covington said pulling from the curb.

"Fuck you...and hurry up and drive because I'm sick of your shit!" Hamilton said.

"Okay, Ham."

"My name ain't Ham, it's Hamilton. Do I need to spell it for you!"

"Yeah, yeah, yeah, chill out man."

"Yeah, yeah, whatever. "You were gonna ask me something before..."

Covington drove with one hand as he searched for his Newports. "Oh, yeah...you seen that guy over in traffic? He seemed kinda odd and shit. He gives out tickets over in a school zone. But yesterday I saw him slip a .22 in a hidden holster strapped to his leg. If you ask me, I think he's shell or something. What do you think?"

"Yeah, I seen him...why don't you just take it to the captain?"

Covington shrugged his shoulders. "Shit...if I see him tomorrow in the gym, I'll talk to him."

"Good luck," Hamilton said with a grin.

***

Later that night on Felix's island, Menage sat alone on the beach with Vapor. It was a full moon in a sea of countless stars. He wondered about the true meaning of love and how the word had so much power and could be spoken at any given time. Many times he said the word without having any true feelings at all. And how could he sleep with another woman and be in love with Chandra? Love...he tried to inject that word into his system, but it just wouldn't stick. He wanted Chandra and he needed to love her, but yet he had so much fear. To him, a broken heart was more painful than any flesh wound. Maybe he was blind to love. He kept more than one woman so he wouldn't get close to anyone; he felt at ease that way, or so he thought. He placed his head on his knees as the water crashed into the rocks to his left.

Chandra had spoken to him about God, and after they had sex she cried and said they both needed to repent and get saved. He was confused. Deep in his soul he had doubts about God. His mom had told him not to question whether or not God was real. She told him to just believe. But why had God allowed all of the recent events to occur? There were too many hard questions and not enough easy answers as far as Menage was concerned. Then there were the people of his own race who said the Bible was just a tool, used to humble blacks when they were slaves—to make them look forward to so-called better days. He took a small Bible out of his pocket and thought about how it said to pray for your enemy. "Yeah, right," he thought. He'd be dead if he did it that way. Then he thought about how it said that God would forgive all sins and how people enjoyed sinning every day, not giving God a second thought. He didn't understand. Did it mean that people could party all night, hit the bars and strip clubs and in the end, get on their knees when they got home? And what about atheists? Did they go to hell? But he had also read that man couldn't understand God's way. He stood up and brushed the sand from his pants as the Bible lay at his feet. He turned and walked back to the mansion, leaving The Good Book.

CHAPTER 6

Can't Hold Us Down

Sunday Morning
Menage clenched the Glock 9 firmly with a two-hand grip and fired off the last five rounds at the target twenty yards away. It was close to nine in the morning when he'd last checked. He was always able to relieve stress at Felix's shooting range. Last night he remembered that he had a built-in system that would automatically record anything off the surveillance camera by the front gate, but he figured that all it would show was what Felix told him about DJ killing the guy in the driveway. However, he still wanted to see it for himself. It was hidden under the sink in his bathroom behind a fake wall. He couldn't wait to see DJ again and thank him for saving his life. But first he had to get off the island. Ignoring the sweat running down his face, he turned and walked back to the Hummer parked in the sand. He knew Chandra would be up waiting for him, upset that he'd left without waking her. Vapor was sniffing a palm tree when he called him. Once Vapor jumped in, he put on his shades and headed back to the mansion. He was glad Chandra had brought some of his CDs from his house. He floored the Hummer down the narrow path as Common pumped from the system. Something had to change, but little did he know it was going to be for the worse.

***

Washington, D.C.
There was an emergency meeting at the White House. FBI agent

Neil Loften, Secretary of State William Peterson, USMC Lietenant General Arthur Coleman and Director of Central Intelligence, Joe L. Troublefield were all in attendance. The only man of color was Joint Chief of Staff, Davis S. Ellis. The room fell silent when he nodded toward the U.S. Marine corporal standing at the door. Seeing the signal, the corporal immediately turned on his heels and went outside the door to stand guard. The door softly clicked and the lights dimmed as a flat screen on the wall showed a picture of an island. Ellis cleared his throat.

"Gentlemen, I'm sorry to have you all in on such short notice, and Coleman, I know you're missing church this morning. But what I'm about to speak on is a matter of national security." Ellis coughed and cleared his throat again. "At twenty-two hundred last night, by order of the President of the United States, we launched a highly classified operation—code name, Take A Look. We dropped six U.S. force recon Marines along with six seals. Once the team hit the ground, they met no challenge and went on with their mission. On that island, gentleman, buried underground by German agents during World War Two, is a massive amount of a deadly Nuclear Biological Chemical. This is unknown, even by the owner of the island, Felix Marchetti. The team carried state-of-the-art chemical analysis systems and I'm here to say that the NBC has lost its power. Troublefield, would you care to finish?"

"Yes, sir," Troublefield replied. "After placing agents in deep cover in the Taliban regime in Afghanistan, the CIA got word that the regime somehow bought information regarding the whereabouts of the NBC from a German agent. The chemical was then going to be stolen by men working for Al-Qaida and transported to a military installation in Iraq. We have proof of plans of the terrorist group wanting to use the NBC against the U.S. That was an action against the U.S. and by tonight, our men will be pulled out of the camps. By order of the President, we will launch a missile strike from the USS John Paul Jones to destroy that installation."

"So they just don't seem to wanna give up, huh?" Lieutenant General Coleman said.

"It seems that way, but I suspect that if the NBC was made active it would have been hell to stop them. We're lucky," Troublefield said.

"Well," Ellis said smiling, "we can call in Scorpion now. It's over."

"What!" Agent Lofton said, surprised that Ellis knew about Scorpion. "Sir, how do you know about Scorpion? He has nothing to do with the NBC. He didn't even know about it until just recently.

Troublefield rubbed his forehead. "You're wrong, Lofton. I'm sorry, but Scorpion is CIA. It had to be done this way and to be honest, he didn't know of the NBC. We used him, hoping that he could get on the island. After that we were going to direct him to the NBC but we had to change our plans, since the FBI was already planning to raid the island. We put our man in...I'm sorry, but you'll have to call him in here."

"You can't be for real," Lofton said as he stood.

"It's true," Secretary of State Peterson said. Lofton was a close friend of his and he figured he could calm him down. "You were given full control, Lofton, but all the calls you had with Scorpion were heard by the CIA. He was told that Felix was dealing with Cuba and I need you to trust me when I tell you that we had no other way to do this. We had to move fast."

"Well...I guess I should understand...I'll make the call," Lofton said as he slowly sat back down. At least he was the only one who had Scorpion's number, but after thinking about it, he knew the CIA had it also. "What about the drugs on the island? I swear I can bring him in with no problem. Felix has to go down for his crimes."

"The President wants a full blackout. We'll make a deal with Mr. Marchetti to quickly remove the NBC from his Island," Ellis said.

"Christ, you can't be for real. How much of it is on the island, and what is it anyway?" Lofton asked.

"It's—" Ellis started to answer him but Troublefield coughed and he got the message. Lofton hadn't been authorized to receive that information.

"Uh, it's a massive amount, and it has go down like this. I'm sorry, but we must all follow the President's orders. And keep in mind that this is still a matter of national security, Mr. Lofton, and cease your operation as soon as possible," Ellis said.

"Yes, sir," Lofton said. He was heated that all of his hard work was going down the drain. The only connection he had to Scorpion, his so-called man, was his cell number, but no one knew his cover—not even the CIA. All he knew was that the man named Scorpion was in Miami. Lofton knew there was a lot that Ellis and Troublefield hadn't told him, and he sensed that Troublefield was not a man to be trusted. The men left the office and Lofton called Scorpion when he got outside. He was tempted to ignore his orders and take Felix down anway, but this was a serious matter involving the Joint Chief of Staff and the President. Lofton was definitely no fool.

***

"So what happened girl?" Benita said sitting on the couch watching Lisa take off her shoes. She had just gotten in from spending the night with DJ.

"Yeah, you was right and guess what?

"Girl, stop playin' games and just tell me!" Benita said with excitement.

"Okay, chill. Tina is the one you saw at the club that night wearing the bracelet. That's Dwight's girl. Dwight's the guy who brought you home from the hospital that night. And she remembered you when you got your hair done, but I didn't tell her I was your cousin."

Benita's eyes widened. "Did ya even ask about Menage?"

"No, but DJ did on our way over to Dwight's place. Dwight

said he was still in the hospital but he didn't say how he was doing, though."

"Damn," Benita said sitting back and folding her arms.

"Chill out. I might be able to find out something when I go in later. And yeah, I'ma call to let you know if I find him, so don't call my job buggin' me!"

Benita looked at her watch. It was almost ten.

"Girl, you trippin'," Benita said.

"Nah, I'm just playing. You know I don't get down like that. That's triflin' and that's not me. Do you have to work tonight?" Lisa asked. Benita shook her head no. "Well, DJ is taking me to work. If you're up, you can come and pick me up after my shift. But I might stay with DJ tonight—depends on if I feel like being with him."

"Yeah, right!" Benita said.

"Whateva! Anyway I'm going to bed, and if he or anyone else calls, don't wake me."

"Yes, ma'am."

When Lisa left the living room, Benita thought about everything that what was going on. Tina and DJ were at the club that night. Maybe it meant nothing, like Lisa had suggested. All Lisa's silly ass had to do was tell Dwight, DJ or even Tina that her cousin was with Menage when he got shot at Bayside. Well, Dwight knew it, but he didn't know that Lisa and Benita were kin. She thought of calling Tina and telling her who she was, with the hope that she could tell her something—anything about Menage—the man who saved her life. What was he doing at this very moment? Why hadn't he called? She couldn't answer these questions. Any other man would do anything to be with her. She finally got the picture that Menage Unique Legend wasn't the average man.

***

It was almost eleven-thirty and Menage lay on his stomach, floating on a water raft in Felix's Olympic size pool. He let one arm dangle in the water, moving it around in a slow circle. Felix was next to him in a chair-shaped raft smoking a Cuban cigar. Chandra and Rosita were sitting on the far end of the pool with their legs in the water. Both women wore skimpy swimsuits, but Menage didn't mind. Chandra wore a two-piece Baby Phat swimsuit. She remembered putting it on and catching Menage looking at her flat stomach. "In due time, baby, I'll be swoll," she had said playfully.

"You sleep, Menage?" Felix asked glancing at him.

"Hmmm…" Menage murmured.

"I like your crazy ass, 'cause I can be myself with you. It's like with everyone else I gotta be big-time mafioso—never smile—business 24 -7…hey, are you listening to me? You can't be still sleep!" Felix snapped.

"Nah, I'm just looking at my eyelids," Menage said hoping Felix would let him relax, but he knew that wasn't going to happen. All morning and even at breakfast, Felix was acting kind of strange.

"Smart ass. But anyway, let's talk about this country…good ol' U.S. of A. Hey, do you know that the Star Spangled Banner was—"

"Written by Francis Scott Key when black folks were slaves. He might have had some slaves himself, talkin' 'bout the land of the free. And he was a lawyer; that should speak for itself—fake-ass bullshit," Menage said.

Felix was surprised. He took off his shades and smiled. "So you know a little history, huh?"

"Yeah, if you say so." Menage turned toward Felix and told him about the tape under his sink.

"Do you think it'll show anything?

"All I think it'll show is what ya'll said DJ did to that guy in the driveway," Menage said. Little did he know that the tape would reveal something more important than that. It had recorded every word between DJ and the hit man.

"I guess so. Anyway, I'll have my nephew stop by and check it out. He'll let us know if he finds anything."

Menage yelled suddenly as his raft was flipped over, sending him under the water. He quickly came back up, treading water to find Chandra gripping his mat. She smiled and dove back under the water. Menage took a deep breath and felt a slight pain in his chest. He went after her anyway. Felix laughed, but not for too long as Rosita gave him the same treatment. Menage finally caught up with Chandra and pinned her back to the edge of the pool. She smiled and wrapped her arms around his neck as her legs encircled his waist. Her hair flowed over her shoulders like a silk waterfall, and since she put on some baby oil before she got into the pool, the water ran off her glistening, smooth skin. At that moment, according to Menage, she was the complete definition of beauty.

"I love you, Chandra," he whispered, his lips only inches from hers. She leaned sideways, looking past Menage and laughed.

"Girl, what's wrong with you?" he said. He turned his head to see Felix butt-ass naked, bending over to pick up a towel. Rosita was still in the pool with his trunks in her hand. Felix put on the towel and looked back at Menage and smiled. Menage shook his head and chuckled. He turned back to Chandra. "God she's so beautiful," he thought. He knew she was the one and only woman for him and even if she weren't having his baby, he would still want her in his life. She closed her eyes and kissed him. He moaned deeply as her tongue ran across his upper teeth. He knew she felt his erection through his boxers, but she didn't stop him when he cupped her ass and brought her closer to his body. And he knew not to get carried away since she did-

153

n't want to have sex again until they were married, but by her body movements he knew it was hard for her to say no also. He could never get enough of her, and that night they shared a month earlier brought back a special warmth between them. They'd always used protection when they had sex, but that night things changed.

She was down for the weekend from school. His bedroom was lit in a deep blue setting as B2K played through the system. He wore silk Gucci boxers and she wore the same with a matching halter-top, but at the last minute before getting into bed, she wanted to change into a teddy. He was sitting on the edge of his bed putting lotion on his knees. He looked up to see her standing naked by his dresser. He got up and made his way over to her. She turned to face him with the teddy clutched in her hand. Taking one more step closer, he pinned her to the dresser. He ran his fingers over her hips and smiled when she dropped the teddy to the floor. He gripped her small waist and lifted her up on top of the dresser. It was the perfect height. She moaned his name as he started to suck her right nipple. Looking between her open legs, he could see that she was sopping wet. His boxers were still on, but she easily pulled out what he had in store for her. It was hot to the touch as she ran her hand down his shaft, causing pre-cum to drip on her fingers. They both looked at the table by his bed where the condoms lay, but both were silent. A tune by R. Kelly now filled the room. He kissed her neck as she arched her back, pressing her hard nipples into his chest. He could feel the heat coming from between her legs, the tip of his penis against her outer lips. They both froze for a moment…and then he slid into her, her legs wrapped around his waist. The feeling of being inside of her with nothing between them shocked him. As she drew a deep breath and tossed her head back he closed his eyes and buried his face in her neck, giving himself to her totally. Sex was like that between them ever since that day, and without words their relationship went to another level.

They almost broke their promise in the pool but they stopped before it got out of hand, and they were back in the room now, having both showered. Still Menage was happy when she took the time to clean him with her slender hands, and he nearly fell when he shot off in the shower. Chandra always managed to take care of her man.

"Baby," he said with his head in her lap as they sat in the middle of the bed, "I promise I'll never leave you and our child. I know it won't be easy, but that's my word and I'll love you all along the way," he added meaning every word.

"Honey, listen to me," she said rubbing his ears. "I love you and I'll never get tired of telling you or showing you how much I do...you'll never have to doubt my love. From the first time I told you up until right now, you are all the man I need. I'm not trying to make it hard for you. I just want to love you the way you need to be loved and you'll always have me. I'm going to be your wife. You are my present and my future." Tears rolled down her face. "I know in my heart we can do this if we really try. I want you in my life and I love you so much. I never told you a lie and I'm not about to start now. You know I had to nearly beg you to let me love you, and I don't want to be without you." They embraced and Menage found himself crying tears of joy. He finally knew what it felt like to be in love.

Later on Menage and Chandra rode down the beach on a pair of ATVs. It was a clear and sunny day and Vapor was with them. He ran down the beach to fetch a stick that Chandra had thrown. Menage thought about how close he'd come to throwing it all away as he watched Chandra and Vapor. "Fuck the fame and playin' the field," he thought. Maybe they'd move to someplace quiet and raise their child—white picket fence and all. Menage smiled. This was the real world—not TV or some novel. He looked up just as Felix's helicopter roared overhead and circled before landing. Chandra blocked the sun from her face with her hand and looked back toward the mansion. She could see Felix waving his arms in the distance. Menage waved back.

"Baby, I think Felix is trying to call you," Chandra said as Vapor came back with the stick.

"What's up with him? All he gotta do is call me on the walkie-talkie."

"You mean the one you got turned off?" she said pointing at the device near his feet.

Menage looked down and saw that Chandra was right. "Damn, my bad. I thought it was on...shit."

"The hell's wrong with you!" Felix's voice boomed when Menage turned on the walkie-talkie. "I been calling you for the last ten minutes."

"Chill out, man. What's up?"

"Come up to the pad."

"For what?"

"We're going to my yacht."

"Good, 'bout time we get off this island," Menage said.

***

Detective Covington walked into MD Beauty Salon. He hoped to find Dwight's girl and he needed a shape-up anyway. He looked at the pictures once more before getting out of his Mitsubishi Montero.

Covington sat in the waiting area looking at the latest Source Magazine. "So what if Dwight's girl is cheating on him; that's not a crime," he thought. But he knew there had to be more to it.

At first he didn't think he'd find her because he didn't see the PT cruiser in the parking lot and he didn't know that Tina had a new car. He was about to put the Source down when a stunning, dark-skinned woman walked into the waiting area to speak with one of the barbers. Damn, she's fine. He he knew he was looking at the woman he saw at DJ's crib. But now he had to find out if she was Dwight's girl. After finally taking his eyes off her body, he noticed a key chain hanging from her waist with a small picture of herself and some man. He couldn't make out the face of the man, but the two names written in black, bold print solved the mystery: TINA LOVES DWIGHT. Covington smiled and put down the Source. He was up next for a haircut. His eyes couldn't help but follow Tina's rear end as she walked away.

"Just a shape-up, round in the back," he said to the barber as he snapped a plastic cape around his neck. He couldn't believe that he couldn't recall Tina's face from the day Menage had been shot. Leaving the salon, he called his uncle and was told that he had left the island. He thought about faxing the pictures, but it still wouldn't prove who had tried to kill Menage. That's all his uncle wanted—not something about a freaky girlfriend...with a fat ass.

Music filled the spacious chop shop as men took cars apart and switched VINs. Two men working on a Porsche Cayenne took a break after removing the front windshield.

"Hey man, I swear. DJ told me to go ahead and tag the DB-7," Xerox said. He looked at AJ with a puzzled look on his face.

"Yo, Xerox, I know we ain't supposed to do out-of-state rides but DJ's the boss. I'll help you after I do the four out back," AJ said.

"DJ got this place wide the fuck open, right?" said Xerox.

"Yeah, but I hope he don't blow the spot up," replied AJ.

"Word!"

The men pulled down their visors and started to grind the paint off the Porsche. What they used to do in a month working for Menage, they now did in a week.

***

"I think it's time we stop having our little late night meetings, DJ, and no I don't wish to talk about our last night together. We could both lose a lot if we get caught, so I hope you understand," Tina said speaking to DJ on her cell phone as she headed down Biscayne Boulevard in her brand new, pearl white Infiniti G35 Coupe.

"Of course, Tina," DJ said. This chick must really think it's all about her, he thought, but he couldn't lie to himself about missing her good sex.

"Okay, I wish you luck and I'll see you around…and have Lisa call me sometime."

She hung up before he could say anything. Tina smiled. It was over and done with. She had fun using DJ, but he was history. He'd be okay. She was sure of it. Menage was still in a coma and she hoped someone would just pull the damn plug, but no, he was still suffering and so was Chandra. Tina pitied her—just a little. But for Menage she felt nothing. Now she and Dwight could get married. Yes, she loved him, killed for him and slept with another man for him. Tina truly believed in the saying, what he don't know won't hurt him. She pulled her Infiniti into the underground parking lot at the Omni Mall. Her phone chimed as she got out of the car.

"Hey, girl," Dwight said.

"Dwight, you sound tired. Are you okay?" Tina said as she headed for the elevator.

"Yeah, it's kinda busy here at the main shop. But remember that lady I told you about that sold us the hair color stuff?"

"Yeah, I remember."

"Well, she wants me to meet one of her partners and have a business dinner tonight, so I might have to take off early and be in late. I think it's in Fort Lauderdale."

"Call me when you get the details. Do you want me to join you?" she said hoping he would say no.

"Nah, it's no big deal. But you can wait up for me tonight."

"Mmmm...I most surely will," she said hoping he wouldn't start talking about Menage. He granted her wish.

By the end of the call, Tina had reached her floor in the hotel above the Omni Mall. She walked down the hall and stopped at room 203. Just moments later, while Dwight was cutting hair and thinking about what size ring to buy her, Tina was in the room with two white men, acting out their sexual fantasy with her. She got a natural high when she went behind Dwight's back. It just felt so good. She faked an orgasm as one of the men grunted on top of her. He didn't even last three minutes. The next guy was just as sorry, but he made up for it when he put his face between her legs. She smiled to herself when she came, thinking about how easy it was to make six thousand for an hour's work. The money would go into a secret account that was now close to eighty thousand. Tina was steadily stacking dough. After the men left, she reached in her bag and pulled out a black dildo. Now she was going to please herself. Then maybe she'd go and buy Dwight something from the mall.

***

"You mean to tell me we got on this boat just to go to Miami! Shit, we could've gotten here a long time ago. But at least I'm off the island," Menage said as the yacht slowly cruised into the port of Miami.

"I have some ends to tie up," said Felix ignoring Menage's statements. I hope you can keep a low profile here. I know it's something you don't know how to do, so please be careful," he added. Menage smiled and patted the two Glock 9s under his arms.

Felix's yacht had been watched for the past three days as it sat in front of his island. Once it moved, a phone call was made and things went into action. Felix didn't take the yacht to the pier. Instead he told the crew to launch a small motorboat to transport them.

"How do I look, baby?" Chandra said turning in a circle for

Menage when he walked into the stateroom. She wore a purple, satin blouse and matching skirt.

"You got that from Rosita, didn't you?" he said wrapping his arms around her waist.

"Yeah, but do you like it?" she said after giving him a peck on his nose.

"A little."

"Stop playing, boy," she said turning back to the mirror to put on her lipgloss.

"Is Rosita feeling any better?" he asked looking at her nice shape from behind. Rosita had been feeling a bit under the weather.

"A little, but she's gonna stay on the boat...and I wish you would do the same, Menage."

"Come on, baby. All I'm gonna do is go get that tape and come straight back. Now go and tell Felix I'll be up soon. And gimme a kiss first." Chandra poked out her lips and he kissed her. Leaving him in the stateroom, she went up on the bridge to see Felix.

Seven hundred yards away, Myrmidon, the head mercenary, peered through a window from the seventh floor of a vacant building. His left eye was glued to the leupold tactical 3.5x 10 variable scope that sat on top of an MK-11 7.62 millimeter semi-automatic sniper rifle fitted with a sound suppressor. Only two inches of the twenty-inch barrel protruded out of the window. The crosshairs centered on Felix's face as he stood with Chandra on the bridge of the 108-foot Leight Notika luxury yacht. Felix gave her a hug and kissed her on the cheek.

"Second target confirmed," Myrmidon said. He lined up the crosshairs on the woman in the purple blouse.

Chandra pleaded with Felix. "Do you think it's a good idea

to have Menage back in Miami? Whoever tried to kill him is still out there...I don't like it, Felix," she said as the breeze blew her hair in her face.

"I know, Chandra, but you and I both know he won't stay in hiding forever. Menage wasn't built that way and it's time we stop playing games."

"Games! This is his life you're talking about, Felix, and it was your plan from the start. I just don't understand!"

Felix rubbed the back of his neck. "Yes, Chandra, it was my plan and maybe it was a mistake. But if it was, then it wasn't my first. I just want him to be safe."

She knew he meant well, and she saw the pain in his eyes. "I'm sorry, Felix. Really, I didn't mean to snap at you."

"It's okay. I understand," Felix said and went down to check on Rosita before leaving the yacht.

The man behind the MK-11 sniper rifle smiled at his luck. The call had come in an hour before, notifying him that Felix was coming to Miami. He was glad because it meant his team of mercenaries didn't have to hit Felix on his fort of an island to take his girl; the fool had brought her along.

"Scorpion, this is Myrmidon. The sun is starting to rise." Scorpion now knew that Felix was on his way with his girl.

"Myrmidon, hold tight till I give the order for plan B."

"Yes sir," Myrmidon said. He watched Felix and his girl head toward the pier, now accompanied by a black guy he didn't know—maybe a do-boy or something. He shifted the rifle back on the woman in the purple blouse.

"So beautiful and full of life," Myrmidon said just before pulling the trigger. The bolt slammed home empty. He would have been pleased to send one of the twenty 7.62 bullets into his target. All that would have been heard was an audible spit from the sound suppressor as the round exited the twenty-inch barrel. It would have taken her head off, tearing through her skull, crushing her frontal skull plate, spraying her cerebral cortex in a fine red and pink mist. He closed his eyes and smiled. The former U.S. Army sniper was fascinated with his rifle and the things it could do.

Scorpion sat in the passenger seat of a tinted green Ford Excursion with two of the five men he'd hired. Two of the other three were across the street in a black Ford Explorer Sport Trac with chrome crash bars. Myrmidon was the only one absent from the group, but Scorpion knew he could pull it off with the four men he had. And he had more control over the mercenaries when their leader wasn't around. They all wore black military issued pants and jackets and bulletproof vests. The two with Scorpion carried silenced Uzis. Scorpion carried a Mac-10 and a Desert Eagle .45. He called the driver of the Sport Trac.

"We'll wait until they pass and see if we can get a chance to snatch the girl." He sat patiently and waited for the stretch Rolls Royce limo.

***

"Look, Chandra, I swear...all I'm gonna do is get the tape and come back," Menage said sitting across from her in the limo. Felix was on the other side on the phone speaking in Italian.

"Everybody in Miami know what you drive, so have somebody else go get the tape," she said. Menage rolled his eyes. It was true what she said, but he had to think of something.

"I'll drive one of Felix's cars. How about that, huh?"

"No," she said frowning with her arms folded. She knew how to work him.

"C'mon, baby, it'll only take a few minutes. I promise," he pleaded. "I love you..."

"Don't try to sweet talk me, boy!" she said. But deep down

she knew she couldn't keep him within her reach 24 -7. "Move out my face!" she added, smiling playfully and pushing him away when he tried to kiss her. She loved him so much.

"Well, now," Felix said hanging up the phone, "that's taken care of. I have to meet a friend today. Hugo will stay with the limo and if you look out back," he pointed toward the black tinted rear window, "you'll see a blue Tahoe. Four of my men are inside to keep an extra eye on things...so I take it you'll go get the tape by yourself..."

"Yeah," Menage said. Chandra sucked her teeth, kicking his ankle.

"I'll send some of my men with you then," Felix said.

"Nah, no need, but tell the men in the Tahoe to stay with the limo since Chandra will be using it, and Hugo might as well go with you."

"Okay. What time will we be meeting up again? My meeting won't be that long," Felix said.

Menage looked at his Rolex. "Let's see...it's uh...one-forty now...let's say two hours." He looked at Chandra and saw her frown. "I mean one hour...or an hour and a half," he said smiling.

"Don't push it," she said pinching his leg.

When they made it to Felix's second mansion, Menage walked towards the garage as Chandra waved at him. The limo pulled out of the driveway with the Tahoe on its tail. He knew she wanted to see her sick aunt and cousins. Felix left moments later with Hugo in a gold bullet-proof Rolls Royce Phantom. Menage ran his hand across a black Porsche Carrea GT, parked in the garage that Felix never drove. He smiled when he saw his yellow Escalade ESV sitting beside his Acura and S600. His new 1300R was parked in the corner. He hated to lie to Chandra, but a man and his wheels were hard to part. Well, that's how he saw it. Sitting in his Gucci Mercedes-Benz S600 V12 AMG, he smiled as goose bumps formed all over his body. Starting up the car, he pulled out of the garage. "CD one, song eight, volume to the fuckin' max." The S600 slowly moved forward as its twenty-two-inch rims rotated backwards while a cut by B.I.G. thundered from the system. He was back in his element. His life was based on materialism to such a degree that it changed his personality at times and made him illogical. And he couldn't be told a damn thing about it. "My world," he said as the sunroof slid back.

CHAPTER 7

All I Really Care About Is

Two Glock 9s!
Scorpion sat tense in the Ford Excursion as it followed Felix's limo on I-95. He knew about the four men in the Tahoe, but that wasn't a problem because he hoped to have the element of surprise on his side. But for now he stayed back and followed the limo and Tahoe at a respectable distance, his .45 loaded in his lap. In the backseat, one of the mercenaries with a cut under his eye was loading the weapons and carefully placing one round in the chamber. All Scorpion had to do was take Felix's girl and demand he hand over the drugs for her return. He clenched his fist when he thought of Neil Lofton. He thought he was joking when he told him the mission was over. At first he laughed, but when Lofton told him he knew about the CIA and Troublefield, only then did he fully understand what was going down. He knew he had to act fast before the FBI and CIA came after him. There was no way they could interfere with his plan. Even the rival crime boss was putting pressure on him for Felix's death. "In due time," Scorpion thought.

***

Menage arrived to his once stunning mansion. He was shocked by all the destruction he saw. The gate was gone, and in its place were orange cones and police crime-scene tape. Stepping out of his car, he looked down the street and toward the beach. It was quiet. Taking a deep breath, he took the Glock 9 from under his left arm. While making sure a round was in the chamber, he ducked under the yellow police tape. Walking up his driveway, he stopped at a dark stain. He knew it wasn't oil; it had to be from the guy DJ shot. He chewed on his lip and started for his house. His stomach turned when he saw the damage done to his eight-thousand-dollar door. The lock and handle were blown away. When he stepped into the living room, he muttered something and nearly fell to his knees. All the furniture had been removed, but hundreds of bullet holes were all over the walls. He could see where some blood had seeped through the carpet and stained the floor underneath. The kitchen was the worst. Chandra had told him how Dwight said he found him in the kitchen lying in a pool of blood with Vapor by his side. He rubbed his nose when it started to itch and tears welled up in his eyes as he thought of Vigor. He got his mind together and went to his bedroom. It too, was empty, so he made a note to ask Felix where his stuff was. In the bathroom, he put his Glock 9 on the black granite sink. He then got on his knees to open the slot under the sink. After two attempts he finally hit the switch to open the fake wall. Pressing the eject button, a small tape slid out of the box. Menage put the tape in his pocket, and he continued to look around when he heard a cracking noise coming from the living room. He quickly picked up his glock and a second later he pulled out the other. He slowly moved toward the bedroom door as he heard the sound again. His fingers were tense on the triggers of the two glocks. Stepping out of the bedroom, he slowly made his way down the hall with the glocks leading the way. Trying to control his breathing, he put his back against the wall and held the glocks at his side. He took a peek into the living room and smiled. The noise was coming from the plastic tarp over the shattered glass door.

When he returned to his car he looked back at his crib one last time before taking off, burning rubber from the rear tires. He couldn't fight the feeling of being back on the scene, riding in the big body Benz, system pumping, rims gleaming. He ended up in Hialeah and stopped at a Jewelry store to buy an engagement ring for Chandra. So much was going through his mind. Maybe he should just move and say the hell with beef. Chandra and his seed were all that mattered. He would surprise her tonight and tell her he was out of the game and fuck the million-dollar dream. He now realized he had something that no amount of money could buy—Chandra's love. Money would be no problem for them and knowing Felix, he'd drop a few mil for a wedding gift. He looked up through the sunroof and squinted from the sun. He wondered what Dwight would say once he saw him again. Gunning the S600 through a red light, he knew his life was headed for better days, and as usual, he used music to express his mood. "CD five, song two, volume max." He slid the tinted windows up and took a sip from a bottle of Old English 800, covered by a brown bag as Snoop Dog's Doggy Dogg World boomed from the trunk. He sang along, word for word as he drove, clearly enjoying himself…"The dog pound rocks the party…all night long…"

***

Scorpion put on his mask as the Excursion closed in on the Tahoe. The Explorer Sport Trac with the other two men was still behind him. They were near the Pro Player football stadium as Scorpion called the driver of the Explorer and told him to make his move. Seconds later, the Explorer slowly passed Scorpion and then the Tahoe. Soon after it was in front of the limo. Scorpion knew he had to act fast and this was the best chance, if any, to grab Felix's girl. As the four vehicles came to a stoplight, the Explorer came to a sudden halt. Traffic wasn't heavy and the light was green, so it moved steadily, not being affected by the three SUVs and limo.

"Now!" Scorpion hissed into his cell phone. The two men jumped from the Explorer, spraying the trapped limo's windshield with a loud, deadly barrage of special tipped rounds from their AK-47s. The windshield cracked, and then gave in as the bullets ripped through the shattered glass. The driver died as glass and spinning lead tore into his face and chest. The four men in the Tahoe reacted fast. At first they waited for the limo to pass the SUV in front of them, but when they saw two men jump out and start firing on the limo, they knew something was wrong. They all jumped out with Tech 9s. Before any of Felix's men could get off a shot, Scorpion's Excursion screeched to a stop, catching Felix's men off guard. Scorpion stepped out quickly and unloaded his .45. The clattering of the Uzis' thirty-two rounds in three seconds drowned out Scorpion's shots. Felix's men never had a fighting chance. The first to die was shot in the left eye by Scorpion. By the time he hit the ground, half of his face was a bloody mess. The next two both took rounds in the chest and neck as the Uzis forced them backward and down onto the ground. The last made it between the Tahoe and limo, but he was trapped. He fired blindly over the side of the Tahoe, hoping it would buy him time and cover to get back into his truck. Quickly he stood up and ran to get inside the Tahoe. From thirty feet away, Scorpion placed two well-aimed shots into his left knee. The man screamed as he fell to the ground holding his bleeding knee, nearly blacking out from the pain. When he opened his eyes, two masked men stood over him with their Uzis pointed in his face. Scorpion ran up to the limo and yelled at the girl to open the door or he'd shoot it open. Chandra was backed up against the opposite door. There was no way she would open the door, but one of the mercenaries up front with the AK-47 reached through the front glass and popped the locks. Chandra screamed as she was yanked out by her hair and then hurled to another man. She was about to speak but Scorpion cracked her upside the head with his .45, knocking her out cold as blood ran from the cut on her forehead.

The gunfire lasted no more than twenty seconds. The last of Felix's men lay on the hot pavement still holding his knee, breathing heavily. Scorpion stopped by his face. "Tell Felix his girl is in good hands and I will be calling him soon." Before the man could reply, Scorpion ran to the Excursion and shortly afterward it sped off, followed by the Explorer.

Once they reached an old warehouse in Northern Miami, the mercenaries switched to a van and took Chandra where Scorpion ordered she be held. Scorpion knew the mercenaries would follow his orders if they wanted to be paid. After changing clothes, he tore out of the warehouse on a Yamaha FZ-1. His day had only just begun.

***

Neil Lofton didn't like the small office at the CIA headquarters and to make matters worse, he was seated in front of the DCI, Joe Troublefield.

"Lofton, Scorpion has gone renegade!"

Lofton wanted to say something smart like, "No shit Sherlock. Haven't you been tapping the calls?" But Troublefield was not a man to be played with. At times Lofton wondered if he had picked his own last name.

"Yeah," Lofton said. You had me in something that was way over my head, Joe, and you know it. When I placed the call and told him to come in, he just flipped—yelling and cursing over the phone. Finally he just became hysterical and then the line went dead. I don't know his cover, so he's down in Miami on his own."

"I see," Troublefield said sitting back in his seat. "I'm sure you remember what the Joint Chief of Staff said."

"What—about this being a matter of national security?"

"Yes, and I'm sure you know this news won't sit well with him and the President, I might add, but we have to find him and deal with him in a very discreet manner. I'll help you the best way I can but before we call the JCS, let's try to handle this problem ourselves."

Lofton almost didn't know what to say. "Are you gonna lay all the cards out on the table this time, Joe? For God's sake, we're on the same team here."

Troublefield smiled. "All right, Lofton, you call the shots. But whatever you do, I want Scorpion brought in—at any cost."

***

Detective Covington couldn't believe his eyes. He was on his way to Blockbuster to return some DVDs when he ran into a roadblock. Since he didn't have a scanner in his truck he didn't know what was going on, but he could see that it was something big. He couldn't even count the squad cars blocking the road. Two Metro Police helicopters circled the area. He wondered why his pager didn't go off and thought that maybe it was someone else's district. He jumped out of his SUV and walked towards the scene. As he approached the area, a rookie cop yelled for him to stop, but his sergeant noticed him and let him through. Covington watched paramedics rush from one spot to another, a few carrying body bags. Quickly scanning the area, he froze when he saw his uncle's limo.

"Oh shit!" Covington grabbed the nearest officer. "What the hell happened?" The officer looked tired and sweat was running down his face and neck. He told Covington that four men were dead—the driver of the limo and three by the Tahoe.

"What about any passengers in the limo?"

"We really don't know yet, but one of the bodyguards is still alive. He ain't saying much..."

"Where?"

"Where, what?" the officer replied.

"The bodyguard you just said who's alive—where is he?"

"Third rescue squad on the left," the officer said pointing behind Covington. Covington left the officer and went to check out the scene as the sun twinkled off the spent bullet shells around the limo and Tahoe. When he made it to the rescue squad, he found the bodyguard lying out on a stretcher in the back of an ambulance. Once he met Covington's eyes, he looked around to see if he was able to speak freely. Covington walked up just as a paramedic stepped away from his squad to stretch.

"Mind if I have a word with him a second?" Covington said as he flashed his badge. The paramedic, seeing the badge, gave him no argument. Covington stepped into the ambulance and swallowed hard at the sight of the man's knee.

"Who'd they take?" he asked. That was all he wanted to know. He could get the full story later when the bodyguard was released from the hospital.

"Th-they took…the wrong girl," the bodyguard said weakly.

"Wrong girl?" Covington said under his breath. He was about to press the man for more answers, but the paramedic tapped on the door.

"Time's up, detective. We gotta rush this guy in…you can ride along if you like."

"No, I'll talk to him later," Covington said stepping out of the ambulance. He ran back to his Montero and tried to reach Felix again. He still wasn't on the island or the yacht and Felix didn't allow his people to tell his whereabouts if he wasn't there.

"Damnit!" he said punching the dashboard. He tried to call Hamilton, but his cell phone said that he was out of the calling area. He looked at the massacre that lay before him, and he knew it was a new ballgame. Pulling over to the curb, he slapped a blue light on top of his SUV and sped down the road, honking his horn at cars that didn't notice it. He called the station and left a message with dispatch to reach Detective Hamilton for him and have him call him right away.

***

Menage sat at a stoplight near Miami Central High School waiting for Chandra to pick up the phone in the limo, but there was no answer. He called her cell phone—still nothing.

"What the fuck!" he said. Then he called Felix's house. Hugo picked up on the second ring.

"Yo, Hugo, you seen Chandra?" he said getting a funny feeling in the pit of his stomach.

"Mr. Legend, Mr. Marchetti said to come to the house as soon as possible."

"Man…shit!" Menage said tossing the phone onto the passenger seat. Ignoring the red light, he floored the S600 and made a tight left turn.

Arriving at Felix's second mansion, he jumped out of his car and raced up the stairs. Before opening the door, he noticed that the limo wasn't there. Breathing heavily, he ran into the large living room. Out of breath, he came to a stop when he saw Felix sitting behind his desk.

"H-hey…man, what's going on…where's Chandra," he stammered. Looking around, he saw that Felix had more guards moving about and all of them carried Mac 10s. Felix looked into his eyes and told him to sit down.

"No, fuck that. Where's my girl, Felix!" he said balling up his fists.

Felix cleared his throat and folded his hands on the desk. Even in the dimly lit room, he could see the fear and anger in Menage's eyes. "Chandra has been kidnapped," he said softly. Menage closed his eyes and lowered his head. Felix started to speak again, but he stopped in mid-sentence when Menage placed a Glock 9 under his chin with lightning, quick movement. Felix's bodyguards were caught off guard, and now Menage had several guns pointed in his direction. He paid them no mind; he was focused on Felix, pressing the glock deep into his neck.

"Put the guns away," Felix said calmly to his guards, but no one moved. "Now!" Felix said firmly. Reluctantly they did as he ordered. "Menage, don't let your anger blind you so."

"Shut the fuck up!" Menage yelled. "Don't play no games wit' me, Felix!"

"Menage, use your head. I don't fault you for your actions, but listen to me…Covington, step in here." Covington slowly walked up to the desk with his hands up, but Menage whipped out his other glock and pointed it toward Covington's chest. Knowing that he wore a vest, Menage raised it to his head. Covington hoped his uncle didn't notice his trembling legs.

"This is my nephew I told you about. Just listen to what he has to say. If you are not convinced, pull the trigger." Covington cut his eyes at his uncle, thinking that he must have lost his mind. Minutes later after Covington told Menage what happened, the two Glock 9s slowly dropped. Covington let out a deep breath and flopped down in the chair. He needed a Newport. Menage sat down and looked at Felix as he lit a cigar. Whoever did the hit took the wrong girl and he was helpless. How could he fully trust Felix? Maybe the same guy or people who tried to kill him knew he was back and were now going after his girl. He did it Felix's way by hiding on his island, and now she was gone. He felt sick, as if he had to vomit when he thought of losing Chandra.

Detective Covington had left minutes earlier and promised to call once he got more info from the bodyguard. Menage sat across from Felix, tapping his foot with his eyes closed. All they could do was wait to see if anyone called with a ransom. What if they really meant to take Rosita and found out they took the wrong girl? Menage shivered. Why couldn't this be a dream? Detective Covington was so happy to have the gun out of his face that he totally forgot about the pictures of DJ and Tina, and the last thing on Menage's mind was the surveillance tape in the armrest of his Benz.

Felix's helicopter brought Vapor to the mainland as a tear ran down Menage's face. He looked at his watch. It was now eight minutes past seven.

***

Dwight pulled up in his BMW and parked behind the blue Lexus RX330. Lydia had called him earlier and said that her sales partner couldn't make it, so Dwight told her to stay put and he would be there shortly. He was still feeling down about Menage but Tina was right. He had to move on. It was a full moon and Dwight searched the sky for the Big Dipper as he rang the doorbell. He was taken aback when Lydia opened the door. She was exquisitely beautiful, wearing a leopard print, silk backless chiffon Chanel dress. He couldn't help but notice the small print of her nipples and he cursed himself when she caught him looking at her cleavage. Her hair was swept up off her shoulders, showing off her slender neck and smooth, brown skin.

"Would you like to come in, Mr. McMillan, or stay outside?" she said. She received the reaction she wanted and thought that maybe she could seduce him into talking to find out more about Menage. Dwight smiled and stepped inside the apartment. As he walked past Lydia she scanned him from head to toe, admiring his Armani suit and black Italian oxfords. She took his coat and placed it in the closet. She could see that he felt uncomfortable.

"Red or white wine?" she said walking into the kitchen.

Dwight couldn't keep himself from looking at her tight, firm butt. "Damn," he said to himself.

"Are you sure it's no big deal that we have the meeting here, Mr. McMillan?" she yelled from the kitchen.

"No, it's no big deal. I have all the forms out in the car for you to sign." Dwight stood up when she came back with the wine.

"By the way, you can call me Latosha." He took the wine and smiled, not knowing what to say. She smiled back. "Let's make a toast...to a good deal and uh..."

"Let's just start out with that," Dwight said still smiling.

Lydia sat next to him and asked him about his salon. He went on and on as she took in his every word while keeping his glass filled. He shivered every time she held her head back to laugh. When he spoke on how the women in his salon gossiped 24-7, she caught him off guard by touching his arm and saying,

"Now I see why they all want to sleep with you, Dwight." Dwight couldn't look into her eyes. He knew it was a pass, but he had will power and he was in love with and faithful to Tina. The woman before him was so beautiful but he had no desire for her. However, why was his heart pumping in overdrive and for God's sake, why was the blood flowing between his legs?

"Yeah, I know they feel that way, but that's life ain't it?" he said shifting his body to a position that would hide his erection.

"Who is Menage?" she said filling up his glass again. "When I was getting my hair done, they were talking about him like he was Don Juan or something." She crossed her legs showing off her toned thighs. Dwight rubbed his face, knowing he had too much to drink. He wasn't drunk, but he had that feeling.

"He's my business partner and best friend," he said with slight emotion. Lydia moved in for the kill. Placing her hand on his shoulder, she asked if he was okay and hoped he wouldn't object to her touch. Dwight closed his eyes, enjoying the feeling of her hand on his shoulder. With a remote device, she turned on the CD player and dimmed the lights. Toni Braxton's Just Be A Man About It filled the room. Dwight drained his glass and took a deep breath. He knew he had to get control of things before they got out of hand, but little did he know that his defenses were already gone. Like R. Kelly said, his mind was telling him no but his body was telling him hell yeah! He didn't protest when she laid his head on her shoulder. Her body felt so soft and warm and he let out a heavy sigh before looking at her cleavage, confirming that she wore no bra. She caressed the back of his neck and closed her eyes. "What am I doing? What about Menage, the DB-7 and the Mayor's son? But what about me and my needs? To hell with it all," she thought. She slowly stood up and Dwight's eyes widened. He was about to say he was sorry, but she placed a finger to his lips. "Shhhh," she said. When he stood up, she replaced her finger with her lips. At first she thought she had misjudged him because he didn't respond, but she was soon proven wrong. It was explosive when their tongues met, and her slender body seemed to vanish when he wrapped his arms around her. She wanted him to take her fully and she was willing to give her all. Part of her wanted to pull away, but her hand was already pulling at his belt to free him. Dwight ran his hand down her back, finding it easy to go under her dress. He rubbed her ass as he felt pre-cum dripping from his throbbing penis that she now held in her hand. She broke away from his kiss to see what she held in her hand and her mouth dropped open upon seeing his size. She led him to the loveseat and slid her dress up around her waist as he pulled down his pants. Dwight watched her as she leaned back and slowly pulled off her thong. One of her breasts fell out just as he got down on his knees. She wrapped her legs around his waist as he rubbed his penis against the folds of her moist opening. Dwight looked down to see himself sink inside of her. The heat seemed to travel through his entire body as he started to plow into her petite frame. Breathing through his mouth, he fucked her hard and fast as her hands pushed against his waist to ease up the pounding he was giving her. Lydia was in a daze. Never in her life had she had such an experience and never had she felt so full. The sound of flesh on flesh slapping together and the moans and grunting from the two sent them over the edge. She couldn't believe she was about to climax, but she did. Her legs locked around him, trapping him inside her. Dwight winced at the pain in his back as he kept going, but knowing that she had climaxed put him in a frenzied state. He buried his face in her neck, let out a deep moan and jerked back and forth as she flicked her tongue across his earlobe. She released her legs from around Dwight's waist and continued to moan as he slid out of her and fell back. Drenched in sweat, he realized what had just happened and he looked at Lydia, still lying on the couch with her legs spread. His mind began to race. Oh, shit, what if she gets pregnant? Damn, why didn't I use protection? Better yet, what in the hell am I doing with another woman? Then he thought of Tina and how she didn't deserve this kind of pain. Lydia stood up slowly, pulling down her dress.

"I...I'll call you...once the shipment arrives," she said looking away. Dwight stood up and got dressed.

"Latosha...Miss Mandrick, I'm sorry about—"

"No, Dwight…it's okay, we…we just made a mistake, so think nothing of it," she said cutting him off as he stood at the door. Then she closed the door in his face. Before he backed out of the driveway, she was already in the shower. "If it ain't one thing it's another," she thought.

***

With her wrists cuffed to a headboard, Chandra slowly opened her right eye. Her left eye was swollen shut. She winced when she parted her lips that were also swollen and covered with dried, crusty blood that ran from her nose. She shut her one good eye and took a deep breath. The room was dark and musky, and the silence didn't bring her any comfort. Everything happened so fast that she wasn't even able to get a call off to Menage before she was yanked out of the car. Trying to move her hands, she moaned out in pain and fright, realizing that she could move no more than an inch. Her feet were free, however, and she was about to see if she could reach the floor, not knowing that her efforts would be useless. But she felt compelled to try to escape because the headboard was thin and weak. Just as she was about to move, she gasped in shock as a hand roughly handled her breasts. Unable to yell, she moaned, sounding like a trapped animal with nowhere to run. Her purple satin blouse was easily ripped from her body. With her arms raised over her head, her breasts pointed upward underneath the black lace bra. The man groping her had no problem finding and squeezing them, even in the dark. All she could think about was her baby and Menage. She had to survive for the both of them. When she felt her bra being ripped off, she clenched her teeth and hoped for a chance to escape, thinking of anything but what the man was about to do to her. She felt no pleasure when his mouth covered her left breast. She crossed her legs and locked them together as his hand traveled down her stomach. Her body quivered as she tried to hold back the tears.

"I'm going to fuck you and you're going to like it!" the man hissed in her ear. Hearing him unzip his pants, she couldn't keep herself from sobbing. She couldn't think of anything to do to stop him, and she knew he would beat her if she fought him. She flinched when she felt something stiff and hot press against her cheek. She smelled his musky scent and realized the man had his penis near her face. Hearing him moan, she realized he was getting ready to rape her. She cried no when he pulled at her panties, his hand roughly cupping between her tightly closed legs. Her mind was made up that she'd fight to her death before she gave up...but her child...maybe if she gave him what he wanted, she would be strong enough to see another day. Just as she felt her legs being pried apart, the light was switched on, exposing her attacker. Still holding his penis with his hands between her legs, there was a look of shock on his face. The man who turned on the light reached for him and tossed his naked body against the wall with ease. Chandra thought she was saved, but when he spoke her world fell back down to hell.

"You fool!" Scorpion said standing over the naked man. "If you want to get your rocks off, go and find some whore house. I don't give a damn about the bitch, but my plan comes first. Now get dressed, get the hell out of here and go check on the others. And let this be your first and last mistake," he warned. The mercenary thought about testing Scorpion's limit, but if he did he might as well had kissed his easy mil goodbye. When he was dressed he slunk out of the room, making sure he got an eye full of what he was missing; maybe he'd get another chance to fuck the girl—yeah, that's just what he wanted to do. Scorpion shut the door and stood next to the bed, looking down at Chandra and her exposed breasts.

"Don't feel thankful because the end result hasn't changed—you'll be dead. But I don't blame that coward," he said reaching down to stroke her left breast. "A coward is one who'll take it, but I can make you want it and like it," he added, caressing her face now.

"Who is this man and why are they doing this to me?" Chandra thought. She glared at Scorpion and he smiled.

"In due time," Scorpion said and violently backhanded her across the face. She was dazed when he left the room. She struggled to not have a nervous breakdown. She closed her good eye to stop the room from spinning but it was no use. She opened her eye and slowly looked around the room. It was so small—no windows, no phone, nothing. The room continued to spin. Then she heard a sound. It sounded like wind whipping against an empty cardboard box. Looking around the room again, she noticed how tiny it was and its odd shape. And she recalled her attacker having to slightly duck when he left. She closed her good eye and the room, once again, began to spin. Chandra heard the strange sound over and over, and then finally, through her broken nose, she smelled seawater and realized that she was on a boat.

Scorpion walked in on the five mercenaries playing cards in a small cabin near the bow. Smoke lingered in the air and a radio was tuned to a rock station. Scorpion glared at the man that he had grabbed just moments earlier. Sitting across from him was Myrmidon, cleaning a deadly looking pistol.

"So when do we make the call?" Myrmidon asked, laying the pistol on the small table to pick up his cards. They were playing five-card stud.

"Soon," Scorpion said. "But first I'll make him sweat—plus I have to tie up a few other things. I'm no longer with those assholes in D.C. but when I call Felix, I'll demand a trade for the drugs and I'll set it up for you to take him and his girl out at the same time...unless you have a better idea."

"Yours seems fine," Myrmidon said, looking at the two kings and three fives in his hand.

Scorpion was pleased with Myrmidon's personal thirty-five-foot cruiser that carried radar capable of sweeping a thirty-mile radius, and he was more than happy to find that the four-stinger launched anti-aircraft missiles. "One must always be ready for anything," Myrmidon had always said. The boat also had a tripod, concealed under a tarp that could hold an M-240B machine gun, located behind a hidden wall. The boat was nothing flashy and if a check was made, the Coast Guard would see that it was owned by a photography company in McKinney,

Texas. Before leaving the cabin, Scorpion talked to Myrmidon alone and stressed the fact that the woman was not to be touched. Myrmidon watched Scorpion get on his jet skis and head back to Miami, which was nine miles away. He rejoined the card game and tried to stay focused but he couldn't; something else was on his mind. He ordered his men to go on watch and prepare to move further south.

***

Back at Felix's mansion in Miami, Menage looked at his Rolex. It was a quarter to ten, and still no word from Detective Covington. He found himself in the same tight spot as earlier. Vapor lay asleep on the floor by his feet. Felix was now upstairs with Rosita. She took it hard when he told her about Chandra and her emotions were sincere.

Menage hated the fact that he could do nothing for Chandra. He thought of the worst, and his stomach turned. He balled his fists so tightly that his nails drew blood from his palms. Sitting on his ass wasn't making him feel any better, and he didn't want to feel better; he wanted Chandra back. Ignoring the tears streaming down his face he stood up, and Vapor got up and stretched his front paws. Felix was at the top of the stairs when he reached the front door.

"Are you leaving?"

Menage stopped in his tracks. With his back facing Felix, he said, "Call me, Felix…and don't hold nothing from me. I don't know if you…we…should tell 'em they got the wrong girl if Chandra hasn't told them by now. I just want my girl back and nothing or no one will stop me from doing what I have to do, because it ain't the same no more." By the tone of Menage's voice, Felix knew there was nothing he could do or say to stop him as he walked out the door with Vapor by his side. The cool breeze outside caused Menage to turn up the collar of his Ecko windbreaker as he made his way toward his Escalade. Taking out the third row seats, he put Vapor in the back. Sitting behind the steering wheel, he sat back and wiped his eyes. Vapor whined and stuck his head between the two front seats to lick his face. Menage got a hold of himself and reached under his seat to feel the steel of the MP-10. Starting up the SUV, he looked back at the mansion to see Felix's silhouette in the doorway. Pulling out of the driveway in silence, he clenched the steering wheel with both hands, trying to control the madness and pain that overtook his body. His temples became tense as he flexed his jaws. The silence was driving him to the point of no return. "CD three, song nine, volume mid," he said turning on the system by voice command. Maximum volume would have been too painful for Vapor's ears, and he now stuck his head out of the window. Seconds later, Smile by Scarface began playing from the four fifteen-inch speakers. The song caused goose bumps to form over Menage's entire body. Squinting his eyes in a hateful gaze, he allowed the words of Scarface and Tupac to seep into his torn soul. With the music still playing, he came to a stoplight and paid no attention to the girls on the corner trying to get his attention. He was on another level—in a zone. Something inside of him told him that his life would never be the same again. Some muthafucka was touching him by taking his girl. He managed to smile as he gunned the ESV when the light changed. He knew he'd see his girl again and he knew he'd see the muthafucka who took her. When he did, he knew he'd ask them to smile for him as he emptied the clip of his Glock 9. Smile for me...won't cha just smile...for me...

***

DJ was laid back on his couch with his feet hung over the armrest, brushing small stems of weed from his shirt. He was on the phone with Lisa, yelling over his loud stereo system.

"So I figure I'll stay with you tonight," Lisa said.

"Huh?" he said searching for his lighter. He was starting to dig Lisa. She didn't bug him if he didn't call or ask him a thousand questions. She was so down to earth and the sex was off the chain.

"Boy, turn the radio down so you can hear me!" she snapped.

"Hold on a sec," he said reaching for the radio remote. "Ok, what you say now?"

Lisa sucked her teeth. "I said I might stay with you tonight. Can you pick me up from work?"

"Yeah, what time?"

"Uh…'bout midnight…is that too late?"

"Nah, I'll be there. Whatcha think—I got a curfew or something?"

"Whateva, just be on time, DJ. Look, they just called me over the P.A. I'll see you later." When she hung up, he wondered if he should have told her about Menage and see if she could find out anything about him. He would have been surprised if she'd told him about Benita and Menage and even more surprised if she'd told him that the section Menage was in was guarded and off limits—even though it was an empty room which was unknown to her. DJ lit his freshly rolled blunt. Pulling deeply on the potent spliff, he closed his eyes and held the smoke deep in his lungs. Moments later, the coke-laced blunt had blurred his vision. Nodding his head to the music, his entire body seemed to pulse rapidly. He seemed to hear new words and beats in the song. Slowly exhaling through his mouth, he looked around his apartment.

"I…I'm the nigga dat floss on dem dub deuce twinkies," he said taking another pull on the coke-laced weed. He smoked half the blunt before putting it out. He felt damn good. There was money in the stash spot, coke was cut and now being shipped to its buyers and a new whip was sitting in the driveway next to his Escalade EXT—both on chrome. He thought of Tina, wishing he could see her one more time. "Silly ass bitch!"

Menage stopped and ran his fingers across the crash bar of DJ's candy red Escalade. Next to it sat a platinum Corvette C-5 convertible with a kit. He didn't recognize either vehicle, but he figured that one of them was DJ's and the other belonged to company. He patted his leg, calling Vapor, and walked up to the door and rang the bell.

***

DJ was in the kitchen warming up pizza and talking on the phone with some young girl that just finished school and thought he was God's gift. She already had a threesome with him, and she found the experience pleasing and fascinating. The older woman that he brought to the hotel did things to her that had her trembling and drained by the end of the day, and she owed it all to DJ.

"Hold on a sec," DJ said sighing angrily. He laid the phone on the table as he went to the door. He left the phone just in case it was another girl, even though he told them to always call first. But the coke, weed and glass of Remy had him slipping. Convincing himself that it was a girl, he smiled and adjusted his erection in a way that caused a print; maybe it was a booty call. He flung open the door without asking who it was or looking through the peephole. His high quickly vanished as he stumbled back and fell on his ass. Menage stood in the doorway with hate in his eyes and gripped his Glock 9 behind his leg. Vapor sprinted into the apartment baring his fangs, emitting a low, deep growl. DJ's teeth chattered and his bladder became weak, warming his midsection.

***

Myrmidon walked into the small cabin with a tray of warm food for Chandra. Closing the door with his foot, he set the tray on a table in the corner.

"I'll take the cuffs off so you can eat," he said reaching into his back pocket for the key.

"And don't bother trying to escape; I doubt you can swim thirty miles to shore—not to mention the sharks. Anyway, I'm not a babysitter but you will talk to no one but me." When the cuffs came off, Chandra rubbed her swollen wrists and tenderly touched the bruise near her hairline. "There's a first-aid kit under the sink in the bathroom...I'll check on you later." As quickly as he entered the cabin he was gone. She listened to him lock the door from the outside. Maybe she could find a weapon—swim-

183

ming was out of the question. She slowly made her way to the small bathroom and looked in the mirror. She was beyond tears now, so what she saw had no major effect on her. Her left eye was sealed shut. Searching for some pain pills, she suddenly realized that she was topless and her skirt was halfway torn from her body. She took off her ripped panties and tossed them in the trash. After searching the drawers back in the small room, she found a pair of sweatpants and a T-shirt. They would have to do for now. After cleaning herself up as best as she could, she tried to stomach the food that was left for her; she needed the energy to go on. She kept telling herself over and over to be strong but she felt so scared, so alone. She faintly called out Menage's name and wished it were all a dream. She prayed for herself and her child until she curled up on the bed and cried herself to sleep.

***

"Yo, son, what the hell wrong wit' you?" Menage said putting away his Glock 9. "Easy, boy," he said giving Vapor a quick rub to calm him down. He walked into the apartment and reached out his hand to help DJ up off the floor.

"You...you...y-you," DJ stuttered as he stood up on rubber legs. He paid no attention to his pissy jeans. "Now dis some shit," said DJ lost for words. "But yo, nigga, we need to talk. And it's a long story." They stepped into the living room and Menage frowned his nose at the odd smell in the air. DJ, still shook, sat down—pissy jeans and all. As Menage told him about Felix's secret plan, DJ looked at him like he was a ghost. Vapor growled repeatedly at DJ and bared his fangs every time he looked at him. Finally the story was coming to an end.

"So, man," Menage said looking off in the distance, "somebody got my girl and don't nobody know a fuckin' thing." He covered his face with his hands and muttered something that DJ couldn't understand.

"So...you been outta the hospital since...Friday?" Menage nodded his head yes. "Uh...so what you gonna do now, I mean—"

"DJ, fuck the chop shop, the dough, fuck all that shit; I'm out the game. I just want my shorty back, yo." Then he asked DJ if he had company after remembering the two cars out front.

"Nah, not yet, but I got this chick coming over tonight. What's up?"

"Nothing really. I just peeped the two rides out front."

"Oh, yeah. I got the truck last week and the 'Vette yesterday."

Menage's mind was on other things besides asking DJ where he got the dough for the whips outside. DJ told him that he could crash in the spare room down the hall. He finally noticed after going to his room that he had pissed his pants. Mad with himself for having allowed Menage to put fear in his heart, he punched the wall and cursed him. He knew that silly-ass Tina would have a fucking fit when she found out that Menage was alive and well. Fuck her. If Menage were out of the game, the chop shop would be his. He just hoped that no one would find out who was behind the two hits. His mind went back to Tina and how she would probably spill it all if she ever got caught in a trap. DJ pondered the possible repercussions of killing Tina while he was in the shower. What would Dwight do?

Menage was in the back room lying across the bed. He was fully dressed with the light on while Vapor lay curled up on the floor. Menage couldn't fully trust anyone and didn't plan on changing that fact. He looked up at the ceiling with his hand behind his head under the pillow, gripping his glock. He tried his best to stay awake, thinking it would do some good to be up for Chandra's sake. His mind said one thing but his body said another. Sleep came easily and about half past midnight he awoke. He rubbed his eyes and sat up on the bed. He took off his holster and then his shirt. He walked out into the dark hallway to go to the bathroom when he bumped into someone and turned on the light.

"Oh, shit," said Lisa taking a step back. "Damn...you scared me."

"My fault," Menage said as Vapor poked his head between his legs to sniff Lisa. She looked at him from head to toe.

"You must be DJ's friend; he didn't tell me your name. Is that your truck out front?" When she saw his bare chest and the fresh wounds, she instinctively reached out to touch him.

"You need to put something on that. Hold on, I'll be right back." Before Menage could stop her, she turned and went back down the hall. By the time he was done using the bathroom, Lisa was coming back down the hall. Menage wished she would just leave him alone. She followed him into the room with Vapor sniffing her feet.

"Do he bite?" she asked.

"Sit down, Vapor." Vapor whined and retreated to the corner. Menage sat on the edge of the bed and reached for his shirt.

"No, just lay back and I'll put this on you," she said holding a tube of ointment. Menage frowned. "Look, I'm a nurse and if you don't keep that clean it can and will get real messy. Now lay back. It won't take long." Slowly he lay back, slipping a hand under the pillow behind his head.

"So that's your ride out front?" she asked again.

"Yeah," he said as she gently began applying the ointment to his chest.

"Bullet wounds...how many times were you hit?" He shrugged his shoulders, wishing she would shut up and finish.

"Well, my name is Lisa." She waited for him to say his name. "And yours?"

"Menage," he said looking at the ceiling. Lisa stopped rubbing the wounds, but her hands lay flat on his upper chest.

"Something wrong?"

"No...uh...the name is just...one of a kind. It's like

menage...you know that sex thang..." she said, but stopped short when she saw that he didn't crack a smile. She knew this couldn't be the same Menage her cousin was stressed out about. He was in a coma. But Benita said he drove an Escalade—check...had platinum teeth—check...and said that he was fine as hell—double check! If Benita weren't her cousin she'd run her hand down his firm stomach, follow his happy trail and see what he was packing between his legs. Hell, DJ was out cold. Menage snapped her out of her sexual vision.

"Are you 'bout finished?"

Lisa looked into his eyes and smiled. "Yes, but I'll leave you a few packs to put on yourself when it gets dry again," she said standing up and wiping her hands on a towel that she'd brought in with her.

"No doubt, thanks," he said getting up and following her to the door. She turned and hesitated.

"I guess I'll see you in the morning." Menage didn't reply. Lisa was telling him on the sly that if he wanted her to come back into his room she would...there was just something about his eyes. He shot her down when the door gently closed in her face.

Now back with DJ, she took off her uniform and got into bed. He was still asleep. So the hero's alive and well, she thought to herself. She knew Benita would flip out once she told her about running into Menage. She sensed that he was in a foul mood and thought that maybe in the morning she'd tell him she and Benita were cousins. It was odd though. Circles within circles—DJ, Dwight, Tina, Menage...oh well... Lisa's thoughts eased as she curled up next to DJ and called it a night.

Sometime during the night, Menage left and went to stay on his speedboat that was tied up at Bayside. He buried his face into the pillow, murmuring Chandra's name as he cried himself to sleep. He was finally learning the true meaning of love.

***

Detective Covington was home in bed with his wife. There hadn't been any calls or leads about Chandra. Detective Hamilton was asleep in the guestroom. For some reason, they both knew that they'd need all the rest they could get.

CHAPTER 8

Song Cry

Monday
Bayside Pier – 6:30AM
Menage sat in the cockpit of his speedboat watching the sunrise as Vapor was curled up asleep at his feet. He had just gotten off the phone with Felix. There was still no news about Chandra and he didn't feel that there was anything good about that. He still felt helpless, but there was nothing he could do but wait. He tried to think of who would hold so much hate for him to try to kill him twice and then take his girl. DJ crossed his mind. He did blow up quick; maybe the chop shop had a good week or something.

On his way from DJ's apartment he had called Dough-Low and left a message on his voice mail. They were to meet at three, but until then he needed to be alone to think. He ran his tongue over his six platinum teeth and stared at the sun from behind his tinted Gucci shades. Spring break was already jumping off. Out on the pier, mostly white girls in skimpy bikini tops and thongs walked back and forth or rode by flashing their tits on crowded boats and jet skis. Vapor woke up just as two college girls walked up to Menage's speedboat. They were astonished by its size and appearance and he could see that they were shocked to see him—a black man—sitting in the cockpit. Vapor ran to the stern, barking and growling viciously at them. They quickly headed in another direction. Menage took off his shades, squinting his eyes from the glare of the sun. It was going to be another hot day with a high of ninety-four.

***

Dwight lay wide-awake in bed with Tina. Last night was hell. He had told Tina he had a headache because Menage was on his mind, but it was really the guilt he felt inside because of what happened between he and Latosha. Tina had cooked a chateaubriand, double thick beef tenderloin steak for him, but he hardly touched it. She sensed a funny vibe and started to fuss with him about how he needed to get over Menage and get on with his own life. At one point he was going to tell her what he'd done, hoping their love was strong enough for her to understand. They ended up having very intense sex and when it was over, Tina had a big smile on her face and told him he needed to come home that way more often. She didn't realize that her comment made him feel as if she wasn't happy with his sexual performance in the past. But he didn't know how to question her; he was the unfaithful one.

"Shit," Dwight said under his breath so as not to wake Tina. He thought of how he had sex with Latosha without using protection. He thought that maybe she was on the pill...he sure as hell hoped so. As he continued to think of Latosha, he was shocked to feel the blood starting to pump between his legs. He had to get her out of his mind but whenever he closed his eyes, he pictured her with her legs cocked open and wet dripping sex. His penis grew. He slowly got out of bed and went to the bathroom. Throwing cold water on his face, he smiled and wondered what Menage would say if he was around. He had his head down with both hands on the marble sink when Tina wrapped her arms around his waist. She licked his back as her hands slid down into his boxers. He was semi-hard, but her soft fingers quickly brought him to fullness.

"Mmm...early bird gets the worm, huh?" she said stroking him. He let out a deep breath and closed his eyes as her thumb rubbed pre-cum over the swollen head of his penis. He tried to turn around but she stopped him and continued to please him with her hand.

"Listen, baby," she said stroking him, "I'm sorry about snapping at you last night, okay?" She went on licking his back and smiled, knowing she was driving him wild. Dwight went to turn around again and Tina let him this time. He began rubbing her thighs and she was pleased by what stood up between her legs.

"It's okay…let's take the day off…just you and me," he said. Tina took off her teddy and smiled. Pulling down his boxers, she dropped to her knees and put his stiff penis into her mouth. Dwight braced himself against the sink as Tina's tongue twirled around his shaft. She wrapped her arms around his waist and took him deeper, causing him to moan out her name.

"Ahhhh…I love you so fucking much, Tina!"

***

"How the hell can we do two cases at one time!" Hamilton exclaimed sitting across from Covington's desk.

"Listen, Ham, the chief said so and I tried to get us out of it…I couldn't," he lied. "But four—no—five people slain at a stoplight in broad daylight—plus a kidnapping…we'll have to split up. You stay on the shooting at Menage's house and I'll see what's up with this…whatever the hell it is," Covington said. He was happy that the chief allowed him to take the case; now he didn't have to worry about anyone else snooping in his uncle's affairs. He also wanted to make sure that Menage's case didn't go unsolved. Menage wanted his girl back, but maybe whoever tried to kill him had nabbed her. However, the bodyguard had said they were going for Felix's girl and it was a mix-up—a big fucking mix-up, so maybe it was no tie to the hit on Menage.

"So what leads do I have to follow up on of any real substance? I mean, all we got is DJ sleeping with all those women. By the way, did you check to see if the girl in the picture was Dwight's girl?"

"Nah, not yet," Covington lied.

"Why the hell not, Covington? Geesh!"

Covington tapped out a Newport and lit it. "The way I see it, it's a waste of time. Just go back to Menage's place and check it out again; maybe we missed a clue or something."

Hamilton cursed and lightly hit his desk with a balled fist. "Now we're going in circles."

"Calm down, man. We can't and won't solve 'em all, so don't sweat it. And that means don't let it bother you," Covington said laughing.

"Ha, ha, very funny," Hamilton said. "So what's with the stoplight thing yesterday—got any leads or anything?"

Covington leaned back in his chair and blew out a ring of smoke. "Ever heard of Felix Marchetti?"

Hamilton's mouth dropped open. "You mean Marchetti as in the Marchetti crime family in New York and over in Spain?"

"Uh huh."

"I heard bits and pieces about the family. But what do they or Felix have to do with the kidnapping? Please man, don't tell me this is the Mafia..."

"No, he didn't do it, but apparently a girl was taken. We don't know who that girl is; no one's talking to the police, as you might guess. But the limo belongs to Felix Marchetti and he hasn't given a statement. We really can't put pressure on him anyway because he wasn't there."

"Criminal against criminal—saves us some time, huh? But good luck. Now back to Menage. After I check his place, then what?"

"Check with the lab and make sure they have all the prints...shit, it's spring break; go down to the beach and relax...get laid or something."

"You can be a smart ass sometimes, Covington, but I just might consider that," Hamilton said smiling.

"Well, Hammy," Covington said standing up, "I'll call you later and if you come up with anything, call me first or hit me on my two-way... I swear I'ma make you the hippest white boy at this station." Covington left the office and Hamilton wasn't far behind. Another day's work was about to begin.

Washington D.C.

"So have you located Scorpion yet? asked Troublefield.

"Well," Agent Lofton said, "I made the call like I said before, but he went ballistic and the line went dead."

"I can recall that!" Troublefield stated firmly.

"We traced the call to a hotel room in Homestead, Florida, but when we got there he was gone and—"

"Did you send the FBI or local police?" Troublefield said cutting him off.

"I informed the FBI down in the area to check the hotel." Seeing that Troublefield was pleased, Lofton continued. "Of course he was gone, but the room was rigged with C-4 and I lost two men, Joe. The Deputy Assistant Director of the FBI wasn't very happy about it. He's going to the Joint Chief of Staff and ask why you used us like this."

Troublefield quickly sat up in his chair and scanned his office before refocusing his attention back on Lofton. "Lofton, I'll come clean with you. Scorpion's real name is

Eugene O'Shea. He's a twenty-nine-year-old highly trained British Special Air Service Commando, but he's been working Black OPs for the CIA in the field. He's an expert in small arms, hand-to-hand combat and a member of a secret counter terrorist team."

Lofton slumped back in his seat. "Why did you hold this vital information from me? If I knew he was like that, I would have had my men warned. But since you and the CIA want to play Double-0-7, two of my men are dead!"

"Now that's uncalled for."

"No, the hell it isn't!" Lofton yelled leaning forward in his seat. "You go tell those two men's wives and kids that it's uncalled for! This whole set-up is bullshit and you know it. If the Director of the FBI pushes for a full investigation, I swear we'll get to the bottom of this."

Troublefield glared at Lofton.

"We're on the same team, Lofton. Scorpion is the cause of our troubles, so let's not lose focus. He's a master of deep cover and that's not the only problem; he's unstable.

"Unstable how, Joe?"

"He has Dementia Praecox."

"Dementia what! What the hell is that?"

Troublefield removed his glasses and took a sip of water. "Dementia Praecox—premature dementia. He has deterioration of his intellectual faculties and emotional disturbance...or simply put, a brain disorder. We have a highly trained government psychotic nut on our hands and I think he may have blown his last fuse. Lofton, by order of the Joint Chief of Staff, we, the Central Intelligence Agency, have been given the go-ahead to terminate Scorpion as soon as possible."

Lofton nodded. "Well, we'll need all the help we can get. I don't know his cover; that's the way he set it up. I guess he knew all along he was going to double cross us, but for what?"

"He's crazy."

"Well why in the hell did you recruit him and then set him up with the FBI for God's sake, Joe?"

"I'm sorry," Troublefield said rubbing his temples. "My guess is that he may be after Mr. Marchetti. Why, I don't know. But we have to find him."

"So what do you suggest?" Lofton asked.

"Call your director and have the FBI Hostage Rescue Team head to Florida. I'll also send a CIA field agent. We can cover Mr. Marchetti in the shadows and wait for Scorpion to bite. And when he does, we'll crush him."

"Does your agency have any up-to-date pictures of him?"

"Yes, but they're no good because he had plastic surgery since then. He was once followed by our friends of the KGB. Maybe they have a more recent picture, but I doubt they'll let us see it; they'll want to know why we want it... and how in the hell we're even aware that they were following him."

"Wonderful!" Lofton said.

"He's smart, but he can only control his mind and actions up to a certain point, so we must act fast before the body count gets bigger." Troublefield opened his desk and handed a thick file with Top Secret stamped on it to Lofton. "Here's his file. You can fax it down to Florida. If we can, we'll take him alive."

"Alive? Troublefield, I'm about to send the HRT out of Quantico on a manhunt and we don't have a positive I.D. It's a mess in the making and I don't like it." Lofton left Troublefield's office, flipped open his phone and called the Director of the FBI. He had to get the ball rolling to put the Hostage Rescue Team on standby.

***

Detective Hamilton knew that he was wasting his time as he walked through Menage's living room. To him everything looked the same—just as he and Covington had left it. Taking off his sport jacket and putting on a pair of latex gloves, he began his second search. First he made sure that all the bullet holes in the wall were empty by poking each one with a thin metal prong. He doubted he'd find anything, because the department had scanned the walls with a high-tech x-ray machine that could look through objects and detect metal or steel. Dried blood was still visible in parts of the mansion. He walked toward the bedroom and stopped at the open door. He couldn't recall whether or not it was open or closed before. Using his shoulder, he pushed the door further open and stepped into the bedroom. It was huge and Hamilton wondered why a man would need so much room just to sleep and have sex. He was about to step out, but he glanced across the bedroom and noticed that the door under the sink was open in the bathroom. He had searched the bathroom before and remembered finding a box of extra large rubbers. He didn't even know that they came in different sizes. Squatting down, he looked under the sink.

"What the hell..." he said when he saw the far wall slid back. He pulled out his small penlight and aimed it at a little empty box. He knew what he was looking at and what was missing. He was aware that the place had a surveillance system but neither he nor Covington could find the tapes—if anything at all was recorded. He knew someone had come and taken the tape and finding who and why just might bust the case wide open. Sitting back outside in his SUV, he tapped the steering wheel. He went over his notes in a hurry, hoping he'd made a note about the bathroom sink—nothing. He grabbed his camera and rushed back toward the house. He slipped and nearly dropped the camera, and that's when he noticed fresh tire marks by the driveway. He flipped through the pictures he took on the day of the shooting and didn't notice the marks in any of the photos. This was proof beyond a doubt that someone had paid a visit to the house since then. After taking a few pictures of the tire marks, he called the station and told them to have a forensic unit come over and lift for prints. He figured that the person whose prints showed up on the device under the sink could answer a hell of a lot of questions for him—particularly about the tape and its contents. He also spoke to the lab techs and instructed them to call no one else but him as soon as possible if any prints were found. Covington put him in charge and he wanted to prove that he was no rookie.

"Geesh, it's hot." Hamilton took off his tie, tossed it onto the passenger seat and headed for the beach. The day, in more ways than one, had started off on a good note. The beach was packed with young college girls who took advantage of every available opportunity to flash their tits and asses. Some even showed more. "Hell, I'm only human," he thought ten minutes later as he gripped the steering wheel while the pale-skinned, petite red-head buried her face down between his legs, sucking him. Beachgoers walked by his tinted SUV, oblivious to what was going on inside the vehicle. "Yes, I'm only human," he thought again.

"Wake up, DJ!" Lisa said shaking him. "It's almost eleven o'clock and you ain't got up yet!" It was only a few minutes that she had been awake herself. Since DJ was knocked out cold, she went in search of Menage, thinking that maybe he was hungry. But after her third knock on the door went unanswered, she peeked in to see that he was gone. She could hear Benita's mouth now. DJ was so tired and high from the coke-laced weed—not to mention the shock of seeing Menage, that he told Lisa to take the keys and drive herself home. She picked up the keys to his Corvette and thought about trying to wake him once more to tell him what time she'd return. She quickly decided against it when he began to snore loudly.

"I'm stompin' wit' da big dawgs," she said smiling to herself as she got behind the wheel of DJ's custom C-5 Corvette.

***

Benita was lounging on the couch reading a book on Greek Mythology. She knew she should be out enjoying herself; it was spring break. And she was still waiting for Lisa to call and prayed that she had some info on Menage. She tossed the book on the floor and rubbed her thighs. They were a little sore from all the dancing she did the night before. The clock above the TV read twenty minutes after eleven. She was about to hit Lisa on her two-way, but she heard a car pull up outside. She got up and looked through the blinds and saw Lisa getting out of her Acura.

"'Bout time you got home," Benita said as Lisa walked into the house.

"Girl, chill. And I got some news for you, so sit down." It took a few minutes for Lisa to gather her thoughts and tell Benita about running into Menage.

"Are you sure it was him!"

"Yes, girl—the platinum teeth, the butter-ass Escalade and that chest..."

"Hold up, hold up. How did you see his chest?"

"Child, please," Lisa said, knowing how Benita's mind was bent. "I had to put some cream on his wounds. His shirt was already off and like I said, when I got up this morning he was gone."

Benita dropped her hands in her lap. "Why hasn't he called me...or come by?"

Lisa could only shrug her shoulders. "Ain't no telling, but look, why sit up in this place and stress yourself? Let's go to the beach and have some fun." The two later stepped outside toward DJ's Corvette wearing matching Fendi string bikinis and fishnet skirts.

"When you 'posed to take the car back?" Benita asked.

Lisa threw her head back defiantly. "When I damn well please, that's when!"

The strip on South Beach was packed bumper to bumper. The sidewalks were crowded with college students, dancing in front of a cameraman who was filming live for BET's Rap City. Most of the shots would have to be censored, no doubt. Lisa had the top down on the Corvette, and at each stoplight she revved up the engine as the crowd urged her on to do a burnout. However, she didn't wish to take a chance of losing control of the powerful sports car. But damn if she wasn't having fun.

"Now that don't make no damn sense," Lisa said as she walked down the beach with Benita.

"What?"

"That!" Lisa pointed out toward the ocean at a huge boat. "Now that's major paper, girl. I wonder how much one of those costs. Got to be somebody famous. What do you think?" Lisa said.

Benita glanced at the boat and then kicked the sand at her feet. "Don't know and don't care."

Lisa sucked her teeth and started to walk again. Seeing that she was about to pass two men, she put an extra sway in her hips as they walked by she and Benita. She got the reaction she wanted when they turned to catch up to them. After a quick exchange of names they paired up, and Lisa stepped off to the side with the taller of the two men. Benita stood with her arms crossed, looking out into the distance. The guy was cute, but she just wasn't in the mood.

"So what's up, you shy or something?" Benita gave him a quick head-to-toe glance. He had a nice smile, even teeth and clean nails. There was no hair sticking out of his nose, and he had nice feet and clean skin. She even noticed his muscle tone; he was perfectly built and proportioned.

"I'm okay…uh, what was your name again?" she asked.

"Alex."

"No, Alex, I'm not shy. It's just a long story, that's all."

"Well, ok, that's cool. Maybe we can sit and talk about it…that is if you ain't seeing someone. But if you are, he's a fool not to be here with you," he said.

"If I did have a man, why would that make him a fool?"

"There's no point in answering that now that I know you're single. Let's move on and talk about me getting to know you, if that's not asking too much." Benita smiled. Alex told her that he was eighteen and she was pleased to find out that he was the starting wide receiver for the South Carolina Gamecocks football team. Lisa pulled Benita away, breaking up their conversation, and Alex walked over to his friend who was the star starting quarterback.

"Girl, ain't they cute? Look, they got a room at the Hilton. Let's go over and chill wit' 'em."

"Lisa, are you for real!"

"Yeah, girl, let's have some fun. Shit, DJ ain't my husband. I see no ring on my finger and he didn't even touch me last night. But anyway, you wanna go or not?" She felt good to attract a man young enough to be her child if she had started early. Benita looked over at Alex who had now removed his tank top. She couldn't help but smile at his body, and she also saw how the other girls were checking him out.

"Yeah, I'll go."

"Now that's my girl. Come on."

Lisa and her date headed for DJ's Corvette as Alex walked Benita toward his sporty pearl black Honda Accord. He asked if loud music would bother her and she told him no. He pulled out behind Lisa and they drove off to the hotel. They let the music play and rode in silence. Benita wondered what she was getting herself into. She knew that going to a hotel only meant one thing—sex, and she felt uneasy as they entered the room. Lisa knew her cousin was uptight.

"You don't feel like doing anything, do you?" Lisa asked her as they stood in the bathroom together. Benita said no. "Look, girl, just go downstairs and wait for me in the lobby."

"Lisa, I know you ain't about to do what I think you're going to do." Lisa smiled and licked her lips. Benita shook her head as she walked out of the bathroom and toward the door to leave. Alex sat at the table with his friend, unable to even look at her. By the time Benita made it to the lobby downstairs, Lisa was allowing the Quarterback to take the first turn at her. She was naked on her back as he grunted and moaned on top of her. Next she mounted Alex and rode him reverse cowgirl style as he caressed her ass. She showed them a thing or two and she was pleased that they didn't waste time in going down on her to taste her sweetness. She was finally able to act out her sexual dream. And it was safe sex, no doubt. Close to an hour later, she walked up to Benita in the lobby.

"About time," Benita snapped looking at her watch.

"Oh, please!" Lisa said. "Let's go. I'm tired and hungry as hell. You drive and let's go to Bayside." Lisa slid down in the seat as Benita started up the car and took off.

"I hope you took a shower!"

Lisa stuck up her middle finger. "Think I'm a slut or somethin'?"

"No, but a nympho, yeah…that's you, the dick-crazy nympho."

"Well, I'ma be glad when you get with Menage. I might put my ear to the door just to hear you yell, 'Oh baby, harder, yes, yes, do me.' "

They both laughed, and Benita didn't respond to the comment about Menage or say anything about how she really felt about him. She was actually still trying to sort out her feelings.

It was ninety-one degrees and the palm trees at Bayside swayed back and forth in the welcome cool breeze. Benita avoided the area where the shooting occurred, but Lisa still bugged her to show her the spot. When they took their seats at the waterfront restaurant, Benita looked out toward the pier, seeing how everyone was enjoying spring break. On a yacht she saw a bunch of white teenagers having a wild party with loud rock music blasting. Jet skis ripped up and down the beach, racing or just showing off doing stunts.

Benita couldn't get over how Lisa didn't have the common

sense to call her last night when she met Menage. She looked at Lisa and rolled her eyes. Stupid! Now he was gone again and she had no way to reach him. She wondered how long he had been out of the hospital and if he was even in a damn coma. She sighed heavily.

"What's wrong with you?" Lisa said.

"Nothing. I'm just thinking about something, that's all."

"Let me guess...Mr. Menage, right?"

"Look, let's just order and eat, okay?"

"Well excuse me, miss don't wanna talk. I guess I'll order but you need to stop trippin' over this guy. He can't be all that. I mean, please, girl, get real!" Lisa picked up the menu and looked for something to fill her stomach with.

***

Menage sat in his Escalade at a gas station in Coral Gables sipping on bottled water. He looked at his Rolex. Dough-Low was running late. Menage drummed on his steering wheel and leaned forward to see if he could spot Dough-Low's Yukon Denali LX or his Hummer H2. He saw neither. Felix had just called him and the news was the same; no one had called with a ransom. He wouldn't allow his mind to think of the worst. He knew someone would call and demand money or whatever the hell they wanted for Chandra's safe return. But they had to call and soon. His patience was in short supply right now, and Dough-Low being late didn't ease him one bit. He was about to page him when his cell phone chimed.

"Yeah," he said as soon as he had the phone to his ear.

"Yo, dun, where the hell you at? I've been here for about fifteen minutes," Dough-Low said. Once Menage found out that Dough-Low was at the wrong gas station, he told him to stay put. He was on his way.

Menage pulled into the BP gas station to find Dough-Low sitting in his Yukon Denali LX. He pulled up next to him.

"Yo, what da deal?" Dough-Low said extending his arm out of his window to give Menage some dap. Menage wasted no time telling Dough-Low about the kidnapping.

Dough-Low was shocked and speechless. Menage knew he needed to be sober, but his music made him high; so as he pulled back into the street with Dough-Low behind him, he dropped all the windows halfway on his Escalade and activated his system. "CD nine, song seven, volume max." Seconds later the SUV shook.

"Dis you?" Dough-Low said pointing at Menage's speedboat. Vapor was on the bow whining and barking at Menage for attention, as he was busy taking off the lines that held his boat to the pier. He then jumped on his boat and took off his shirt.

"Damn, it's hot."

"It's true!" Dough-Low said. Menage went about the task of starting up his speedboat as a crowd started to form on the pier, waiting to see what his boat could do.

"How fast this thing go?" asked Dough-Low.

"Fast enough. You might wanna strap in," Menage said as he pushed the red start button. The engine seemed to have a growling beast within it. Dough-Low frowned and looked at the stern of the boat as it slowly moved away from the pier. The speedboat now pointed in the direction of the open sea. Menage made sure Vapor was strapped in his special seat and he strapped himself in as well. He put on his shades and voice mic as he saw people gathering near the shore just to get a closer look at his boat. He gripped the throttle and a feeling of power went all through his entire body. He thought of Chandra as he slammed the throttle forward. The stern dipped into the water and lunged forward with great force. Menage steered the boat to the right, sending up a wall of water as he headed out to sea. When the boat's digital speed counter read ninety knots, he eased off the throttle.

"You wasn't bullshittin'!" yelled Dough-Low. He found it hard to believe that a boat could move so fast over water. The bow was raised up high out of the water, but the way the speedboat was built, it felt as if they were riding over a level surface. When a wave high enough to reach the bow hit the boat, the Skater cut through the wave with ease and landed back hard on the water. Menage navigated the boat on a straight path, ignoring the speed limit now. He knew the Coast Guard's speedboat could only reach up to eighty miles per hour. They'd bring out the helicopter for anything faster.

"Hey, I thought you said you had the fastest boat out here!" Dough-Low yelled pointing over his shoulder. Menage gripped the wheel and took a quick look behind him. Coming up fast and on his tail was a sleek thirty-foot Donza speedboat. It pulled up next to them, matching Menage's speed. The driver of the Donza looked over and smiled as his two male passengers mooned them. Then with a quick burst of power they pulled away, leaving a giant rooster tail behind.

"Dat's fucked up. If I knew the police wasn't out, I'd set fire to their pale asses…oh, it's true!"

Menage watched the boat speed ahead while Dough-Low shook his head in disgrace. "Not today," Menage said. "Today I won't lose. Yo, Dough, have I ever lied to you?" he yelled.

"Nah."

"Well, I ain't about to start. Hold on!" He slammed the throttle forward to WOT (wide open throttle) and as the speedboat reached 99.1 knots, they eased up next to the Donza. Dough-Low looked to his left to see the surprised look on the driver's face. The two boats ripped through the water at blinding speed. At 100.2 knots, the Donza was still side by side with Menage's Skater 46. The Donza began to stagger at 110.3 knots. Dough-Low stuck up his middle finger as he and Menage left the Donza in the dust. Menage eased off the throttle after increasing the speed to 128 knots. As the speed decreased to 60 knots, he saw Felix's luxurious yacht come into view.

***

Menage and Dough-Low boarded Felix's yacht and were led toward the front of the vessel where Felix sat with Detective Covington.

"I see we have company," Felix said nodding toward Dough-Low.

Menage looked at Dough-Low and motioned for him to take a seat. "Yeah, this my man Dough-Low. Dough, this is Felix and…" He looked at Detective Covington, not knowing how to introduce him. Detective Covington extended his hand toward Dough-Low.

"Just call me Covington," he said. Dough-Low didn't shake his hand but made a fist and bumped it up against Covington's instead.

Felix lit a cigar and inhaled deeply. "I didn't get much sleep last night—been waiting for a phone call with demands or whatever, but first let's lay all our cards on the table." Dough-Low was shocked when Felix revealed that Covington was a police officer and also his nephew, but family came first. Now that Covington could speak freely, he did.

"I have my partner on a goose chase by sending him back to your house but as Felix said, nothing's come up about your girl…sorry." Covington informed Menage about how they would be able to trace the call once they got it. With so much going on, he forgot to tell his uncle about Dwight's girl and the pictures he had. And the last thing on Menage's mind was the surveillance tape.

"The question is," Detective Covington added, "do we tell them that they have the wrong girl." All eyes were on Menage. Dough-Low could see his jaw muscles become tense as he balled up his fists. Menage had been thinking about this from the beginning. What if it was a mistake? What would the kidnappers do if they knew they had the wrong girl? He knew Felix had to be willing to give up anything just as if it was his girl they were holding. Would he?

"No...it will only make them mad...we'll just try to see what they want, and that's the end of the stick you're holding, Felix!" he said looking directly into Felix's eyes.

"I'll meet any demand they come with," Felix said. No one spoke. Only the sound of a few seagulls up above broke the silence. One of Felix's bodyguards walked up to the table and whispered in his ear. He placed a cell phone in his hand and everyone at the table knew it was the call they'd been waiting for. Menage clenched his teeth and glared at Felix, giving his all not to lunge across the table and snatch the phone. Detective Covington was already on his way to the lower deck to make sure the small plate of the art-tracking device was up and running. Felix knew he had to keep the caller on the line for a certain amount of time in order for the call to be traced. Every second counted. Felix answered the phone and Menage focused on his lips, as he spoke in hushed tones. All he wanted was for Chandra to be alive and well.

"Yes, I understand," Felix said. "But how do I know she's not already..." His voice trailed off and he looked into Menage's eyes and nodded his head. He continued, and asked the dreaded question of whether or not Chandra was still alive. The man at the other end of the line ignored his question.

"Ten o'clock tonight, Mr. Marchetti. I will call you again at nine-thirty to let you know of any change. Once I get the shipment, you'll get your girl back. It's as simple as that. Now have a nice day, Mr. Marchetti."

"No...wait...hello...hello..." The phone went dead. Felix made a gesture toward his bodyguard, who gave him the call earlier, to come and get the phone. Felix took a deep breath and wiped his forehead with a silk cloth. He quickly told Menage what the deal was; some guy calling himself Scorpion wanted him to give up two hundred kilos of pure coke in exchange for Chandra.

"How is she?" Menage asked.

Felix cleared his throat. "He didn't say. He plans to fly in by helicopter to pick up the drugs and I'm supposed to meet Chandra at an airfield, but he didn't say which one. I'm sorry...but like I said, I'll meet any demand to get her back...it goes down at ten tonight."

"What about dis trackin' shit ya'll 'posed ta have?" said Dough-Low.

As if on cue, Detective Covington reappeared, running up to the table gasping for breath. He made a mental note to cut back on the Newports...for the umpteenth time.

"Good news...and bad news," he said, not knowing whether to sit or stand.

"No time for games, out with it!" roared Felix, slamming his hand on the table nearly tipping over his drink.

Detective Covington winced. "Sorry...we got a fix. The device has a lock, but I won't have the exact location until the next satellite passes, which will be at seven. That's something I don't have control over. Only the government can control those real-time satellites they have in orbit, but I'm doing the best I can."

"So at seven we'll know their location?" Felix asked.

"Yeah."

Felix sat back and folded his hands. "They want it to go down at ten but he—or they—will call again at nine thirty. We'll know how to find them...and hopefully Chandra as well at seven. Menage, it will be up to you on how we move on this, but my offer still stands to make the trade."

Menage stood and looked at Felix then Covington. "Just call me when you get the location," he said turning to leave the boat. Felix got up from his seat, but he knew it was pointless to call after him. He could see the pain that Menage tried to hide.

"Take care of him," he said turning to Dough-Low.

Dough-Low shrugged his massive shoulders. "He's a grown-ass man," he replied before turning to follow Menage.

***

"So what's the plan?" yelled Dough-Low over the roar of the speedboat engine.

"We just wait...time will tell."

TO BE CONTINUED.

Made in the USA
San Bernardino, CA
05 December 2012